City Noir
General Editor: Timothy La

BUDAPEST NOIR

ILONA GETS A PHONE

Alison Langley

Budapest Noir

Ilona gets a Phone

Dedalus

Published in the UK by Dedalus Limited,
24-26, St Judith's Lane, Sawtry, Cambs, PE28 5XE
info@dedalusbooks.com
www.dedalusbooks.com

ISBN printed book 978 1 915568 42 7
ISBN ebook 978 1 915568 49 6

Dedalus is distributed in the USA & Canada by SCB Distributors
15608 South New Century Drive, Gardena, CA 90248
info@scbdistributors.com   www.scbdistributors.com

Dedalus is distributed in Australia by Peribo Pty Ltd
58, Beaumont Road, Mount Kuring-gai, N.S.W. 2080
info@peribo.com.au   www.peribo.com.au

First published by Dedalus in 2024
Budapest Noir: Ilona Gets A Phone copyright © Alison Langley 2024

The right of Alison Langley to be identified as the author of this work has
been asserted by her in accordance with the Copyright, Designs and Patents
Act, 1988.

Printed and bound in the UK by Clays, Elcograf S.p.A.
Typeset by Marie Lane

THE AUTHOR

Alison Langley was born in Missouri, but grew up in Minnesota. After graduating from the University of Minnesota, she worked as a journalist in Connecticut and Maryland before moving to Europe in 1986, where she covered events in Germany, Hungary, Austria and Switzerland. Most recently she taught journalism in Vienna.

She lives in the Swiss Alps with her husband and their dog.

Budapest Noir is her first novel.

Acknowledgments

So many people encouraged and spurred me on that my head spins. Thanks to Lynn Shockley and Ella Shields for reading multiple versions of this story, and letting me bounce ideas off them. Zsofi Antoni and Bettina Fabos helped me get the Hungarian language, culture and history right: Köszönöm szépen! Please check out Bettina's website, Proudandtorn.org. Sarah Shields read the first version — and still didn't dissuade me from continuing. Will Wolfslau, Caroline Bishop and Derrick Eaves provided important critiques at crucial moments. Chris Shields, Val, Reece and Najaa gave me personal insights into what it means to be an artist. Hesse Phillips has allowed me to bug her endlessly. Betty Stenson from the Irish Writers Centre gave me that encouragement every new author needs. My co-finalists of the Novel Fair Class of 2022 have continued to be incredibly supportive — thanks, guys. David Butler pointed me to Dedalus — thank you. Finally, to Mike, my love, my rock, thanks for never giving up on me.

Ezt a könyvet Gedeon Anna
emlékènek ajánlom

I dedicate this book to the memory
of Gedeon Anna

BUDAPEST, 1991

If she strained her eyes while peering out of her bedroom window, Ilona Kovács could see the car park six floors below. For the last fifteen minutes she'd only spotted a handful of cars — Ladas, Wartburgs and Trabants mostly — but no telephone van had yet entered the car park that served their four buildings.

Ilona got the letter a month ago notifying her that her application for a telephone had been approved. *Finally,* she thought giddily. She telephoned the Post Office from work the next morning — she insisted on speaking to the manager's manager, of course — and arranged to be the first customer installation of the day. She knew well that she'd lose a whole day of work otherwise.

Now, the telephone man was late. She sighed and stared out of the window, oblivious to the capital city's skyline with its colourful rooftop tiles on the horizon, recognisable just beyond the trees which lined the Danube on the Buda side. She looked at the three blocks of flats on the right side of her building. The ones that blocked the sun in the afternoon. There were more around the other side. Monoliths of concrete, all erected by the Soviet-backed government after the war, each side identical, no-nonsense, unimaginative. They contained none of the elegant flourishes or impressive opulence of the buildings a few blocks down that had been spared the bombs of World War Two.

Why couldn't the telephone man arrive on time?

As she scoured the broad boulevard below, her eyes caught sight of the two street cleaners in their orange jumpsuits, leaning against their brooms, smoking cigarettes. When the communists were in power, there would have been five workers, what with full employment and all. Nowadays, these two men would take most of the day just to finish her block of flats, and even then, the playground would still wind up with more cigarette butts than it started off with in the morning.

Ilona tugged at her sleeve, then walked briskly back into her living room, her house shoes slapping the soles of her feet — *clip, clip, clip* — and checked the dark walnut table for crumbs. There were none. More than an hour ago, she had finished her breakfast of tea and toast, washed the plate and cup and put them away. She kept the tea bag to use later that evening. She even had time to vacuum up any crumbs. Then, she dusted the flat thoroughly while she waited. This was on top of the cleaning she had completed the evening before. Ilona prided herself on keeping her flat spick and span.

For the third time that day, or was it the fourth, she checked the bottle of *pálinka* on the side table near the door, turning the schnapps so that the workman would see the label as soon as he entered her flat. It was a quality brand that had set her back a few forints, but Ilona knew he would appreciate it and ensure her installation would be done correctly.

Since she was in the room, she again polished the side table that she had readied for the phone, including a space one shelf below for the phone book, which she had requested. After replacing the duster in its place, she returned to her bedroom window — *clip, clip, clip* — and peered out again. The street cleaners were stubbing out their cigarettes with their toes. The sun was peeking through from the building across the way, and still no phone man.

Ilona darted out of her flat, careful to leave the door open so she could hear the buzzer, and knocked at Erzsébet's door across the tiled hallway. Erzsi, whose blue flowered house dress draped over her large frame, was just getting around to washing her breakfast dishes. Since Erzsi's husband Péter died last year, Erzsi took her time getting dressed in the morning.

'Good morning!' Erzsi said, her voice echoing down the dark, narrow hallway. Honestly, sometimes Ilona jumped when Erzsi spoke. Erzsebét's hands were still soapy when she opened the door. Boxes were piled up in the corner of her living room. As she walked in, Ilona wondered for a moment what Erzsi was selling this month. A few weeks ago, she had given Ilona a good price for a nice silver chain, which Ilona attached to her reading glasses, so they hung like a necklace. Very handy at work.

On the kitchen table was a newspaper clipping. From where Ilona stood in the kitchen doorway, it looked like an advertisement of some sort. Sections of the *Magyar Hírlap* were lying next to it, read but not folded back properly. The scissors were still out. Erzsi shared recipes, stories, crossword puzzles, job notices and quotes with neighbours, friends, family and her son István.

'Look,' Erzsi said, pointing to the article with an elbow. She held her hands in the air like a surgeon. 'There's going to be a second auction of restaurants! Maybe István could buy one of those, too!'

'I know, John wrote a story about it.' Ilona liked to remind Erzsébet that she often knew all the news first. She worked at a news agency, after all! It was her way of reducing the sting of Erzsi's comment. In her heart, Ilona knew Erzsébet wasn't bragging about her son, still, Ilona could feel a pang of resentment. Back when their boys were young, Ilona had always assumed her Emil would be the more successful of the two, what with his swimming prowess. But, well.

'The telephone man is late.'

'He'll come.'

'They promised I'd be the first installation.'

'You know what they say, 'you pretend to pay me, I'll pretend to work. He'll come eventually.' In the thirty-five years they had been friends, Erzsébet learned how to calm Ilona's nerves. 'Would you like to read my paper?'

Ilona shook her head and turned on her heels.

'I need to get back.'

As she closed the door to her flat, Ilona decided in that instant to stand next to her buzzer. Up close, she wondered whether it, too, needed a dusting. She tugged once again at her sleeve.

If she was not mistaken — and Ilona rarely was — she was the only person in her block of flats without a phone. Back in 1960, when the Telephone Company began wiring the building, she was humiliated when her flat had been bypassed.

Ilona guessed it was because of the way her husband Laci had died. Under the communists, though, you never knew why anything was done. Explanations were not their thing. Back then, Erzsébet had waved it off.

'Never mind, you can use mine whenever you want.'

'That's not the same.'

Ilona was still on the waiting list when she and her mother had moved into a smaller flat — this one across the hall from her friend and one floor down from their old place. That was back in '74, after Emil left. Even that hadn't fazed Erzsi.

'It just means we'll see one another more often!'

Now the telephone man hadn't come and it was seven minutes past nine. As Ilona pondered whether she should peek out of her window again or dust the intercom, the buzzer bleated loudly. She jumped, when it pierced her ear, which, admittedly, was a bit too close.

Ilona knew it would take a while for the workman to reach her floor — one of the lifts was out. She patted down her beige summer wool skirt and checked the mirror to make sure all the strands in her light red hair — not a single grey thanks to her hairdresser — were in place. She personally thought she made a very young sixty-one-year-old. No one ever guessed her age.

She waited for him in the hallway, shifting her weight and tugging at her sleeve while staring at the lift's light that indicated which floor it was on. It seemed to take forever before the number 6 lit up.

'I'm so pleased you were able to make it,' Ilona said as the lift doors opened with a ping.

The workman, startled, nearly dropped his black faux leather work case. 'Mrs. Kovács?'

'Yes, pleased to meet you,' Ilona said again. 'My flat is over here.'

She directed him toward the open door with her hand. 'I've cleared a space for the telephone.'

'You're Mrs. Kovács?' he said. He looked confused. Still not moving.

'Yes, yes,' Ilona again pointed him toward her door.

'Oh. I wasn't expecting — I mean, usually these kind of requests —' He stopped.

Ilona was sure she could guess what he was expecting: the people who hadn't had a phone installed tended to be dissidents blacklisted by the communist party. Passing her over for a phone back in 1960, years after her husband was killed, was as wilful as the not-so-subtle lack of a pay cheque at her factory office when Emil disappeared in 1974. Never an explanation of course. All she knew was that Laci's death had left her with no phone and her son's defection left her without a job. Ilona collected offences the way others collect spoons.

But it was 1991. All that was in the past. Ilona didn't want to dwell on it. Especially now. If only she could get the telephone man to get working, she'd finally be getting a phone.

Ilona smiled sweetly at the man, who smelled of stale cigarettes and aftershave.

'I'm so glad you could finally make it. I mean, I believe your boss possibly might have mentioned I needed to be at the first installation today because I must get to work. I work at an important Western news agency.

'You are my first job of the day,' his voice was flat.

'Well, yes, and I'm so pleased,' Ilona said, her smile remaining frozen. 'Of course I hadn't expected to wait until after nine.'

'That's when I start work, at nine.' He looked at her stubbornly.

'Of course, you do!' Ilona said, almost pushing him through her doorway. 'Many of us start work a bit earlier than that, and naturally I hadn't fixed the *exact* time with your supervisor. No worries! You are here now and this' — she waved dramatically at the side table — 'is where I'd love the phone to be installed.'

'Your place is nice.' The telephone man put down his bag so he could take off his jacket.

Ilona tried to relax, even though this man clearly was not one to be rushed.

Not long before her mother passed away, Ilona had purchased embroidered cloth from Tura, where she grew up. She draped them on the armrests of the sofa and settee to hide the threadbare spots. She thought the bright colours added sparkle to the decor. Ilona hoped the workman also noticed the mothballs in the wardrobe when he pushed it out of the way to install the line. Proof of her good housekeeping abilities despite her lack of money.

The telephone man took out a piece of white wire, which he nailed along the moulding trim. Ilona stood over him and watched as he marked off a space where he would need to run the wire to the main line. He pulled out a drill and inserted a bit. A slow whirr emitted from the machine as he began to squeeze the handle, when Ilona tapped him on the shoulder. The telephone man sighed.

Ilona recognised that sigh. She had a sense that she irritated people — that they thought she was pushy or even nagged too much. But it wasn't like that at all. She had learned that to get what she needed in life, she had to nudge a little.

'What do you think? Should I get my vacuum cleaner out?'

'No, it's a small hole,' he said.

'Of course,' she said, her voice a tad too loud. 'I can always clean up after you leave. It won't make me *that* much later for work!'

She noticed that he rolled his eyes, so she knew not to go too far.

'Go on! Don't let me disturb you!' She tried to sound jovial. Then she tugged at her sleeve as she watched him work.

As he packed up his tools, Ilona couldn't suppress a smile as she admired her new phone. The receiver was flatter, lighter and sleeker than the old models her neighbours had. Ilona checked for a dial tone and was excited to hear that flat *rrrrr*. It worked. She had a phone. As he left, Ilona presented the workman with his reward.

'For me?' He asked in surprise as he accepted the *pálinka*.

'You did such a careful job, so just a small thank you'

She was aware that the lines did tend to get disconnected from time to time and she was likely to see him again. She waved goodbye as she shut the door behind him.

Ilona hoovered the drill dust up and wiped away his fingerprints from the table and her shiny, new phone. It had ten square buttons to press — instead of a rotary dial — which made calling faster. Hers was the most modern device she could afford. She couldn't wait to show it off. She called Erzsi, even though it would cost her. It was worth it!

'Ahhhh, it came!' Erzsi yelled into the receiver, when she

heard Ilona's voice on the line.

Erzsi hung up before Ilona could say another word and hurried across the hall.

'That's it,' Ilona said triumphantly. 'Here it is.'

'Ooh, such a beautiful colour, and I love that new design.'

'I thought cream would brighten the room better than black.'

Erzsébet picked up the wide handle. 'With buttons!'

Ilona nodded, proudly.

The dial tone was the same as on all phones, but Ilona was grateful Erzsi pretended it was special. She nodded when she heard it. Erzsi carefully replaced the receiver in its cradle.

'So, it came! I knew you'd get it. I'm sure you'll be so happy to finally have a phone of your own.'

The friends admired the telephone in silence for a minute. Then Ilona said, 'I'll give John my phone number so when he needs to reach me for work he doesn't have to call you.'

'Ilona, it's never been a bother. He has rarely called.'

'Now I can arrange a Sunday tea with Judit!'

Erzsi didn't think much of Ilona's childhood friend. 'And you can also call Emil.'

'Yes!' Ilona's face muscles felt too stiff, her voice too cheery.

'He'll call when he has a number, Ilona.' Erzsi patted her shoulder. 'Well, I need to get going. I really am pleased you have your phone, Ilona. What a special day for you.'

After Erzsi left, Ilona, chuffed, stared silently at her phone.

When the telephones were being installed for the first time before the war, people worried about privacy. Good Lord, anyone in the room could hear what you were saying! A letter, naturally, was more discreet. After the war, as Laci put in an application for a phone, he had said he didn't worry about privacy anymore.

'I know they're going to listen!' He had winked at Ilona conspiratorially. 'That's progress.'

She had laughed. They were newlywed; they had just moved into their new flat.

Each week as they waited for their phone back then, the *Népszabadság*, the local paper, would dutifully report on the percentage of households in the capital with telephones. That was after they had dutifully reported how quickly the Soviet Socialist government had built People's Housing, like the building complex she and Laci had moved into. A steel playground was created after the debris had been cleared away from where there had once been a copse of trees. Back then, she and Laci dreamed of the day they would be visiting that playground. Those newspaper reports of advancements aside, Ilona had not been fooled. She knew that many of the houses in Tura, only an hour away, didn't even have hot water. Then 1956 came, Laci died and the government never approved her phone application.

Now it was 1991. The communists were gone and she had her telephone. Ilona took a step back from the side table so she could admire it. It really was there! She couldn't manage to stop grinning.

Ilona took a moment to reflect on the wonder of it. For most people, a telephone was just a communication device waiting to ring. For Ilona, the marvel lay in its mere existence in her flat. It was redemption; proof that she outlasted the communist bastards, as her father would have said if he had survived. For her, the magic was even more than that. It was a machine that converts sound waves that might bring back the voice of her son. At the thought, Ilona could feel her eyes starting to burn. She hoped Erzsi was right, that Emil would call once he knew her number. His letters had been getting less frequent.

She noticed Erzsi's fingerprints on the phone and once again Ilona took out her duster. She wiped tiny circles on the sleek, smooth surface. It didn't feel much different from the black Bakelite phone the foreman had screwed to the wall in the foyer of her home when she was a girl. The Pálffy's estate was the largest in the region, so her father felt it was important to keep up with technical advances. Ilona must have been ten or eleven when her parents were the first in their village to get a phone. The entire family, along with their housekeeper and nanny, gathered to admire it when it was installed. There was a separate hook on which the receiver could be placed without disconnecting the line while the maid would run to fetch Ilona's father or mother.

'A phone can create from mere electrical pulses the sound of a human voice,' Ilona's father declared as they admired the new-fangled machine. It was before the war, of course. Before she lost her father; before they lost their estate. She had lost so much.

Now, fifty years later, she stood in front of her sleek cream-coloured telephone with its long curly wire. She had got her own phone. She sighed, feeling a mixture of contentment and delight.

Then, slowly, her smile froze; the edges around her face turned pink.

How foolish she must have looked to the telephone man and to Erzsi. So thrilled to get a phone. Animated, like a child at her birthday party, jumping from foot to foot waiting to open a present.

Ilona could feel her face begin to burn. That phone wasn't a miracle. It wasn't a milestone or a technological advance for all its buttons and stylish colour. It was simply an appliance that every other citizen in Budapest had acquired decades earlier.

She thought back to the telephone man and the way he had glanced at her. Had it been a look of pity? Had he been embarrassed for her? Had Erzsébet simply humoured her?

Mortified, Ilona took a step back and looked at her sofa with its tattered armrests covered by the embroidered pieces of cloth, her duster still in her hand. Is this it? Is this what my life has come to? To get carried away over a telephone? Over the hope that maybe someone might think of me long enough to call?

Really, aside from Erzsi or her friend Judit, who was even left to call? Laci and her father were long dead. She had only recently buried her mother. Her brother — well, no one knows what happened to him. Her aunt had moved to Debrecen ages ago, so they only got together once a year at most. And Emil? Well.

It was mid-morning. Ilona could hear the hooting of car horns in the distance. Someone at the far end of her floor slammed a door. Ilona heard the lock turning and the key being pulled out. In the quiet of her flat, she could hear the radio from her upstairs neighbours. She thought she could also hear the ticking from the kitchen clock hanging on the wall of the next room over. Marking time. Like her life now.

Ilona looked once again at her new phone. Now that she had a phone, who would call?

Ilona felt exhausted and nearly too tired to move. She could feel her jaw clenching; her breath shortening, her forehead wrinkling, her shoulders tensing. Then, she did what she had done so many times in her life. She took a long breath, straightened her back and reminded herself to smile. Ilona waved the duster at nothing in particular and stood up. She smoothed her skirt and patted her hair. She was late for work.

INTERCONTINENTAL HOTEL, 1:30 PM

Ilona tugged at her sleeve as she cleared her throat. She and her boss John were sitting on beige padded folding chairs at the Intercontinental Hotel waiting for a press conference to start; and Ilona was supposed to be his interpreter. She was not happy about that, because the speakers were going to be talking about economic things, concepts which she didn't always fully grasp. She re-crossed her legs and let out a long sigh. *Venture capital, privatisation of nationalised lands*, *blah, blah, blah.*

Western businessmen like the ones organising this press conference were falling all over themselves trying to buy companies being privatised. The Soviets may have nationalised the whole country into collectives; this new government was selling it off like a giant fire sale. *New era! Synergies! Blah, blah.*

Now the sales would include the *kastély*. It had not escaped Ilona that with each business deal announced, another mansion in the leafy part of the twelfth district seemed to be erected by some government official driving a new Western car.

John cracked his knuckles as he read the notes she had prepared for him. Cracking his knuckles was a sign that he was no happier to be there than she was. He tended to be nervous when he had to write articles about the economy. She had once overheard him say that he had felt the agency put him out to pasture after having spent his career as a war correspondent: 'Who cares about the economy?' he had said.

John, an Irishman, was nearly as old as she was, so Ilona felt she understood him. Only, she wished he would take more care of his appearance. She had never seen him without rolled up sleeves, for instance, and he looked like he had a permanent sunburn on his face. He was hunched over. Worst of all, he spoke too quickly for Ilona to understand everything he said, so she often just provided information she thought he needed to know. She almost didn't take the job because he had told her he was a Cork man and she thought that meant he drank. It wasn't the last time he had perplexed her.

She'd been working for John only for about a year; Ilona was grateful for the job, although translation was not her strong point. Before the Iron Curtain fell, she worked for a variety of Western journalists as a fixer, setting up appointments, helping get visas and such like. That's what she liked doing.

Ilona and John had arrived at this press conference nearly a half hour early. John often did this, and Ilona approved. She loathed being late for anything. His slow and deliberate movements occasionally irritated Ilona. She didn't believe in dawdling, and he seemed to enjoy chatting with everyone, which was exhausting. Still, coming early meant they could sit in the first row, or near to it. Another trait that suited Ilona. They were sitting in the front for the press conference.

'Let's see,' John said, shuffling notes on his lap. 'The Hungarian aristocracy owned these estates —'

'Yes. They adopted the word *kastély*, because only the emperor could live in a castle, a *palota*,' Ilona said. It was a charming titbit of information that few knew.

'Worked the peasantry like they were slaves, did they?' he said perhaps a bit too snidely, adding. 'When the communist government took over in the 1940s, it created cooperatives and gave the land to the people, is that it?'

'Well yes, except, not all aristocrats were so bad —'

'Oh, is that so? *Noblesse oblige* and all that?'

Ilona pursed her lips. In all the seventeen years she had lived at her family's *kastély*, the Pálffy de Tura, Ilona had never seen her father act incorrectly. Before the Soviets confiscated it, he farmed about two hundred hectares of land. The Soviets turned all of it — the orchards and rapeseed fields — into a collective. The *kastély*, a small castle really, with its patriotic Habsburg yellow façade, was currently a home for the elderly. Ilona hadn't been to it in years, although she could still remember its ornate beauty.

This was in stark contrast to the decor of the Intercontinental, where they were waiting for the press conference to start. It was built during communist times, so of course it was drab and all grey concrete. That podium looked like it would collapse with the slightest touch.

'The aristocracy were left without titles after the First World War, then they were left penniless when the Soviets came along in the 1940s and took everything,' Ilona felt compelled to add.

'And now they want it all back.'

'Yes, there is a political movement to do that. They are also monarchists, and want to restore the titles and go back to the way things were. They have invited Otto von Habsburg to reclaim the throne, even! He's declined so far, though.'

John muttered under his breath something which Ilona didn't understand, so she added, 'Otto von Habsburg is a member of the European Parliament now, but of course, he's next in line if the empire was to be brought back.'

John kept shuffling through the papers.

Ilona let out a long sigh. As she stared at the podium, she wondered how much anyone in the country, including the new government officials, knew how much people had lost.

John, though, never seemed that interested. Oh, the stories she could tell him.

'So last week the government announced that anyone who can prove ownership of land in the 1940s — when the Soviets took it — can have it back? Providing they can maintain it, of course?'

'That's what I understand, yes. However the big caveat is that they need to compensate the current residents.'

'And these current residents? Who are they?'

'Oh anybody, really. A *kastély* can be a home for the elderly, an orphanage, a technical school. The smaller ones were taken as government residences around the country. Soviet officials kept a few *kastély* as their summer holiday homes, you know…'

'So how will they compensate them? I mean, how will that work practically?'

'Well, that's the big question, isn't it? I think that's what this press conference will address.'

Ilona wanted to add: it's all a ruse. How could she afford to take back her family estate? How would she make amends to the old people living there now? In her eyes, this government's scheme was just another plot for the bankrupt nation to get more money from Western businesses. It wasn't meant for people like her. People with no one left.

Thinking about it put her in a bad mood. She shifted in her seat. They still had a few minutes before the press conference would start, and Ilona needed to use the rest room. She got nervous when she had to interpret for John and this long wait wasn't helping. To make matters worse, the hotel had already turned on the air conditioning, even though it was only May. She pulled her sweater tighter around her neck.

A confident man in a dark blue suit walked briskly from the back of the room toward the podium, smiling at different men sitting in the audience as he walked by.

'*Guten Tag*!' he said in a loud, vibrant voice to one man.

'*Ja*, hello!' he greeted another.

Ilona and John exchanged worried glances. Neither of them spoke German.

The man tapped the microphone. It screeched. Ilona winced.

'Hello everybody and thank you for coming.'

Ilona's bladder calmed down once he spoke in English. She guessed it was probably because of the man who walked up next. Ilona nodded to him from her front row seat. The man with the bowtie nodded back as he took a seat behind the German.

'You know him?' John asked Ilona.

'Oh yes, that's Matt Nelson, the US ambassador. He

demonstrated on the streets next to the dissidents a few years ago, and he let East Germans sleep in the American embassy after the West German embassy was full —'

'That was part of the trigger for the wall to fall in Berlin,' John whispered.

'Right, but that was later. I arranged...'

'Can everybody hear me?' The German spoke loudly into the microphone. It was his way of making sure the audience hushed, Ilona knew. He introduced himself as Albert Sabo and said his parents had fled Hungary before he was born.

'I'm now returning to my roots,' he announced. He held his arms out rather grandly. 'I would like to announce that we have put together a new venture capital company dedicated to Eastern Europe.'

Ilona guessed the name on his birth certificate was probably Béla Szabó. Hungarians often changed their names to fit in with whatever country they moved to. She wondered if Emil used a different name in Ohio. Ilona re-crossed her legs and settled in for a long press conference, grateful not to have to interpret, although she was not happy that she had to sit through it all. This press conference wasn't likely to be anything Ilona hadn't heard before. *Money, joint ventures, blah blah blah.*

'Our fund will purchase some of Eastern Europe's greatest treasures: the old castles and villas,' Sabo said.

There it was, Ilona thought, just as she expected. She hoped Sabo noticed that she was glaring at him. She crossed her arms in front of her chest and gave him the best dirty look she could muster.

'We will be partnering with some of Hungary's oldest families to convert their once beautiful estates into bespoke hotels, spas, resorts, golf clubs and perhaps, for the city locations, hotels, nightclubs or office space. Our focus will be on Poland, Czechoslovakia and Hungary.'

Wait a minute! *What*? Ilona sat up straighter in her chair. *Partnering*? *What exactly would that mean*?

She was alert now, her heart pumping harder. Imagine: her *kastély,* only an hour from Budapest, as a grand hotel! She thought about the hunting grounds and the small lake in the Western corner of the land. Perhaps a resort might be more suitable. She liked the thought of that. *Partnering*.

Ilona's mind was racing as she puzzled it all out. That's the point of this new law. The government wants to raise money by selling off the *kastély*. They can't simply do that because so many families want them back. Yet the families can't afford to maintain them any more than the government. That's where these investor people come in. Partners!

Ilona had uncrossed her legs and was now leaning forward, her bottom at the edge of the folding chair, her right hand on her chin.

The ambassador took the microphone next and announced that he, too, was joining the board of investors. John lifted an eyebrow.

'That's your "very good man"?'

Ilona nodded, pleased. 'Oh, yes! He's been helping Eastern Europe for years.'

John stared for a moment at her, then raised his hand to ask a question.

'Isn't it a bit dodgy to represent both a country and a business venture?'

'Well, first, the fund will invest in all Eastern European

countries, not just Hungary,' the ambassador said. 'We are merging forces for the good of the region. Our investors of course include prominent Eastern Europeans. But, yes, I have resigned my position from the State Department.'

John grunted under his breath.

As they left the conference, Ilona asked, 'Did you understand how those investors were going to pick their partners? I mean, they will need the former owners, right? The families whose properties they were in the first place?'

'They didn't really say. I'm guessing they have that all lined up. These guys don't leave much to chance.'

'I wonder how others can join this group.' Ilona mused. 'You know my family once owned a *kastély.*'

'You're going to become a businesswoman now with the ambassador, are you, Ilona?

'What's wrong with wanting to make money?'

'Nothing, as long as it's legal, ethical and moral.'

The two walked in silence the few streets back to the office. John, probably thinking about what he would write in the story; Ilona wondering if the ambassador and the fund manager could help her get her estate back. And she was grateful that they would be able to call her at her flat now.

'Oh John, the phone installation went well today,' Ilona said.

'Yeah, glad to hear it.'

It was hard to talk on the street, the traffic was loud and they needed to concentrate on not stumbling over the cracks and buckles in the pavement. The remnants of cobblestone on the side streets showed through past Soviet efforts to modernise. Now they were more a walking hazard than practical.

As they neared the door of the office, Ilona could smell the savoury, meaty scent coming from the American hamburger joint that had just opened on the street level of their building. Next to a Dunkin' Donuts.

'So many changes!' Ilona said. 'I love these new dough-nuts. Have you tried them? They are so sweet!'

John stared hard at her as he pushed open the door to their office building.

'You know, Ilona, change can be good, but it must be the right changes. Money doesn't make you happy.'

Ilona let out a surprise 'Ha!' and looked at him amused. 'It doesn't hurt either.'

Ilona felt important walking into the office building. It, too, was once a *kastély*, and its grandeur proved she had status once again. She liked the way her heels echoed against the marble walls as she strutted across the matching marble flooring of the lobby. The carpeted upper-level hallways seemed muffled when she stepped out of the recently installed lift.

While John was typing up his story, Ilona set to work writing the Daily Digest. She usually got it to him early in the morning, but what with the telephone installation and all, she was late.

Since she started at the agency, Ilona's first task each morning was to read all the national papers and summarise the important items in English. On her first day, it had taken her well past five to do it. The report she had proudly handed John was nearly twenty pages long. It was very difficult to do; her written English was rusty. John stared at the thick tome, looked up at her red in the face, and promptly threw it in the waste paper bin.

'Well, it is terrible, I know, however it is my first day. I will get better and you will get only the best in the future. An important agency like yours deserves…'

John waved her away and sent her home. Ilona's hands were shaking. What had she done wrong, specifically? She desperately needed to keep this job as no Hungarian company would give her work.

Since John had not explicitly fired her that first day, she came back the next morning, two hours earlier than when he would arrive. She gave a box of chocolates to the cleaning woman to let her in. She had a hot cup of coffee and a ten-page report waiting for her boss when he walked in. He told her it needed to be five pages.

Now, Ilona knew to skip the women's and celebrity sections (which she read later), sports (which she avoided anyway) and not to repeat the same information, but to add any details another paper might have missed. It had all been very difficult, however now she had the report prepared by the time the boss arrived at nine. Along with his coffee with milk, not cream, and no sugar.

This afternoon, though, she was not really concentrating on the Daily Digest. She was thinking about her phone, the family *kastély* and partnering. Everything in this country was happening so quickly.

She thought of Erzsi's son, István. He had bought a restaurant in Budapest where he had been working for years. Maybe he would know how to help her buy the *kastély*. Ilona stared at the page in the typewriter. She had only written a few paragraphs. The words blurred.

She hadn't thought of the family estate in years. She was seventeen when the Soviets had stolen it. But, well, why not get it back? If she got back her estate, maybe Emil would come back and live in it. He could run it the way her father had. Employ the people in the village to work the fields as before. Of course, Emil would bring his wife and little girl. Ilona could teach them Hungarian. She smiled to herself at the thought.

They would need money, of course. *Backing* they called it these days. She had learned something from sitting in on the press conferences. That is where foreigners like that Albert Sabo man came in. Except that Emil lives in America now, so he has probably got quite rich now. And friends with money, too. She had seen photos of the home where he lived after he escaped.

'How's that daily round up going, Ilona?' John's voice snapped her out of her dream.

'Nearly finished!'

Ilona translated an excerpt from the business page of *Népszabadság*: Prince Charles was making a private visit to the Puszta, the European great plains, where his ancestors once owned an estate. *Well! That settles it*, she thought. *If Prince Charles can return to his roots, then Emil can too*.

By the end of the day, Ilona had a plan. She had a *kastély*, István knew how to buy these things and Emil could give him the money. That West German might be able to help, too!

When John left for the day, Ilona phoned the businessman Albert who had hosted the press conference. She explained that she was a Pálffy by birth and that she thought she had first right of refusal to an exclusive *kastély*. She emphasised the word for him. She was not exactly sure if she really did have first right of refusal, but Ilona was someone who believed if you said something with confidence, it was true.

'We can be partners!' Ilona's voice almost twittered.

'And do you have the deed to your estate?'

'Well, we are working on that. Shall we meet tomorrow? After work?'

'And who lives there now?'

'It is an old people's home. They have taken very good care of it,' she assured him. 'So shall we meet, say, at seven tomorrow?'

'I have my secretary contact you, *ja*?'

'*Ja*,' Ilona said. She made a mental note to start brushing up on German. '*Auf Wiedersehen*!'

That went well, Ilona thought, as she put down the phone.

On the tram ride home from work, although Ilona stared out of the window, her mind was back in Tura. Ilona imagined the Pálffy estate as hers once again. She knew right away she would take her grandmother's room. It had the most beautiful tiled fireplace in the house. Its windows looked out onto the woods. Emil's daughter could have her old room!

As the tram rumbled across the Danube, Ilona could glimpse Lady Liberty, that bronze statue who stood forever erect and proud on Gellért Hill, head slightly tilted skywards, holding a palm frond in her two hands for all the world to see. For years, Ilona hated that thing. The Soviets had built it to commemorate liberating the Hungarians from the Nazi occupiers.

The new government had removed the Russian plaque

and rededicated her to the memory of those who sacrificed their lives for freedom, like her husband. Now Ilona could look at it with pride. Each day, when Ilona's tram gave her a brief view of the freedom statute, Ilona thought of Laci.

Maybe freedom finally had come, these were indeed heady times and she could believe the new president. Arpád Göncz was a poet, a gentleman, kind. He had been someone, like her, who had been blacklisted. She wondered if he also had to wait to get a phone.

Göncz was there for the rededication of the liberty statue, urging his countrymen and women to embrace the changes and continue the work for freedom and prosperity. Could the *kastély* be her way toward prosperity? Regaining the Pálffy de Tura *kastély* certainly would be the ultimate revenge on the Soviets.

She wished her mother were alive to see it. There is a reason liberty statues are women, Ilona thought. They are the ones left to hold their heads high. They are the ones who had to remain resilient.

At her stop, Ilona climbed down the tram steps with the bearing of a queen. Or, at least, landed gentry. Ilona smiled to herself as she walked the rest of the way home. Normally she would trudge heavily up the street, trying not to breathe the leaded petrol exhaust fumes emanating from the cars clogging the boulevard. On this day, there was a lightness to her step. She swung her handbag a little, and noticed the leaves on the trees lining the street were nearly in full bloom. She had a project! So many details to work out! She felt a frisson of patriotism, heeding the call of her president.

At her block of flats, Ilona pushed the button to call for

the lift, and while she was waiting, contemplated the best way to approach István. Maybe she could pretend to just run into him right here in the lobby. She let the lift go when it finally arrived and fiddled with her mailbox for the next few minutes. A woman pushing a buggy with a crotchety toddler in it walked in and pressed the UP button. When the lift came, she held the door open for Ilona. Ilona was embarrassed. She wondered how often she would have to let the lift go before István came. So she walked in and pressed the button for her floor.

Perhaps to get Isi into the right mood, she should make him dinner. It was card night for Erzsi, so she knew István would be at home by himself. *Oh Isi, I made too much csirke paprikás, come in and have some.* To be honest, she usually just had a bread and cucumber sandwich for supper. She rarely cooked for herself.

As the lift rattled its way up, Ilona decided the best way to approach Isi. She hurried to her flat, and after she carefully hung up her cardigan, she pulled a photo album from the bottom drawer of her sideboard. Years ago, Emil had taken snapshots of the Pálffy *kastély* when they had a picnic on a Sunday in Tura. He was maybe twelve or thirteen then and crazy about Laci's old Zorki camera. He took pictures of everything. Trees, cloud formations, the lake, stray dogs. It nearly bankrupted her paying for the film to be developed. She finally had to limit him to one roll of film per year.

That day they had taken the bus to Tura, Emil, Ilona, and her mother. Ilona had made a pack lunch and Emil brought his swimsuit and the camera. It was a hot August morning, the kind when the air was so thick even the insects seemed too exhausted to fly. They walked through the dusty town with its neat gardens in front of identical houses while Emil trailed behind the two women, uninterested in their stories of days gone by. A bored almost-teenager, stuck on a hot Sunday with his mother and grandmother. Most of his friends were still on holiday at Lake Balaton or at the Young Pioneers Camp, but Emil had returned early for swimming practice, and Sunday was his only day off. This was clearly not the way he wanted to spend it.

The lake Ilona remembered as a child was more the size of a pond that parched August day. There was a footpath that led to it from the street; visitors like them had flattened the grass. They could stroll around it in fifteen minutes. Ilona's mother scowled when she saw the unkempt grounds and overgrown flower beds.

'The boxwood has gone wild! The roses are scraggly. The azalea bushes need clipping,' she complained as she and Ilona spread out a tablecloth to sit on. Clearly the old people were too frail to care! Emil had already trudged off to explore the outside of the *kastély*, the camera strap around his neck, his right hand steadying it so it didn't swing as he walked.

Ilona found the photos he had taken back then in the black leather album. There were four of them on the page; glossy squares rimmed in white, tucked into triangle fasteners. The first showed the front view of the mansion from the gravel driveway. Its single turret cut off from view. Ilona was not sure whether that was due to artistic licence or just that Emil could not fit the whole building into one frame. He shot a close-up of the front door, with its Pálffy crest and *1859* etched into the stone. That was the year her great-grandfather had completed the renovations. The estate was much older, she knew. The lower left photo showed a side view, with a close-up of the bevelled glass in what Ilona guessed was the billiards room. The last picture was one Ilona did not remember. It featured an upstairs window. The silhouette of an elderly woman was looking out of it, oblivious to the young photographer below. Ilona knew that the view from that window was only of trees, but the woman's gaze could have been on anything. A family reunion, a lover's tryst, the cradle of a sleeping child long grown. Emil's photo somehow caught the loneliness Ilona, at the time, did not understand. Now, she was struck by its depth of meaning. Beautiful, to be sure, however it certainly was not what she was looking for to show István.

Instead, with the carefully filed nail of her index finger, Ilona pried the first photo out of the page, and holding it like gold, walked over to Erzsi's flat and greeted István with a wide smile.

'You want me to buy your *kastély*?' István was sitting at the kitchen table, a plate of half-eaten *gulyas* in front of him. Ilona was still standing, so she could see that Isi's hair was starting to thin in the same place his father lost his hair.

'It's an investment, like your restaurant.'

'I just got the restaurant. All the money I have goes into it. I don't have the time or the money to buy your *kastély*. Besides, what would I do with it? What happens to the old people who live there now?'

'We can get backers, that means —'

'Ilona, I know what that means.' He shovelled a large spoonful of stew into his mouth and wiped his lips with a napkin. 'Sorry, but I need to go back to the restaurant soon.'

'Go ahead, Isi. I can eat at home.' Ilona smiled sweetly as

she pulled out a chair. She put the photograph in front of them, so he could admire it. 'This is the Pálffy *kastély* by the way.'

A few of the boxes that had been in the corner of the living room earlier in the day were now on the kitchen table. Ilona surreptitiously peered in: they looked like cassette tapes. Nothing Ilona would be interested in. She tugged at her sleeve. István glanced briefly at the snapshot.

'Ilona, your place is very nice, but look, I don't have the money or the time to help you out. Practically all the money I earn is from lunches eaten by these foreign businessmen. I know all about them. I'm telling you, every *forint* I earn has to go back into the business.'

'Well —' Ilona stopped herself. István didn't understand her plan. 'It works this way, Isi, we partner with the businessmen who will give us money —'

'Us?' István raised his eyebrows. 'Are you going into property speculation now, Ilona?'

Ilona pursed her lips and stared at István, a hulk of a man whose thirty-four years of life she knew better than he did. She remembered when he could barely walk across the room, when he was toilet training and when he got frustrated when the older boys wouldn't let him join in their football game. She wanted to tell him she didn't like his tone of voice, like she did when he was twelve. Instead, she sighed.

'Well. I just wanted to help you out, István,' Ilona shifted her weight onto her hands, which were on the table, as she stood up. 'It's a great opportunity.'

István jumped up and held out his arms. Ilona didn't like the smile on his face. To her, it looked more like a smirk.

'*Ilona néni*,' *Aunt Ilona*. He hugged her. She patted

his back.

Back at her flat, Ilona absentmindedly picked at a small tear on the armrest of the sofa with her left index finger while she held the photograph of the *kastély* in her right hand. Even though she had placed the antimacassar over the tiny hole, she knew it was there, and it was the place her fingers found when she had thinking to do. *Financial backers, privatisation, foreign investments, current account deficits, trade deficits, bonds, markets.* She had to learn these terms so she could translate for John; that didn't mean she understood how it all worked, though. She did know one thing: she wanted the family home back. Someone had to help her.

The flat darkened as the day waned. She had not yet turned on the lamp, but her living room was so familiar to her she didn't need the light as she sat picking at the bare spot on the armrest. Her eyes surveyed her small flat: the television, the sideboard in the dining room, then back to the side table next to where she was sitting. Her telephone, with its stylish cream colour, seemed out of place. It did not seem to fit in yet with her flat or her life. No one except John had the phone number.

Erzsebét was right, she needed to call Emil in the United States. Ilona tried to think of what she would say when she called. She had spent so much energy preparing for the arrival of the phone, she had not thought about what she would do with it.

Hello, dear, it's your mother!

No.

Though they had been apart for as long as they had been together, Ilona's longing for her son had not diminished. Her heart still ached that he had left her and had not told her why.

39

She often replayed their last months together, searching for clues. She found none. If he had been signalling a message, she had not picked up on it.

In the ensuing seventeen years he had graduated from an important university in Ohio, but she could not share in the celebration. He had married an American woman, but Ilona could not attend their wedding. He had a baby whom she could not hold. She missed him terribly and she wanted him to say the same to her.

Her fingernail found a thread and started scratching away at it. Maybe Emil could help out. The *kastély* could belong to him, too, after all. It's high time he came back.

THE NEXT MORNING

Ilona squeezed into the yellow tram heading towards the city centre. It was late as usual. Ilona held tightly onto the leather strap hanging from the ceiling, her court shoes planted firmly so she wouldn't fall through the wooden slats on the floor. Her stop was the third after the *Nyugati pályaudvar*, the Western Station, where most of the commuters got on, so there was rarely an empty seat available, even this early.

She had not slept well; her mind replaying the conversation with István; the mockery in his voice amplified in the silence of the night. Each line repeated every so often with a slightly more exaggerated sneer of his lips, as if her mind enjoyed the torture. *You going into the property market now, Ilona?* As if that was beyond the realm of possibility, which at 3:00 am and only then, she knew probably was true. Except... she was tired of having men tell her what she could and could not do.

Ilona stared pointedly at the young man sitting on the seat next to where she was standing, as if his existence there, on that seat, demonstrated the unfairness of her life. He resting comfortably while she, easily decades older, swayed to and fro with the gyrations of the ancient tram, clutching the leather strap to keep her from falling over.

He didn't look up. She cleared her throat and continued to glare. Then she coughed. The elderly woman with the window seat saw Ilona, then quickly planted her elbow firmly into the young man's ribs. He jumped up.

'Please,' he said, indicating at his seat. Ilona smiled pleasantly in his direction as she sat down.

'For me? Oh, thank you!' She didn't look at him again. Why would she?

She and the elderly woman nodded a greeting to one another. The woman smelled of fresh soap and toothpaste. It was reassuringly familiar.

'It's a beautiful day,' the woman said to Ilona, looking out of the window. The Danube glistened in the morning sun as the tram rumbled over the green Szabadság Bridge, with its art nouveau design that features winged mythological creatures.

'Yes,' Ilona agreed. 'Beautiful day.'

Ilona remembered when Emil would sit on her lap and point them out. '*Anyu*, look, birds!' he said once. She thought of her son and birds when she crossed the bridge.

István and the young man temporarily forgotten, Ilona settled down to enjoy the rest of the journey. She had lived in Budapest her whole adult life. Ghosts huddled in every corner she passed, whispering memories of a life she had not picked for herself.

The tram lurched for a moment, tossing Ilona into her neighbour. The two women steadied themselves by each putting a hand on the seat in front of them. The parliament was off to the left, but Ilona rarely took it in. The sight of the most beautiful and majestic building in all of Europe, perched on the banks of the river, still caused her pain. It was there that Laci had been killed.

She looked out as the tram passed each of the large *kastély* on the Buda side of the river. Ornate, green tiled roofs, bowed windows, some still with stained glass, the few that had withstood the tremors from the bombing. Once city residences to the members of the emperor's court, the mansions now were government offices, some housing restaurants or shops on the street level; once white, the stone now blackened from the fumes of the Trabis, Wartburgs and diesel lorries that clogged the streets. Parts of their façades were missing in places, gargoyle heads shot off, or more recently, fallen off by neglect. So much of the city had been neglected.

Still, the buildings somehow managed to retain their dignity, like a grand dame whose fur coat was riddled with moth holes. Ilona could see the beauty of what they once had been. What still could be. Like the Pálffy, her childhood home. She had taken Emil there when he was a boy.

Because it had room to expand in the countryside, where land was more readily available, her childhood home was just that much grander. A blue-tiled roof, not green. An extra wing. And a gilded cross on the spire on top of the turret. Her grandfather had planned on adding a chapel, she knew, so when that had not happened, her father added the cross. There was still space on the east side of the *kastély* to build the chapel; it was currently used as a car park for the old peoples' home.

The tram screeched to a halt. Passengers jostled past Ilona as they hurried out the folding doors. Ilona's bad mood had returned.

Few people ever took Ilona seriously, that was the problem. Why was everything so difficult? Clearly her family estate could be bought if only people would listen. Why couldn't Isi?

Of course, the solution was Emil. He was in America now, so he would understand, like the Western businessmen at the press conference. As she stomped down the steps of the tram, Ilona knew that he was pivotal to her plan. She would need to call him. Yes, she told herself, she would telephone him.

Even as she told herself that, she felt her stomach twinge; her nerves acting up again.

Because Ilona typically was the first to arrive at the news agency office, she stopped at the kiosk on the corner to pick up the newspapers. Every morning, she and the man at the newsstand always exchanged a few pleasantries. His wife was about to have gallbladder surgery.

'Beautiful weather, today,' he said, as he handed her the large load. He held a cigarette in his lips and he winced to keep the smoke out of his eye. The bundle of papers was heavy but she pretended it wasn't.

'Pleasantly warm,' Ilona nodded a goodbye.

There is an art to walking on low court shoes while carrying a heavy load, and Ilona had perfected it.

The news agency rented a large office on the third floor. Its floor-to-ceiling windows and open plan had jarred on Ilona the first time she entered. She had tried to convince John to order upmarket office furniture, walnut wood, and proper armchairs, yet he chose modern white desks and black swivel chairs.

Now, a year on, it was worse. With each new purchase came more clutter. Piles of newspaper clippings, press releases and notebooks overwhelmed the desks; unwashed coffee cups and ashtrays half-buried in between. A telex machine, enclosed in its own glass box to dampen the noise, constantly typed away, spewing copy on the floor. Ilona decorated her desk, which was located in the front, with an African violet so she could greet visitors as they entered.

As Ilona hung up her cardigan, she decided she would write a letter to Emil and give him her phone number; soften him up a bit. He could call her when he was ready. Besides, she convinced herself, it would cost less if he called her. If she wrote, she could mention the *kastély*.

'*Jó reggelt!*' John said that every morning. It was practically the only Hungarian he knew. That, and a collection of swear words, which he learnt from Janos the photographer.

'Good morning,' she smiled back. She had his coffee ready.

After she handed John the Daily Digest, Ilona dawdled, rolling up the copy from the Telex, tidying away the newspapers on her desk while she waited until he and the other journalist, Kálman, left for lunch. When the coast was clear, she inserted a fresh piece of paper into the electric Olivetti.

She often typed her letters to her son because it looked like she was working, and no one would be suspicious when she mailed the letter from the office. Not that Emil wrote back very often; she supposed he was busy.

Erzsi's blood pressure is under control, she wrote. *My own health is fine. Of course, I might have a slight circulatory problem, but nothing to worry about, I'm sure. I've started taking something for it. István has purchased his old restaurant, and he is hoping to buy more at auctions. Do you remember our kastély in Tura? It turns out the new government is allowing owners to take back property stolen from them! If only that could be us! Imagine! I decided to get a phone, too. It was installed this week. Here's the number…*

Akárhogy! Anyhow! I do hope you, Melissa and the baby are also doing well. I will enjoy seeing any pictures you might want to send me, if it's not too much of a bother.

Much Love!

Ilona calculated it would take about two weeks for the letter to reach Cleveland. So exactly two weeks after mailing the letter, she raced home to wait for Emil to call.

The phone didn't ring.

Nor did it ring at the weekend.

Well! Ilona reasoned; the Hungarian Post is very unreliable. It could take a month for that letter to arrive in Cleveland. She settled in for the wait.

Waiting was something Ilona did every day. She waited for the tram, stood in line at the grocer, queued at the post office to pay her bills. Sat in a chair staring at the flame next to the curling iron while the woman before her got that last mist of hairspray to hold down a recalcitrant lock. Back in 1974, it had taken a month before the Red Cross informed her that her son was in Italy waiting for a sponsor, likely an American who would take him to the United States. That was how she got confirmation that Emil had indeed escaped. There was some sort of organisation in Ohio that helped escapees from Hungary, she had learned. Apparently, that was how it worked: as a minor, Emil would have to have a family agree to take care of him. She was grateful that he wouldn't be left to fend for himself, and hoped the family would be kind.

Now, here she was again, seventeen years later, still waiting on Emil. A few times she picked up the receiver to check the dialling tone. Once, she got out her black address book and turned to the page for Emil's details, but she never called the number.

About a month after she had sent her letter, Ilona did hear from Emil. It was on a day she had been dreaming about how she would decorate the *kastély* interior. It was something she had taken to. During her free time — on the tram, waiting for a press conference to start, standing in line to pay bills — she reconstructed the *kastély* room by room, restoring it so it looked as it once had before the war. In her mind, she walked through each room, noting the wallpaper, the colour of the paint, the furniture and the paintings. She could even remember where the wall sconces were situated. While she knew it was important to restore the building back to its former grandeur, she felt it would need a few of her own touches, too. Modernise a bit.

On this evening, she was so preoccupied with the colour scheme for the reception rooms, pale cream or a warm yellow? She nearly forgot to check her post box. Her mail wasn't usually very important, anyway. Her birthday was months away, so she was likely only to get bills. What she found instead was a letter with a familiar return address from Cleveland, Ohio, USA.

To be honest, Ilona was disappointed. It would have been nice to hear Emil's voice again. Emil, in her memory, still sounded like a yodelling teenager, but he would sound like a man now. She wondered if he was a baritone or a tenor? She guessed baritone, like his father. The smooth tone of Laci's voice had always soothed her. Of course, a letter from Emil was always welcome. She could feel her heart pound a little faster as she waited for the lift. Did he want to set up a time for a telephone call? Maybe he was interested in learning more about the buyback scheme. She quickly hung up her cardigan, washed her hands and pulled the letter opener from her desk drawer. Then she sat on the edge of her sofa and she stared at the letter. It was square in a thick envelope.

In earlier days, Emil had sent thin blue letters that, when folded correctly, also acted as an envelope. She had to be particularly careful opening those, or the letter didn't unfurl properly and she was left turning the paper around and upside down to get the order right. In the early years, once the Red Cross had placed Emil with the Molnár family, he sent long, rambling letters describing: his sponsors: *their name is Molnár, but in America they spell it Molnar. Mr. Molnar is very nice. He's an engineer. Mrs. Molnar is a nurse. Their sons are Sándor and Tamás, but they like to be called Sandy and Tom. Sandy is my age, but in the year above me in school. He plays a lot of different sports. Tom is in ninth grade. He plays in the school band. He brings his trumpet home with him like it belongs to him*; his High School: *they thought I'd learn English faster if I went back a year. It's very easy*; and America: *the house is a villa! I get my own room! There are lots of motorways! The cars are huge. The Molnars bought a new 'Town and Country' Station Wagon and didn't have to wait. They even got to choose its colour. They picked turquoise with wooden side panels.*

48

Once, Emil sent her a newspaper story about the Hungarian émigré who had beaten a college swimming record. It showed a tall man that Ilona almost did not recognise as her son. He had only grown a little, yet his body had filled out; the muscles on his arms bulged. Still, that was not why he looked unfamiliar. In the photo he did not wear that same ecstatic look he had worn when he was younger and had won a race. He looked tired, and Ilona fretted that they were not treating him well. After that letter, he was quiet for a long time. Ilona worried so much she lost a kilo.

The letters did not always divulge everything their recipient wanted to know. Ilona became a sleuth, attempting to detect a mood; follow a meaning; gather clues to his life from phrases stated too glibly, pictures not sent, words not written. On a telephone call, she could ask him questions he could not avoid in his letters or postcards.

Sometimes Emil would send a package of photos from Ohio — of the Molnar family, their house, which to Ilona, did indeed look like a villa, their station wagon, and their trees. All were photographs Emil had taken with a camera the Molnars had given him his first Christmas. Ilona was stunned by the wealth of this family. *This*, she thought, *could have been us*.

Now, sitting at the dining room table, Ilona slid the letter opener into the slit at the top of the envelope and pulled out the latest card Emil had sent.

She carefully turned the note over to the front and frowned. It was a photo in black and white, and featured a child undressed from the waist up, its enormous eyes staring at the camera without blinking. No colourful background or cheery greeting. To be honest, Ilona preferred cards with pink flowers winding around the edges. Pretty, to put the reader in a pleasant mood. She sighed — never mind — and opened the card.

The message inside was in Emil's familiar heavy scrawl. And, typical for her son these days, it contained only a few sentences. She had noticed through the years that his Hungarian was getting rusty.

We're coming to Budapest in August and hope to stay for a year. Can we live with you? Do you have space? Melissa and I don't mind sharing Grandma's room with Tünde. Can't wait to see you! Love!

He added flight details.

The letter was direct, there was no small talk about his new baby, his wife or of Ilona's plan to buy the *kastély*. Ilona re-read the note for clues, thought about it all for a minute, then decided she would need someone to help decipher it.

Erzsi's kitchen table had not changed since she and Péter had moved into the flat in the 1950s. Because it was pushed against the wall, only three chairs fit around it. It was the site of birthday parties and funeral dinners, low-volume debates about whether to flee to Vienna and money exchanges when Péter got a shipment of watches or jewellery to sell on the black market. There were multiple water stains and scratches, of course, and in one prominent spot István had carved his name when he was a rebellious teenager.

On the back of the table near the wall, there was a small indentation on one side where Ilona could make out the image of a swimmer. Emil must have scratched it out with his knife at a boring dinner. She often fingered the outline of it. It was hers, that small scratched drawing of an arm above a wave and a mouth gasping for breath. His legs in the frog-kicking position. Had he been thinking about a new stroke or had he just been doodling? When had he made it? Ilona had no idea, but when she sat at Erzsi's table, she often placed her finger on it to make sure a part of Emil was still in Budapest.

Erzsi made tea and washed her hands before admiring the front of the card.

'What a sweet little face,' Erzsi said. 'Look at that pout.'

'Read it, Erzsi,' Ilona said. She tugged at her sleeve impatiently.

Erzsi opened the card and read the message twice. A large grin spread over her face.

'Oh Ilona, this is wonderful! Emil is coming!'

Then Erzi's brow furrowed as she re-read one sentence. 'Grandma's room?'

Erzsi looked at Ilona, laying the note on her lap.

'He doesn't know you moved into a one-bedroom flat? Almost seventeen years ago?'

'When was there an appropriate time, Erzsi? First I was waiting to make sure he was okay, then he was excited about moving to Ohio.'

Erzsébet paused to let that sink in.

'It's wonderful they are coming, but where will they stay? And for a year?'

Ilona had no idea; she hadn't thought that far ahead. Still, she sure wasn't going to let a lack of a bedroom get in the way of her son's homecoming.

'Of course he won't really *need* to stay with me for a year. I'm sure he means until he finds a villa or something,' Ilona said. 'I don't mind sleeping on the pull-out sofa.'

'Ilona, you slept on that thing for more than ten years when your mother was alive. It killed your back.'

Ilona ignored her.

'After all, it couldn't possibly take a year. Emil and his new wife will fall in love with the *kastély* immediately and get things moving to buy it. Of course, I can help with the red tape…'

'*Kastély*?' Erzsi said. 'He doesn't say anything about a *kastély*. Ilona, what are you going on about?'

'Erzsi, you know that the government is allowing us to get our old properties back. You know how wealthy the Molnars are. Maybe Emil has heard and wants to come to reclaim it.'

'How would he have heard, Ilona?'

Ilona ignored the question.

'Maybe he'll want to join István.'

'Join István! Ilona, can't you be content that Emil is coming for a visit? That you will see him for the first time in who-knows-how-long?'

Ilona wasn't listening, she was mentally starting her to-do list.

'August is only a couple of months away. How are we going to arrange everything in time?'

Erzsi reached for a notepad.

'Will we need bibs? Bottles?' *How could she afford all this*? Ilona worried. 'Do you know anyone we can borrow a cot from?'

'What about that nice family down the hall? Their son

must be too old for a cot now.'

'What do you think an American wife expects? Does she know Hungarian flats are small?' Ilona asked, half to herself.

At the thought, Ilona smiled. 'Maybe that's not such a bad thing as the cramped quarters would force Emil and his wife to see the necessity of getting the *kastély*?'

'Ilooona,' Erzsi sounded a warning.

Ilona felt embarrassed.

'What's important is that Emil is coming back. With his American wife and baby girl.' Ilona said it as though she meant it.

'That's right,' Erzsi patted the top of Ilona's hand.

Ilona, sitting at Erzsi's table, read the card a third and fourth time and felt chastened. Erzsi was right. Ilona imagined coming home from work to a flat full of people, eating dinners around her dining room table — not Erzsi's — with all its chairs occupied. Then the dining room in her mind morphed into the main hall of her *kastély*, eating on family china that she no longer owned. Then she had an image of herself sweeping through a chandeliered restaurant of her own Grand Hotel de Tura, greeting guests as she passed by. Emil and his wife standing at the front door grateful that Ilona had been so clever to encourage them to invest.

It all seemed so logical to her now. Emil had to leave Hungary in order to make a fortune he never could have made if he had stayed in Budapest. With that money, he could buy Ilona her *kastély* and restore her good life. They could be as wealthy as the Molnars! It seemed to her as if that had been God's plan all along. Emil had left in order to redeem the family. To reclaim its name.

With a *kastély* and a son, she would no longer feel the empty space that had opened in her stomach when the Soviets took her home in the first place. That space that had expanded into a great hollow in 1956 when army tanks ripped off her husband's face. That space that had widened into an abyss when Emil abandoned her. Now, everything seemed to be so clear to Ilona. It was all meant to happen. Emil was meant to swim away from her, to meet this wealthy family, to attend an American university, to marry an American wife and make an American fortune, with which he could then return to Hungary and to her. Buying back her *kastély* would complete the circle. It would make those years of loneliness all worthwhile. This was the plan all along.

As the weeks ticked by, Ilona's flat filled with items for her grandchild: an ancient cot from the family down the hall squished into the bedroom, a high chair borrowed from the daughter of a friend that Ilona rolled to the spot at the table closest to the kitchen. Ilona purchased an adorable pink bunny.

'How old will the little one be?' Erzsi asked.

'Two.'

'Such a sweet age.'

It was a Saturday. The two friends were at Erzsi's flat drinking tea, even though it was nearly lunch time. István stumbled in wearing just his trousers and reeking of last night's cigarettes and beer.

'Good morning, sleepy head,' Erzsi said, as István poured water to make coffee.

He grunted. His eyes were barely open.

'Goodness, Isi!' Ilona said. 'Are you just now waking up?'

'Yeah. My manager is opening the restaurant today. I'm still focusing on getting this new nightclub off the ground. Today I need to hire some new staff, so I have to go in soon. I won't be back until late.'

'New nightclub?'

'Yeah, I was able to get this place around the corner from the restaurant. It was a wreck with the ceilings collapsing and lots of structural problems, I've hired some Romanians to do the renovations. A lot cheaper than Hungarian workers.'

He slurped his coffee as he leaned his back against the counter. He was awake now, relishing the chance to talk about this new life he was making.

'They work for about a dollar a day. Found out about them from my financial backer. He's using them to renovate a hotel. Imagine, it's cheaper to hire Romanians to haul bricks up a ladder than use machinery.'

Erzsi looked down at her empty tea cup, crimson skin creeping up her neck, her lips tight. Ilona studied István for a moment. He used to be so kind, she thought. She wondered if this new, hardened Isi was an act. Like that time when he and Emil were teenagers and tried desperately to look tough. That was when they started smoking cigarettes and Isi let his hair grow long. Emil, because he was swimming, had to keep his head shaved. Both were such softies, though, it was an impossible act to keep up.

István continued: 'I've learned a lot about maximising profits from this guy. Before, when I was just managing the restaurant for the state, we didn't care about making money like that. We just made sure customers got food on their table before the plate got cold.'

He chuckled. 'Sometimes even that didn't happen.'

Ilona was quiet for the slightest second, then her eyes widened almost imperceptibly.

'I have an idea. You should write a business proposal. Maybe Emil would like to become an investor.'

István gave her a withering look. 'For your *kastély*?'

'No, your business.'

'You think Emil would do that?'

'István, have you seen pictures of the house the Molnars live in? Of course, he'll be coming here like all the other returnees, looking for opportunities. You've seen all these people.'

'Oh yeah. Their Hungarian is terrible! Some of the expressions they use; like they're still back living in the 1950s.' Then István turned serious. 'Ilona, do you really think that's why Emil is coming? Do you think he'd become a partner?'

Erzsi shifted in her seat.

'Ilona, Emil didn't say why he was coming to Budapest. Isn't he a photographer?'

Ilona waved her off. 'Of course, he'd be interested, István!'

István nodded. 'Yeah, I can write something up.'

'It probably needs to be in English. I'm not sure how well the Molnars speak Hungarian anymore.' Then, seeing István's scowl, Ilona added quickly, 'I can help with that.'

Ilona knew that Erzsi had bought a Teach Yourself English Course and that she and Isi were learning English from it. They already were on Side A of the second LP, but their written skills probably were still limited.

Then she added: 'Maybe we can add a chapter about a hotel. You know, down the line. Once the nightclub is running.'

István slurped his coffee.

'Anything more I can add to the To Do list?' Erzsi asked Ilona.

'We need to organise a welcome dinner. I guess I can make it,' Ilona mused. 'Of course, I would need to get to the grocer and the butcher before going to the airport. That probably would mean I'd need to take a taxi, because otherwise I would be late…'

She paused a moment, considering logistics. István was cutting some bread for breakfast. His back was to the women. Erzsi seemed to be preoccupied with the To Do list. Ilona continued a little louder.

'I remember that time you, Péter and István arrived back from visiting Czechoslovakia after István had finished school. And I made you that special dinner so I could hear all about your trip. I can use that same recipe.'

István was spreading lard on the bread, clearly not listening to the conversation, however Erzsébet took the cue.

'I can make dinner for you all.'

'Oh no. That's too much work for you. I couldn't dream of imposing on you. Perhaps,' Ilona said, demurring, 'we could go out to eat.'

She paused and waited for Erzsi and István to consider that option. István was adding peppers to his meal. When there was no reply, Ilona shook her head gently.

'Oh, that would be expensive… no, I'll get up *very* early and be the first in line at the grocer.'

'Perhaps István could reserve us a table at his restaurant?' Erzsi said. István turned around, holding the plate in his hand, when he heard his name. He was holding the salt shaker in his hand.

'Huh?'

Ilona smiled.

'Well. That's a great idea, Erzsi! István, we can eat at your place and show it to Emil. That would really give him an idea of what a special restaurant you have. Erzsi, I'm so glad you thought of that.'

August

Ilona arrived at the airport gate thirty minutes before the plane was scheduled to touch down. She wore her best summer skirt, with a cardigan draped over her thin shoulders and secured with a small chain clasped on each side so that she would make a good impression. She got there early because she worried the plane might land early and she wouldn't be there to help Emil get through customs; something Ilona was familiar with because she'd been there many times as a fixer, meeting journalists. It was a point of pride that she greeted them at the gate. Few of the new reporters noticed the difficulty in meeting them *before* visa control, so she always made a point to tell them that she had made an extra effort to pull some strings so they wouldn't have any long waits. Westerners rarely were aware of these things; they needed it explained to them.

Of course, she didn't mind inconspicuously tucking a few extra *forints* into her passport for the border control guard this visit, explaining to him that she was picking up her *American* son and his *American* wife and child. The official waved her past without a word, discreetly stashing the bills into his shirt pocket. In past trips to Ferihegy Airport, Ilona would carry a clipboard with the name of the person she was waiting for on it. She would hold it just right, so that she didn't look pushy, just discreet, as she searched for whichever journalist she was expecting to arrive. She usually could pick them out quickly. Reporters tended to look scruffier than the diplomats and businessmen who shared the plane with them.

That's why Ilona was certain she would recognise her son. He had sent only a few photos of himself recently — most were of the baby — even though he claimed to be good at taking pictures. The older he got, the more Ilona thought he looked like Laci, however, their bodies were different. Laci played soccer, so he had been wiry. The butterfly stroke had given Emil an elongated V-shape body, with broad shoulders that tapered down to a small waist and skinny legs. When he swam competitively, he had cropped his thick brown hair, but she knew that was grown out now. She would know her son anywhere, or at least she thought she would. She tugged at her sleeve and fussed with a handkerchief she had tucked in it. She suspected Emil would act more like someone from his adopted country: bold, brash, loud and confident.

When the plane taxied to the gate, Ilona knew from experience it would take a few minutes for the mobile steps to be pulled up next to it. Even so, her heart jumped with excitement. She felt herself standing a bit straighter and focusing her eyes as much as possible. She shifted her weight back and forth. She tried to think about what she would say to him first, but, really, she was too distracted by the events unfolding in front of her to worry about that: the doors had opened and the first passengers were ducking out onto the steps.

First there seemed to be the businessmen in first class who walked briskly across the tarmac. Ilona ignored them; they were easy to spot, with their briefcases and no-nonsense gait. They knew the airport routine well. Then came a couple — she, with her blonde hair in a bun and sheer stockings gleaming under black high heels, he wearing a dark suit. Both of them carried briefcases. Ilona stared at the man. He was tall enough to be Emil, yet he didn't have Laci's features and there was no child, so Ilona kept straining to see who would come next. It seemed to her that the whole plane had emptied out and still no sign of Emil. Instinctively Ilona took a few steps closer to the gate door, peering out of the large glass windows at the plane. A stewardess came out, blinking a few times in the light.

What if they weren't on the flight? Ilona's heart missed a beat. What had happened to them? Oh dear. Ilona tugged at her sleeve again.

She peered once again at the passengers still coming out of the gate. People were hugging. Others shaking hands with guides holding clipboards. Should she ask at the desk? Her eyes darted again back to the plane.

Then she saw that the stewardess was helping a couple with their bags.

Ilona was not expecting to feel so breathless and agitated when she finally saw him walk down the plane steps and onto the tarmac. It's just that Emil's gait was unmistakable. He lumbered slowly and softly, like he didn't want to take up tarmac others might want to use. He nodded a thank you to the stewardess as he took the bag from her. Then he, too, began to strain his neck in search of someone.

There he was, finally, after seventeen years, her son. Emil.

'Oh.'

Ilona gasped a small, almost inaudible, sound; her eyes began to burn as tears welled up. She quickly dabbed them dry with her hankerchief and tucked it quickly back up her sleeve as she walked even closer toward the gate door to meet him.

'Édesanyam! Mother!' Emil said, smiling. '*Nagyon örülök* — it's so great —' but then Emil stopped, too overwhelmed to continue speaking.

Beaming, Ilona gripped her son's arms tightly, breathing him in deeply. She wanted to smell him, touch him, feel him. To make up for nearly two lost decades. She held him back from her for a minute to take him in. He was heavier and maybe a bit taller than she remembered. His hair, indeed longer, was starting to grey at the temples. Her son with grey hair! Then she grasped him close to her again, ignoring the bag that was in the way. In the past he was rarely without his swimming gear, so she was used to it. This time he held what might be a bag for nappies as well as a camera bag on one shoulder. She didn't mind. She took in his smell and rocked him side to side.

'Ohh,' was all she could say. 'Ohh.'

She didn't want to let go. Then she heard another voice beside her.

'*Jó napot kívánok!*' It sounded like, '*YonaPO KEEvinok!*' A loud unmistakably American voice, which is why the greeting was pronounced incorrectly.

Ilona understood the gesture. She had heard it often with other foreigners. At first glance, Ilona thought the petite woman next to Emil looked like a tall, thin girl. She wore socks with her sandals, which looked like they were men's with two wide suede stripes over her feet. She was beaming a huge, toothy smile, holding her arms out ready to embrace her mother-in-law.

'You speak such excellent Hungarian already!' Ilona was practised at this. It's what she told all her clients. Ilona made sure she always spoke the Queen's English, like she heard on the BBC World Service. Like she had learnt from the Scottish au pair when she was young.

'You must be Melissa. I'm so pleased to finally meet you.'

Ilona stretched out her hand, but Melissa leaned in for a big hug and wrapped her arms tightly around her mother-in-law. Ilona was not sure what to do. She patted Melissa's back until the hug was over.

A second glance at her daughter-in-law revealed she had no dress sense, wore no make-up and her hair was a mess. *No wonder he rarely sent photos,* Ilona thought. The strange contraption she wore on her back held a small child. Ilona wasn't sure what more to say, but Melissa filled in the gap.

'I'm so happy to finally meet you too! I've heard all about you! And this —' Melissa said, pointing to a slouched body over her shoulder with a flourish, her voice still a tad too loud, '— this is Tünde, your granddaughter. She was awake the whole flight and only decided to sleep after we took off from Vienna. What a flight! I felt like we walked the aisles with her the whole nine hours. We are so excited…'

Ilona wasn't listening.

She peered over the chattering woman and stared at the top of the little head. Her grandchild. The thin wisps of hair were dark brown like Emil's and Melissa's. She had a stubby nose and her mouth was open slightly, lending her an innocent, peaceful look.

'Ohh.'

Ilona could feel her eyes well up again. She wanted to hold her granddaughter. Kiss her. She couldn't take her eyes off this sweet little person that seemed so soft and gentle.

'Ohh,' Ilona said again.

It felt like she had seen that face before, it was so familiar. The face in her dreams, she supposed. The face in the photos Emil sent. As she studied it, the little girl woke up and deep brown eyes penetrated her grandmother's soul. The eyes were unmistakable. This was the child, the face on the postcard Emil had sent. He hadn't mentioned it was her granddaughter. In other pictures, she had been a baby wrapped in a blanket. They grow so fast.

'Hello,' she said to her granddaughter. The little girl tucked her head shyly into the papoose.

Although Ilona wanted to savour the moment, to touch the baby, she found herself following Melissa and Emil to visa control instead.

With all their luggage, video equipment and such, they decided to take a taxi. Emil was surprised when Ilona gave the driver an address of a restaurant.

'I thought you'd be hungry,' Ilona said in English so Melissa would understand.

'I think we're more jet-lagged.' He yawned, to prove his point.

Ilona pretended not to see Melissa poke her husband in the ribs as he settled into the back seat of the taxi. Ilona was in front to make sure the driver drove directly to the restaurant and not around some back neighbourhood a few times. She knew their tricks.

'A quick dinner would be great,' Melissa said politely. Then she turned to her daughter on her lap. 'We are hungry in Hungary!'

No one laughed.

'It's *István's* restaurant,' Ilona turned around to chat with Emil 'He *owns* it now. He's very successful, you know.'

'Hey, that's great,' Emil nodded his head.

'He's looking for opportunities to open more.'

'That's great,' Emil repeated. He didn't sound excited.

The couple hadn't exchanged money yet, so Ilona was forced to pay the taxi driver. She counted the money exactly.

As they entered the old-world restaurant, each family member blinked several times, adjusting their eyes. White linen tablecloths; heavy brocade curtains; oil paintings of the Hungarian Great Plains. In the taxi, Ilona worried that István might not allow Emil and Melissa into his restaurant because they were wearing jeans, yet Isi didn't seem to mind.

'So?' István's face lit up when he saw Emil.

The two men leaned in for a hug, wound up catching themselves, so they ended up just patting each other on the back instead; poked each other's bellies, laughing a bit. István was portly around the middle. A hulk. He slouched. Emil was softer than he used to be, but still had an athlete's build.

'Hey, where's your hair?'

'Where did the brown go on your head, old man?'

'At least I still have mine.'

'*Háát*!' They shrugged in unison. Then they laughed at their synchronicity.

Erzsi, who was waiting at the table, gave Emil such a

giant squeeze that he nearly lost his balance.

István let Melissa embrace him as he said to her. '*Kezét csókolom*.' I kiss your hand.

Ilona noticed István gave Melissa the once-over with his eyes. Ilona then gave him a warning with her eyes, which István ignored.

'And dis is baby?' he said, gallantly, as Melissa held the toddler up for inspection.

'Her name is Tünde,' Melissa smiled as she said it.

István knitted his eyebrows together, like he was confused. 'Tünde?'

Emil said in Hungarian, '*Tünde*. In America they pronounce it differently.'

'*Persze*.' Of course, Isi said. He smiled and turned to Melissa, and in English, said. 'She look just like fairy.'

Ilona noticed Isi seemed to be growing into his role as the new owner of one of Budapest's top restaurants: courteous and diplomatic. The restaurant, Ilona knew, had a reputation for its discretion. Once, when John had treated Ilona to lunch, Ilona thought she saw a Swiss pharmaceutical salesman and a health ministry official in a *tête-à-tête* at a table in the back. She had asked Isi if she was right, but he stayed mum. None of the restaurants' guests, István once told her, acknowledged one another. He wouldn't either. His was the place where deals were made, and he liked that.

For his American guests, István chose a front table, close to the peripatetic musicians who he knew would, at some point, come into the restaurant to play the accordion. The foreigners like that sort of music. István had asked his chef to prepare American-style Hungarian Goulash for them in advance. It wasn't as spicy as the restaurant normally served the dish.

Melissa looked at the layer of grease floating on top, and holding a spoon full of meaty-stew, gave Emil a smile across the table. Then she turned to her host.

'Everything looks so delicious, István!'

Ilona was pleased. The couple will probably want to help István in his business venture too, she thought giddily. Then Melissa spoiled the moment by taking off her jumper, revealing a black tank top underneath.

'I had forgotten Europeans don't use air conditioning! It's nice and cosy in here,' Melissa wiped her brow. She left her jumper in a heap next to her chair. One of the waiters discreetly placed it on top of the pile of luggage stacked in the corner.

Ilona was certain that, what with the jeans and those sandals, Isi would certainly ask them to leave. István did not seem to mind, though. She saw that he was ogling Melissa, who didn't notice. Her eyes were surveying the room.

'And these paintings!'

Melissa studied a horseback rider in a traditional cobalt-blue smock fastened at the waist with a thick leather belt. His blousy sleeves looked almost like wings as he galloped across the great grassy plains of Hungary, a long feather in his flat, black felt hat.

'Are those Cossacks?'

Ilona scowled. 'They are plainsmen, dear. Magyar.'

Erzsi chuckled and reached into her handbag, pulling out a thin 'Welcome to Hungary' pamphlet she had found at a tourism office and handed it to Melissa. Then she looked over at the boy who had swum away and sighed.

'I can't believe you're back. You look just the same!'

Erzsi said in Hungarian as she placed a hand over Emil's.

Emil smiled back. Remembering Melissa, Erzsi switched to rusty English.

'So. Vat brings back for year? Vat going to do?'

'Well, I got a grant from the Fulbright Scholar Programme in Fine Arts. Officially I'm here as a professional photographer and as an academic to research and document the role of media and art in Hungary. I wrote the programme pretty broadly so I have some freedom to dabble,' he said. 'I'd like to work with video, too. That's a new medium for me.'

'And I'd like to explore Hungary,' Melissa said. 'See where Emil grew up. Give *Toondah* a sense of her heritage from her father's side!' She tried to pronounce her daughter's name like the Hungarians were doing.

The other dinner guests nodded in quiet agreement.

Ilona tried to get a handle on the meaning of it all.

'So Emil, will you be taking pictures that will help your stationery company? Make note cards like the ones you send me, or will you be looking for other business ventures, too?'

Melissa snorted. Emil ignored his wife and looked earnestly at his mother.

'Well *Anyu*, the note cards are for you and Melissa's family. My work — with my photography, I aim to do a little more than that,' Emil said.

Melissa jumped in: 'As his *gallerist* likes to say, when someone looks at Emil's photographs, "you feel like you do when you want to read a line of poetry twice".'

'Well everyone reads poetry and looks at pictures in their spare time,' Ilona said, quickly adding: 'It's also helpful to find ways to earn a bit of money, though, isn't it? And there are so many opportunities opening up now! Would anyone like more goulash?'

Within a half hour of arriving at their flat, Melissa and Tünde had gone to bed, the jet lag had got to them. Ilona didn't mind, she wanted her son to herself. Ilona sat in the living room with her son drinking tea.

'It's so wonderful to see you again, Emil,' Ilona said, grateful she could switch back to Hungarian.

'It's good to be back. I missed you.'

Ilona's heart skipped a beat. Those were words she had been waiting to hear for seventeen years. She sighed with contentment. Ilona didn't want him to walk behind the bedroom door, fearing he'd disappear again. She wanted to keep him there, in front of her, so she could look at him.

While she had been expecting Emil to be older, she hadn't anticipated him to be, well, bigger, filled out, expanded. He wasn't that awkward teenager anymore, which was the image she had kept in her head. Now without meaning to he took over the whole living room. His legs seemed too long for the settee. She loved all of him.

'So, are you going to be okay on that couch, *Anyu*?' he asked. 'I didn't know you moved.'

'It's only for a year.' She hadn't brought up the *kastély* yet, deciding that it was best to speak of it once his jet lag was over. 'Melissa seems nice.'

'She's the best thing that's ever happened to me. Really. She helped me find my way in college and figure out what I wanted to focus on. She's been amazing. Her brother is my best friend. That's how we met, actually. Through him.'

Emil smiled faintly, like he was remembering something. There was so much to learn about her son and she didn't want him to hold back the memories. She wanted to hear all his stories all at once, but Emil had never been talkative. When he was a boy, she'd ask, 'how was school?' He always just answered, 'fine'. She never got any more details.

'I noticed a lot of medicine in the bathroom. Are you ill?'

'Oh no. Melissa takes them for her epilepsy. It's no big deal.'

'Epilepsy?' Ilona's eyes bulged. She brought her hand to her throat. 'You never mentioned she has fits.'

'She doesn't have fits. They are called seizures. And anyway, as long as she sleeps well, eats well and keeps her stress levels down, she's fine.'

'You don't let her stay alone with the baby, do you?'

'Yes, mum. She's fine. Her seizures are under control. Don't worry about it.'

Ilona tried to come to terms with that information. It was all so difficult. She didn't know Emil had married an epileptic. What did it all mean?

'Eat well? You'll have to tell me what food you want me to make,' she said, figuring it best to change the subject. 'Anything you missed?'

'Oh, wow. No. The Molnars eat Hungarian dishes all the time.' Ilona noticed he pronounced their name with an American accent, the vowel sounds were wrong; the *l* and *r* were too pronounced, like he chewed them. 'Don't worry. Just make whatever. Melissa will probably do a lot of cooking. She usually cooks vegetarian. I mean, she ate the goulash today, except she normally doesn't eat meat. I cook a lot, too.'

'Vegetarian? That's ridiculous,' Ilona said. 'The meat here is the best in Europe. She'll learn.'

Emil said nothing.

Ilona didn't want that woman to spoil her time with her son, so she changed the subject yet again. Goodness this was going to be complicated.

'Emil, I'm so happy you are here.' Ilona found that she couldn't stop smiling. She'd been grinning so much she thought her cheek muscles would start to hurt.

'I'm really happy we got to make it here.'

'So, tell me.' Ilona put on her best serious-mother voice. The one she used when Emil hadn't confessed to going out with teammates after practice. 'What will you be doing this year? I can help you set up appointments.'

'Oh no *Anyu*. Thanks. I don't think that'll be necessary. The university and the Fulbright committee helped me a lot,' Emil said. 'Like I said earlier, I want to get the lay of the land. See for myself how the country has changed. I mean, I haven't been here in seventeen years! My goal, though, is to try to document Hungary's transition to a democracy.'

'Well, part of that *transition* is the government's privatisation scheme. Have you read about that?' Ilona asked him. 'I might have written to you about it. There are some great opportunities…'

'Oh yeah, well,' Emil shrugged. He poked his finger absentmindedly through a gap in the upholstery under the antimacassar.

'— István has a number of business ventures planned. And I thought we could look into taking back the Pálffy. You remember our estate in Tura.'

'Right. Right,' Emil said, nodding his head vaguely. 'I remember all the stories you used to tell me about growing up on the Pálffy estate. Next time I find a few million hanging around, I'll think about buying a castle in Hungary. Anyway, I'm really happy for István.'

Ilona kept her smile steady.

'When you are away so long, you forget who you are,' she said. 'Don't forget that you are a Pálffy, too. Not just a Kovács.'

'Never.' Emil smiled at his mother, then with a flourish, he straightened the piece of embroidered cloth on the armrest, stood up and stretched his arms as he yawned. He leaned down to where Ilona was seated and wrapped his long arms around his mother. Ilona couldn't remember the last time she had been held like that. She breathed in contentment.

'Thanks again for putting us up. It's great being here again.'

He brought their tea cups into the kitchen.

Ilona let Emil use the bathroom first.

'Good night, *Anyu*.'

'Sleep well, Emil.'

He closed the bedroom door gingerly behind him. It wasn't late.

Long after Emil went to sleep, Ilona remained seated on the couch next to her phone.

It was silent in the flat. She could hear traffic on the street below. The TV was on in the flat above her, but Ilona couldn't make out the programme.

A telephone rang somewhere on their floor; the sound barely audible. The quiet in her flat had a different quality now that it was full of people. Sounds didn't bounce around. They were more muted, less echoey.

She had some thinking to do. Tünde was shy and a bit whiny, which Ilona put down to the long flight. *Melissa was sick, an epileptic; maybe that had to do with being a vegetarian*, she thought. Ilona feared what would happen if Melissa had an attack.

Emil, though, was the same; maybe more confident. Definitely happier, she could see that. He used to be a moody teenager. It was hard imagining him as a family man, but he seemed so natural and relaxed around his daughter. She wondered what kind of father Laci would have been.

Ilona was disappointed that Emil hadn't come to the country ready to invest. So many foreigners were arriving to do just that. The country had been isolated for so long, Ilona assumed they had been forgotten. It was as if the Soviets had erected barriers and they all had fallen asleep trying to escape a bad dream.

When the Iron Curtain fell, she had been certain all the young people would leave. It hadn't occurred to her that all the people who had fled in 1956 would want to come back. It's why the hotels were fully booked and new ones were being built to house all the people flooding in. They came wearing tennis shoes made of real leather and speaking a formal version of Hungarian that she hadn't heard in decades with expressions that had long since fallen out of fashion. They spent money so easily; flaunting their wealth in ways they weren't even aware. So why did Emil pretend he had no money and didn't seem at all interested in the Pálffy estate? This was going to be more difficult than she thought.

The long summer sun had finally set. The traffic outside was thinning out and the TV upstairs was still on. Ilona could tell it was the news. Her hip joints were stiff when she stood up. It only took a few steps to the bathroom to get them moving again. She knew as she unfolded the sofa bed that it would be a long night, not just because the springs poked into her ribs. She had a lot of thinking to do.

She'd have to plan this carefully. Eventually Emil will come around. She was sure of it.

LANDSCAPE OF CHILDHOOD

'See this?' Emil picked up a white bag from the refrigerated section of the *csemege*, the corner store where, as a boy he'd run to get items they had forgotten.

He held the small bag in two hands as if it were a slippery fish about to flip away any minute. Tünde reached for it playfully to touch its cold moist surface. The word *tej* was written in bold black letters, otherwise there were no pictures to indicate the contents. Melissa looked at it curiously.

'Milk,' Emil answered her unspoken question. 'All the packaging for products here in Hungary just have their names on.' He grinned at her astonished face. 'No pictures. No brands. You wouldn't believe how confused I was when I moved to Ohio.'

'What about skimmed?'

'Nope. Just milk. That's what you get. The real deal.'

'*Vaj*?' Melissa tried out, pointing to a small square package.

'Butter.'

A matronly woman carrying a green plastic basket

squeezed by the three Americans who were taking up the aisle of the small store. She smiled wanly at them; Emil apologised and stepped back to allow her to grab a litre of *tej*, which she dropped unceremoniously into her basket.

'*Joghurt*! That's one I know!' Melissa laughed a bit too loudly for a small store. The woman jumped slightly as she moved on. Emil thought she had a faint smell of sour milk.

Melissa bent down over the refrigerated shelves and screwed up her eyes in concentration. Next to the yoghurt in the same white container was another item marked *túró*.

'What's that?'

'Oh, umm that's...' Emil was stumped. 'It's like ricotta cheese, but it's not. I guess it's like cottage cheese, but it doesn't have that consistency. It's... I don't know what you call it in English. I don't think you have it.'

'What do you use it for?'

Emil had to think for a moment. 'In cooking, there is a great fried dish that uses it.'

In the next aisle, Melissa considered the gigantic golden loaves of bread. 'Is that it? Just one kind? I mean, no wholemeal?'

Emil shook his head. 'You'll survive.'

In the ensuing weeks, Emil savoured those moments when he could show his wife Hungary so she could get a glimpse of what his life had been like. Part of that was nostalgia; but another part was Emil's need to get Melissa to understand that Americans lived in a bubble.

He wanted Melissa to see her world through his eyes; why he wasn't excited about some new product the way she was. That his life had been fine without new improved secret formula shampoo or laundry detergent or even beer. Zero calories, lite, no fat, no salt. Food was a joke in the US. Worse, the packaging in America was abhorrent, he thought. Huge boxes were shrink-wrapped in plastic three times for one tiny bottle that Emil could buy without any packaging in a store in Budapest. There never was that kind of waste when he was growing up.

He felt the same way about raising Tünde. The number of toys that kid had shocked him. In Ohio Melissa's friend had held her five-year-old's birthday party at Cedar Point Amusement Park. The Berenstain Bears greeted the kids who then played in a roped cage filled with balls at King Arthur's Court. It must have cost that family a fortune, and for what? In Budapest kids played outside.

Too often people in the States spent so much money entertaining their kids. Emil wanted to prove to Melissa that when he was a kid, he never felt poor. He had the impression that Melissa somehow thought his childhood had been deprived, even though she never actually said it in so many words.

Emil's favourite places to go as a kid were *Margit-sziget*, the long island in the middle of the Danube, and the city park. When he and his mother visited these green spaces on Sundays, they had a whole day of having fun with swimming, running, and picnicking. Emil was pretty sure his mother never paid a lot of money to enjoy their time there. His mother always brought a picnic. When Emil was homesick in Ohio, he thought a lot about *Margit-sziget*.

He wanted to show them the vivid colours of Margaret's

Island. The lush, green lawns, the verdant copses of trees, the riot of flowers in meticulously kept flowerbeds that framed the gravel path. Their thick scent mixed in places with the acrid fishy smell of the river or the chlorine of the huge swimming pool, depending on where they were. Add to that the slight breeze wafting from the Danube and the laughter from the picnickers and frisbee-throwers; the quacking of ducks in the pond. All that, to Emil, was the essence of his childhood.

There was so much to see on that island in the middle of the Danube, and Emil was excited to show it all to them, so he suggested they rent a red pedal car to drive around. It had two seats, four handlebars, a red-striped canvas roof and bicycle pedals. Emil was certain nothing on it had changed in the last two decades.

'It's a Flintstones car!' Melissa had squealed.

Emil was relieve — he was certain the pedal car wouldn't pass American safety standards, what with its red steel bars in the front serving as a seat for kids. It was eleven o'clock and already the sun beat down. Emil had to test the metal first to make sure it didn't burn Tünde's thighs before helping her into the seat. She wiggled her legs in excitement.

'When in Hungary do as the Hungarians do!' Melissa hopped into the passenger seat. 'I hope you know how to steer this thing.'

Emil rang the bell, Tünde clapped her hands at the sound and they pushed out into the gravel path. Budapest was hot in August, but out here it was somewhat cooler. Gulls circled hungrily above. He felt heavy in the heat as he manoeuvred the pedal car around families laden with towels and baskets searching for an empty spot to make their own for the day.

78

Melissa reached over and rang the bell too many times; picnickers strained their necks, watching the foreigners accelerate down the path.

'Watch out! We don't know what we are doing!' Melissa yelled out in English to people they passed.

Emil was surprised at how many people waved back. Had he forgotten how friendly people were, or were they, as Westerners, still exotic enough to be tolerated? He wasn't sure. He wasn't paying attention, when an errant football rolled into their path. Emil swerved sharply to avoid hitting it, nearly tipping the pedal car.

Tünde squealed as she flipped over, nearly being thrown out of the pedal car. Both Emil and Melissa managed to grab her.

They went up a small hill; Emil's forehead was sticky with sweat. He circled a large fountain, making sure to get close enough to feel the spray, cooling them off a bit.

At the far end of the island Emil drove them over to the ruins of Margaret's convent, and he pointed to a bench.

'My first kiss was right there,' he told Melissa.

He avoided the hotel and spa, choosing to stay next to the inner part of the island, where they could see the rose garden, the water tower, the lilies and mermaids in a small pond.

It didn't take them long to go round the whole island.

'I always thought the island was huge,' he had said as he paid for the pedal car rental.

'You were little!' Melissa nudged his shoulder playfully.

They walked away down the path into a copse of trees to find a secluded part of the riverbank. It was humid. Emil was grateful the canopy of trees blocked out the sun. Melissa spread out the cloth she usually used as a papoose for Tünde as a makeshift blanket for them to sit on while Emil collected a handful of stones and threw them in wide arcs into the flowing current. Tünde found more stones for Emil to throw, delighting in the loud dull sounds of the heavier rocks, marvelling at the ripples. They threw a stick onto the water and saluted it on its journey to the Black Sea.

As they settled down to enjoy their impromptu picnic, Emil couldn't help but feel a deep sense of contentment. He leaned back, so that his head was lying on the grass, blades tickling his ears. He combed his fingers through the grass. Emil picked a dandelion and put it to his nose breathing in the earthy scent. He closed his eyes. He could hear the river's soft, soothing murmur, the low hum of a barge somewhere downstream and quiet giggles from Melissa and Tünde. A slight breeze cooled his arms, the dense river smell wafted in. Emil dozed; at peace. He was home. Melissa broke his reverie. 'Tünde's getting sunburned; we're exhausted. I think I've had enough sightseeing for one day.'

Emil opened his eyes, stretched his arms above his head. He took in the leaves overhead as they fluttered slightly.

'We're not sightseeing. This is living.'

SEPTEMBER

Emil and Melissa had asked Ilona to take Tünde to the park so the couple could meet with the university to get their residence permit sorted out and help Emil move into his studio. The money Emil was saving on accommodation had been set aside to rent the darkroom, studio space and a part-time assistant.

Ilona could have arranged for them to easily get their visas. She had done it dozens of times before for foreign journalists, but she didn't offer. She wanted her granddaughter to herself. Ilona was trying hard to get the child to play with her, but the little one was shy.

Ilona refused to call her by that ridiculous name, *Tünde*. Did Emil even tell Melissa that it meant fairy? Ilona got around the stupid name by calling her *kisbaba*. My little child. It would be her nickname for her granddaughter. No one had noticed.

Ilona planned to take the toddler to the playground just after 9:00 am, when she knew Erzsébet was likely to go shopping on Wednesday.

Ilona was spot on in the timing. She and the *kisbaba* were

holding hands, waiting for the lift when Erzsi waddled out of her flat. Ilona smiled proudly as Erzsébet walked slowly toward them, her dress swaying with each step.

'*Ohhhh, de édes*,' Erzsi said. How sweet. Ilona thought Erzsi smelled of washing-up liquid. Her voice echoed slightly in the concrete hallway.

'Emil and Melissa are getting their visas in order, then Emil will be setting up his studio at the university later today,' she told her friend. 'I'll be taking care of the baby all morning!'

'That's wonderful,' Erzsi said. 'Melissa and Emil seem to be settling in well. I noticed Emil's Hungarian is coming back quickly, too.'

Ilona nodded in agreement. She looked up to see if the lift was coming yet.

'And how does Melissa like Budapest?' Erzsi asked.

'She loves it, of course,' Ilona said. 'She's always off to some corner of the city. She keeps telling *me* about Hungarian history and art.'

'That's sweet.'

'And she has an important meeting next week with the Hungarian National Ballet. No doubt she will be dancing for them soon. She asked me to set it up.' Ilona leaned conspiratorially towards Erzsi and added: 'I won't be surprised if they end up staying longer than a year.'

'The ballet? I thought Melissa was a modern dancer.' Erzsi said.

'Melissa asked me to set up an appointment with some "friend of a friend" from Cleveland, Ohio. She tried to do it herself, but no one on the other end of the phone line could speak English, so I helped her out.'

Ilona had made the call at work; no point in running up a phone bill at home. Ilona fundamentally believed that going to the top was always the most effective way to accomplish one's aim, so she didn't bother seeking out Melissa's 'friend of a friend'. Instead, she arranged a personal interview with Gyula Szabó, the first principal and choreographer of the ballet.

Ilona told the press relations contact of the National Ballet that an important American was visiting Budapest from Cleveland and wanted to meet him. She let it slip that her daughter-in-law 'danced in Cleveland'. The spokeswoman naturally would know of the Cleveland Ballet. It was founded by a student of Anna Pavlova, and if memory served, was currently being run by two Hungarian-Americans.

'I'd be pleased to arrange a meeting with this important Amerikai dancer,' the press relations officer had told Ilona. Since the fall of the Iron Curtain, the National Ballet was starved of funding. The spokeswoman clearly saw dollar signs, hard currency and venues for a foreign tour; Ilona did not disabuse her of this notion.

'I haven't told Melissa I arranged the meeting with the director; I want it to be a surprise,' Ilona told Erzsi.

The lift door opened with a ding, but there were too many people crammed into the small space. Ilona and Erzsi had to wait for it to come back. The second lift was still not working.

Erzsi nodded, still, Ilona could tell Erzsi's mind was elsewhere. She was looking at Tünde, who was standing bravely next to her grandmother, her fingers in her mouth, her sunhat covering the upper part of her face.

'She has beautiful eyes,' Erzsi said. 'Just like her papa. And grandfather.'

Ilona froze. That is where she had seen that look. From László. How could she have forgotten, but Erzsi didn't? Laci, whose eyes had made Ilona go weak at the knees the first time she saw him. Laci who was quick to smile. When Ilona got upset — a bill not paid; a joke she thought was being played on her; life taken too seriously — Laci's dark eyes would peer deep into her heart. 'Sense of humour, my dear,' he'd say. 'Sense of humour.' The eyes that winked at her from across the room. The eyebrows that rose quickly when he wanted to leave a party but was too polite to say so. The eyes that seared into anyone who annoyed him.

They were the same eyes that bore witness to the Soviet tanks that rolled into Budapest while the world's gaze was fixed on the Suez Canal. Those were the eyes that were blown away when shrapnel from Soviet munition destroyed the upper part of his face, making him unrecognisable to everyone except Ilona, who quietly claimed his body when it was all over. He had already been placed in a cheap wooden coffin and she didn't have the money to pay for anything more appropriate. His eyes could not be closed; they were simply gone, along with his forehead, an ear and his nose.

Ilona looked down at her granddaughter with those deep brown eyes and said in Hungarian, 'Édes, take your fingers out of your mouth. You'll get bad teeth.'

Ilona was grateful when the lift finally arrived. She regained her good mood when they stepped outside in the warm September sunlight. Only a few cloud wisps dotted the sky.

To Ilona's surprise, Erzsi walked into the playground with her and sat herself on a bench where the two friends had the best vantage point of the sandpit, a spot they knew from experience toddlers loved the best. But Tünde didn't go to play, instead she sat down near Ilona's feet and put her fingers back into her mouth.

'Do you remember the hours we spent sitting on this bench chatting while the boys played?' Ilona asked Erzsi.

The playground had become run down since the two women last sat under the single tree that provided shade. The grass was gone; clouds of dust kicked up when a few of the children happened to run by. Red paint had chipped off the metal frame of the slide. The only new items were three cutout animals on wide tight springs that rocked when children pretended to ride them, yet even their colours were faded now.

'Isi tried his best to convince the older boys he was big enough to play football with them, but Emil was happy to sit on that digger in the middle of the sandpit, moving tiny rocks from one pile to the next.' Erzsi dabbed her eyes with her handkerchief.

Ilona remembered. She had worried that Emil was too much of a loner. She had urged him to go play with the other boys, only, Emil, who was small for his age, hated to run. He was shy; he liked to build things; to draw, to sing.

One summer, Emil grew, and then miraculously got picked to be on the swimming team. Swimming was the only sport he had ever liked. Though he hated to run, he loved the water. Once Emil began to train with the national swimming team, Ilona loved to regale Erzsi — and anyone who would listen really — about her son's successes. She became an expert in stroke technique, push and pace. She followed all the top swimmers in the other national teams and kept track of their progress for Emil and his coaches.

She displayed his ribbons and trophies on the sideboard, so they would be the first thing a visitor would notice. She included all of them until there got to be so many she limited the display to the first place cups, ribbons and medals. The remaining ribbons and citations were carefully glued into a scrapbook along with the occasional newspaper article. After Emil escaped by swimming to Trieste the scrapbook was torn apart by the police as they rampaged their way through her flat looking for clues as to why he left. She had put the book back together again as best she could, barely able to see the ripped spine through her tears. Then she put it away, took a deep breath and never mentioned it again. In the end it was István, not Emil, whose progress was noted regularly by the two women. Isi's promotions were a great source of pride for his mother, and Ilona was happy for her. It's why Ilona thought it was so important now for her to point Emil in the right direction for success. Her life had been littered with making-do and compromising. She wasn't content with that anymore.

Ilona stared down at her granddaughter. Emil had a child now; it was time for him to grow up.

'Go play, darling,' Ilona said to Tünde.

The little girl peered up at her grandmother, legs splayed out in front of her; sunhat partially hiding her face, but didn't move.

'She's shy,' Erzsi said.

Ilona heard Erzsi sigh. Ilona knew that Erzsi had wished she had been able to have more children. *Háát*, what can you do?

'It's so nice to have a little one around. István is too busy

86

to have a girlfriend,' Erszi said.

Then she added, 'Oh! I didn't tell you. Guess what? István won that auction for four places around Lake Balaton and the border with Austria! He has an investor! They are looking for even more locations!'

'Well,' Ilona said. 'Emil is very busy too.'

'No, no, no. That's not what I mean,' Erzsi said. 'I'm happy for both boys.'

'Isi has a restaurant and *four* nightclubs?'

'Five, actually. Don't forget that bar near the restaurant. He wants to open a chain of places all over the country. That's why I'm taking my time this morning; I want Isi to get some rest. He got home at two this morning.'

'Three,' Ilona corrected her.

She had heard the lift doors open in the small hours, István's heavy shoes clomping down the hall, echoing on the concrete walls.

'Of course, it doesn't bother me to wake at 3:00 am nearly every day. I can eventually get back to sleep in an hour or so. It's fine,' Ilona added. Her back did not touch the park bench; Ilona chose to sit with her back straight and her feet planted firmly in front, knees together.

She decided it would be cruel to mention that sometimes Isi's smell of sweat, cigarette smoke and alcohol wafted through the front door into her living room. She'd seen him recently, his greasy hair combed forward to hide his receding hairline, and his eyes puffy. His skin a sickly pallor, the gold chains he wore around his neck emphasised the opaqueness of his skin. She guessed this was the fashion for bar owners, but hoped that he didn't wear them to the restaurant.

'He works at the restaurant during the day and spends the night learning how to run a nightclub. He hardly has time to sleep. I was shocked to see him this morning,' Erzsi said. 'I told him, 'the restaurant staff can open for lunch without you today.' István grunted something about making an order and needing to meet some people but then stumbled back to bed.

Erzsi dabbed her forehead with her handkerchief and slipped it back in her dress pocket.

'It will be hot today.'

Ilona glanced over.

'I have news too. I finally got a date arranged for us to see the Pálffy *kastély*. I'm still waiting to hear from Albert, though. You remember that investor I told you about.'

'Oh? Does Emil know why you want him to see it?'

Ilona ignored the question. 'It's going to be fine. Emil and Melissa will fall in love with the Pálffy *kastély* immediately. How can they not? Then they can go into business, like István.'

Erzsi looked down her nose sternly at her friend.

'Ilona, you just told me Emil was setting up a studio and Melissa had a meeting with the ballet. What do they want with your *kastély*?'

'Sometimes one needs to be persistent to become successful.' Ilona did not meet Erzsi's gaze.

Erzsi said nothing. She, too, stared ahead, watching the children play. Her jaw seemed to tighten.

'I have an idea…' Ilona turned on the bench and looked directly at Erzsi. 'You said István needed a break, what if you two joined us? We can have a picnic down by the lake!'

She could see Erzsi hesitating, pursing her lips, so Ilona added, 'I'd love to have the two boys spend more time with one another. Emil doesn't know many people here these days. Just the people at that university. It will do Isi good to be out during the day. We'll have fun.'

'I'll ask him, but I'm not sure he'll have time.'

'Good,' Ilona said, like it was settled. Then she added, 'perhaps István wouldn't mind driving us.'

Erzsi rolled her eyes. She found a sweet as she tucked her handkerchief back into her pocket. She unwrapped it and handed it to Tünde, who popped it into her mouth, tasting the sugary cherry flavour with delightful surprise. Tünde seemed to be getting used to strangers offering her sweets; far more than her mother knew. It was one advantage to being wrapped papoose-style. Tünde spat it onto her hand and examined the beautiful red colour, then stuck it into her mouth again. She did this repeatedly, in between keeping tabs on the children in the playground. Red syrup trickled down her chin. The palm of her hand was pink and sticky, but Tünde didn't mind. She seemed particularly fixated on the children who looked like they were flying.

'Should I push you on the swing?' Erzsi asked her in Hungarian, then a second time in rusty English.

Tünde's head nodded.

'I think this young lady is going to learn Hungarian very quickly!' Erzsi extended her hand; Tünde grabbed the woman's finger and hauled herself up. Ilona looked alarmed. She was the grandmother, after all.

'Here, let me do it.'

Erzsi sat down again as Ilona made a beeline to the swing, unsteady as her court shoes sank into the sand. Tünde half-crawled, half-toddled behind her grandmother. Her hands, sticky from holding the sweet, were coated in sand and dirt by the time she reached the swing. She tried to wipe them on her dress, but Ilona stopped her, scowled, then leaned forward and took off Tünde's dress so it wouldn't get dirty. She helped her granddaughter climb onto the swing and secure a safety bar across the toddler's belly. She gently pushed the little girl a few times. Tünde — her round, pink belly exposed to the wind, her sunhat nearly completely covering her eyes — smiled shyly at first, then began to giggle.

'Again.' She said, in English, only it sounded like: 'Agn.'

Ilona understood and it brought tears to her eyes. It was the first time the *kisbaba* had spoken to her. As Ilona pushed a little harder, she glanced over to make sure Erzsi was watching.

Erzsi was standing up to leave, she straightened her dress and hitched up her stockings and waved goodbye. She was pleased to see Ilona finally happy. After Laci died all those years ago, Ilona's grief had unnerved Erzsébet; it made Ilona weak and passive, traits that she never thought would describe her friend. Back then, Erzsébet had urged Ilona to flee to Vienna, but for Ilona, about to give birth, the thought of even packing a bag was too overwhelming. She resolved to stay near her mother and Laci's grave, which she visited often. Erzsi knew it became a part of Emil's childhood routine. Ilona never seemed to enjoy life as she once had. The bitterness increased after Emil swam away. Now, seeing her pushing her granddaughter on a swing, Erzsi saw a joy that had long been missing.

'I'm off to the *csemege*! I heard they got in a shipment of raisins today,' Erzsi called out. She picked up her handbag.

'Buy some for me if there are any,' Ilona yelled back.

'The *kisbaba* loves them.'

Ilona watched Erzsi's back as she opened the gate and sauntered out, unhurried. Erzsi had a husband who had lived a good life and a son who was well on his way to making his fortune. Erzsi had a two-bedroom flat, a summer cottage on Lake Balaton, a car and a phone. Ilona had watched Erzsi's accomplishments stoically for decades. Now she, Ilona, had a beautiful little granddaughter and surely, soon, she would be able to convince Emil to get a real job.

Just to hedge her bets, she had spoken with John and János, the agency photographer. She had suggested that Emil could come in and chat with János. János agreed and Emil, surprisingly, was amenable to talking with him.

'That would be great! I want to check out their archives,' he had said.

Ilona knew there was no money in that, but she also was aware she had to tread carefully with her son. If she played it right, maybe Emil could sign on at the news agency and make some money until the sale of the *kastély* went through. She had seen the commercials on the Austrian TV channel that broadcast now in her living room. She knew how wealthy these Westerners were, what with their modern homes and new cars. Emil could not fool her.

This year was her chance to make Emil see sense. Of course, this is what happens when he's without parental guidance for all those years. You can't live on art. Emil was thirty-five now, and had a wife and child. It was high time he grew up.

EMIL

István knocked on Ilona's door, holding a bottle of Williams-Birne *pálinka* in his hand. Emil was suddenly aware of how the flat looked to a Hungarian. Toys were strewn across the living room; a cassette tape of children's songs boomed from a newly purchased boombox. Beyond the living room a mass of clothes spewed out of suitcases in the bedroom: they had been there a few weeks but neither he nor Melissa had got around to hanging anything up. In the kitchen, Ilona and Melissa were washing dishes. Tünde was sitting in the middle of the floor surrounded by her building blocks; her finger stuck in her mouth while her other hand moved a square about.

'Come over for a quick drink?' István asked Emil.

'Does it have to be quick?' Emil followed Isi across the hall.

Erzsi had gone out for her card night, a ritual she had adhered to since István and Emil were kids, so they had the place to themselves.

'So, you're a family man now,' István placed two shot glasses on the table next to the schnapps bottle as Emil settled

92

into his seat.

'Pear? Not plum?' Emil asked, looking at the bottle. Without a thought, Emil sat in the same chair he had occupied as a boy.

'No. I like pear brandy.'

'Noted. *Egészségedre!*' Cheers.

Emil had forgotten how hot his throat felt when the brandy slid down his throat.

It was reassuring to see that Erzsi's kitchen looked the same as it had, except perhaps for a few more trinkets — a new napkin holder, more magnets on the refrigerator, an extra framed poster wishing everyone a great morning and an even greater day.

Erzsi's kitchen surfaces were so filled with gadgets and spices that Emil wondered where she cooked. Ilona, who as far as Emil could tell, rarely cooked, had plenty of available space. Emil was surprised to see that boxes had been piled up in the living room. A staple of his childhood, those boxes; he always wondered where they came from. It occurred to him only now, as an adult, that their contents had paid for that holiday home on Lake Balaton, and a car.

'Yeah, Melissa's great,' Emil said. 'How about you?'

'No, I'm working too much to have a steady girlfriend.'

'So what do you do for fun these days?'

'I haven't really done anything more than visit bars over these last months, scouting for the ones with the best locations,' Isi's eyes darted over to the green kitchen surface.

István had placed his business plan there, ready to present to Emil at the right time. As promised, Ilona had corrected the English grammar and re-typed it for him. She even added a chart, to make it look professional. Isi had already presented a copy of it to the German investor who gave him a loan to bid at the auction of the nightclubs near Lake Balaton and encouraged him to look for other locations along the border. With Emil's help, though, they could go bigger, he thought.

'Most people can't afford to eat at a restaurant, so the customers tend to be foreigners or sometimes, government officials.'

Emil nodded. For him, business talk was boring. When his US 'family' got together at Thanksgiving and talked about stock markets, Emil would usually switch off. Now, he just took another sip of the *pálinka*. He'd only been a teenager when he left — and one who spent most of his time in the swimming pool — so he hadn't had much practice knocking back the hard stuff. At art school, they preferred grass over alcohol. Nowadays, he rarely drank anything stronger than a Miller Lite and smoked weed only occasionally.

István, on the other hand, didn't seem to have any difficulties imbibing. Emil remembered how, when they were teenagers, Isi and his friends drank on the banks of the Danube. It made sense he was into running bars and stuff. Emil was surprised to see thin red veins creeping up István's cheeks; he hadn't noticed them until today. Maybe the fluorescent lights of the kitchen had something to do with it.

'So...' István lit a cigarette and exhaled slowly. Then more boldly, he smiled at Emil and got straight to the point. '...why are you here?'

'Why am I here?'

'I'm guessing you're like a lot of people, coming back and looking for a good deal.' István stretched his body so his arm could reach the business plan with its blue transparent cover on the counter. With a flourish, he presented it to Emil. 'I've got some great ideas. We could partner —'

'— Oh István, that's a nice thought, but really, Melissa and I are just here for a year, to see Hungary. I have to put together an exhibition as a condition of my grant. That's all.'

Emil smiled at his childhood friend whose thinning hair and slight paunch made him seem decades older. 'Plus, I wanted to come back and see you, buddy.'

'That's all?' István looked at Emil, like he was staring at a child who needed things explained. 'The government is practically giving away the country and you want to take pictures? I know this guy. Together the three of us can make millions.'

Emil looked down at his nails. His fingers were red raw from photo developing chemicals. Emil, not yet a month back in Budapest, was surprised that all people seemed to talk about was getting rich. The cigarette smoke in the small kitchen made him nauseous.

'I'm not interested in business.'

István refilled the two glasses. He tilted back his head.

Emil tried to smooth things over. 'So do you still play any football?'

'No. I don't have time.'

Surprisingly, in spite of his easy-going nature, Isi still had his menacing look, which Emil suspected would come in useful in the restaurant business. When he glared like that, Emil could see his veins protruding from his neck. Emil would have liked to photograph him.

Isi softened his voice. 'Emil, what happened?'

'I just snapped when they told me I wasn't going to the Olympics. Wait. You never heard that, have you? Why I escaped? Actually, I hadn't planned it at all, you know I have a quick temp...'

'I don't mean that. I mean why are you so... so... *soft*?' István stubbed out his cigarette with force, grinding the stub into the ashes. 'This is the time, man. We can all get rich. The opportunities are out there for anyone with the energy to make it happen. We can partner. There's this guy I know. He's given me a loan and wants to make more deals with me, but I need some money to put down. Plus I have other ideas...'

He paused to breathe for a moment before continuing, his voice passionate.

'I see deals being made every day at the restaurant. Funny how my clients think we restaurant managers are invisible. With your money and my connections, we'd be a perfect match. Emil, we have to act fast before it's all gone.'

Emil looked up, surprised. 'My money?'

István continued: 'Dunkin' Donuts and KFC just opened. Some second-generation Hungarian-American yuppies from New York started a bagel shop — what the hell are bagels? Competition here is really fierce.'

Emil drained his glass and didn't look up, he could feel himself drifting off like it was Thanksgiving and the Molnars were talking about the stock markets. He felt like he had once again failed someone else's dreams. Isi continued to ramble on.

'McDonald's came in before the curtain fell. Wow, that sure was a game changer,' István's eyes grew wide. 'No one had seen anything like that. Large windows, airy, light,

bright, clean. The servers behind the counters *smiled...*'
István punctuated the word by smiling himself. 'Food came
fast. It was like the City Grill,' István said, looking up. 'You
remember City Grill, right?'

Emil nodded.

'Except McDonald's *shined*. And that,' István said with
pride, 'is the kind of business I want us to run.'

He slapped the table with the flat of his hand. He leaned
forward, staring at Emil intensely. Emil could smell tobacco
and alcohol mixed with ambition.

'My place, the restaurant, is an institution; I can't change
a lot. Maybe modernise a little. The new nightclubs won't
have brocade curtains or linen tablecloths.'

For emphasis he tapped a finger on his forehead. His eyes
twinkled.

'I want my new places to be as *classy* as McDonald's,' he
said. He was grinning from ear to ear. 'Are you in?'

'No.'

Emil stared intently at his glass, not daring to look up,
unsure whether he was going to laugh at his friend or belt him.
'I don't think you were listening. We don't have any money,
Isi. Besides, if we did, we'd spend it on making art. Melissa
and I aren't into business.'

István blinked a few times, then lit another cigarette.

'So what are you doing here?'

'I'm trying to see Hungary; photograph it, video it,' Emil
said, then shrugged his shoulders. 'Maybe document your rise
to fame.'

István didn't see any humour.

'I thought anyone could make money in America. Why

are you back here sleeping on your mother's floor? Why aren't you at the Kempinski Hotel or the Gellert? Americans don't scrounge. They order more food than they can eat; they over-tip.'

Emil shrugged. 'I like photography.'

There was a pause. Emil poured this time. They both tilted back their heads in unison.

'Shit,' István said. 'I've been on the fucking waiting list for a car for God knows how long. I hate my Lada, but it's gotta keep running for a few more months. You can just walk into any dealership and get a BMW.'

'Are you driving your dad's Lada?' Emil said, deciding to sidestep the fact that he knew he was not likely to ever be able to afford a BMW. He could feel his head starting to buzz from the schnapps.

'What else am I going to drive?'

'It's still running?'

'Yep.'

Emil was surprised by the answer; he could see István was surprised by the question.

'*We* can't buy cars every year,' Isi said. '*We* can't just walk in and get whatever we want.'

'There's a wall of ketchup at our supermarket in Ohio and Americans aren't any happier for it.'

'We don't *have* supermarkets.'

It sounded like an accusation that startled Emil. The two men locked eyes for a moment. Emil could see István's nostrils widened; his chest heaved. Then his voice softened.

'Last year, after the travel restrictions were lifted, I drove to Vienna, just to see it. When I got there it felt like another world. Jesus, I don't know what surprised me more — the pop music in the grocery store or the shelves packed with cat food.' István's lips tightened. 'It didn't matter, though. I couldn't afford to buy anything.'

He looked up accusingly at Emil: 'Hungarian cats eat chicken necks.'

Emil wanted to leave. He'd had enough.

'My mother said yesterday that Carrefour is buying the ABC food stores. Then you'll have all the French products you'll ever want.'

'And no money to buy them.' István said. Emil could practically taste the bitterness in his voice. 'Not now anyway.'

Emil took a final gulp of schnapps, then stood up.

'I have one life to live. I've learned to appreciate what I have,' he looked intensely at Isi. 'Don't waste your time worrying about what you don't have.'

István didn't look up.

'Look.' Emil said. 'We never know when we're going to die. I don't want to put off what I want to do in life just to have a BMW and a villa in the twelfth district.'

István raised an eyebrow, and with a slightly bemused smile that almost looked like a sneer, asked: 'How about a *kastély* an hour from here?'

EARLY OCTOBER

István's Lada was cleaned, polished, vacuumed and with a full tank — Ilona made sure of it. She asked him at least four times. She had prepared everything in advance, ensuring there were devilled eggs, salted radishes, peppers, tomatoes, cucumbers and cold chicken for the picnic. They would go to the lake at the west end of the property, she had told Erzsi. The one she had once taken Emil to decades ago. The one she and her brother swam in as children, while their mother and grandmother visited the thermal springs at the neighbouring town.

As the Americans were getting dressed, Ilona packed the food and blanket, placing it next to the door so nothing would be forgotten. She even had time to pick up fresh bread, the wholemeal kind that was so expensive, but Melissa insisted it was the only kind she would eat.

It was just as well that she kept busy. Ilona could barely look at her daughter-in-law in the morning. She, Ilona, never would show herself unless properly dressed. First thing every day, Ilona put on her face. Melissa, on the other hand, walked around for hours before she even bothered to unsnarl her tangles. No bra under a black half top that didn't even hide her belly button. Wide, baggy, shapeless slacks with a red pattern on them. Rainbow socks. Sometimes she had milk stains on her shirts as she was still breastfeeding. This for the mother of a child nearly two years old.

Ilona washed up the breakfast dishes and straightened the living room, unable to talk above Emil's music. Tünde, she could see through the door, was playing with a stuffed animal, not dressed. Ilona sighed. For something to do, she walked across the hall to Erzsi's flat to make sure her friend and István were ready.

'Isi, you're sure you have a full tank?'

'Positive.'

Erzsi, who was washing up the dishes, pointed an elbow at some flowers on the counter.

'I thought we could stop and put those on Laci and Péters' graves.'

Ilona froze momentarily, considering the idea. She hadn't put any on Laci's grave for a week; with Emil and Melissa's arrival her schedule was off-kilter. Still, she didn't want to be late. Everything needed to be perfect for the Pálffy. Her hands and stomach felt prickly. She tugged at her sleeve.

'We'll have to leave quickly then.'

As an afterthought, Ilona stopped at the door and added, 'Thank you.'

Back at her place, Ilona was vexed to see Emil wearing jeans and a T-shirt. The same one he had worn when he arrived in August. The same shirt he wore nearly every day. *Grateful Dead Summer '89* was written in a circle.

'Oh,' Ilona said, when he sat down for breakfast. 'Did you forget to do the washing this week?'

Melissa's thin white dress barely reached her thighs and had large flowers stamped on it. She wore white lace anklets and pointy black shoes. It was difficult to disguise that they once were tap shoes, even Ilona could see that. Her jeans jacket was in her hand. She was wearing a large floppy hat as if she was in some theatrical performance.

Tünde ran around the coffee table naked.

'C'mon Tünda,' Melissa coaxed, as she inspected her appearance in the bathroom mirror, not bothering to close the door. 'Do you want to wear a pretty dress like Mommy?'

Tünde stared mutely at her mother, then started to run around the dining room table.

Ilona sat with a stiff back on the sofa, her hands fidgeting on her lap and waited.

'It's okay if we're late,' Ilona said to no one in particular. 'I guess.'

Once they finally got down to the car park, it took a bit of persuasion to convince Melissa that the *kisbaba* didn't need a baby seat.

'If we used one, we won't all fit in the Lada,' Ilona said. She made a point to check her watch.

István winked at Melissa.

'I drive good.'

Melissa eventually acquiesced and got into the middle, holding tightly onto Tünde on her lap. Ilona and Erzsi took their places next to each of the doors. The stems of Erzsi's bouquets poked Melissa's thighs. No one had room for their elbows. Ilona watched as Melissa leaned forward to stare wistfully at the two men in the front.

'So why is it that the men always get the most comfortable seats?' Melissa asked, only half joking.

'Long legs,' Emil said.

Ilona slammed her door shut, but Erzsi kept hers open. She reached over Melissa and Tünde and handed Ilona the flowers, then got out again. She leaned into the car.

'Oh Melissa, I sit in middle so you and baby can look out of the window.'

Melissa demurred.

'Oh goodness, is it ten o'clock already?' Ilona said, loudly.

István turned on the ignition.

Erzsi squeezed into the car again, placing her handbag on the car floor between her legs. Then, before she closed the door, she leaned over to fetch something from inside her bag, forcing Tünde and Melissa to squash Ilona further against the door with the door handle digging into her ribs. In a moment Erzsi straightened up with sweets in her hand and offered them to Melissa and Tünde. Melissa politely shook her head.

'We don't believe in eating processed sugars.'

Tünde looked disappointed.

'Well dat's nice,' Erzsi said, patting Melissa's thigh. She closed the car door.

Ilona leaned forward and tapped Isi on the shoulder. In Hungarian, she said, 'István, you're sure you know where to go?'

'Yes, Ilona *néni*.'

Eventually the Lada pulled out of the car park.

'We're going to stop quickly to see your father,' Ilona told Emil in Hungarian.

Emil swung his head toward the back seat. 'I'd really like that.'

At the cemetery the group quietly walked to Péter's graveside, then turned the corner to an older part of the grounds and found Laszló's grave. Ilona's mother was buried next to him. Erzsi picked up the dried flowers that were in the small vases on each grave and dropped them in a waste bin at the corner of the row. Meanwhile, Ilona arranged the fresh flowers so they made a good show. No one spoke.

Some birds chirped and tweeted in the nearby trees. Tünde pointed to the flowers, then stuck her fingers in her mouth, leaned her head against her mother's chest. István lit a cigarette.

'*Anyu*, tell us about Dad,' Emil said.

'He was the best man I've ever met.'

Erzsi nodded. 'Very lively. He always had a smile on his face.' Then Erzsi patted Emil on his shoulder. 'You have made him very proud. I know it.'

'But, what was he like?'

'Let's talk in the car, shall we?' Ilona said.

Along the way, Melissa peered over the seat and out of the front window as best she could at the little villages they passed. Ilona tried to imagine how her country would appear to an American. Ilona had never been to the US, but she had seen pictures of the large house Emil lived in at the Molnars. In the front was a tall tree, a manicured lawn and a few bushes that lined a brick walkway to the house. Curiously, there were no flowers unlike in Hungary, where it was a matter of great pride to have the best flowerbeds.

'The countryside is dustier than I expected,' Melissa said.
Ilona placed her hand on Melissa's knee.

'The air in Tura is so fresh,' she said. 'Not dirty like it is in Budapest. We often took lovely strolls through the orchards and along the shores of a lake — well, a pond, really — that was on our property. That's where we will have our picnic today.'

'Oh nice,' Melissa said, using the voice she reserved for her parents' friends.

'Occasionally, my mother threw *soirées* even though times were difficult just after the depression,' Ilona said. She herself had only heard about the dances, but she felt as if she had attended them all.

'Right now it is the middle of harvest, so everyone will be busy, very busy. When I was a girl, after the harvest was in, my parents would have a lovely party for the workers. They would break out the cider, wine and schnapps; roast a pig…' Her voice drifted off.

Ilona did not see Emil, who seemed to stiffen.

'*Anyu*, don't you think you are rewriting history a little? The aristocracy treated the peasants like shit. The townspeople near your fields were probably half-starved despite the rich harvest,' he said.

István nodded agreement. 'De landowners taxed hell out of dem, while dey pay no taxes at all. Who set taxes? Landowners and clergy, because dey only ones who could to vote.'

The men couldn't see her, but Ilona shook her head 'no' in disagreement at Melissa. After all, they weren't there, how would they know?

The car was quiet a moment, before Emil said: 'I'd forgotten these special earthy olive hues. I think I associate it with Hungary. Almost sepia.'

He pinched his index finger to his thumb to form a circle, which he held up to his eye, framing the passing countryside. He often did this, imitating a viewfinder, to see what he might capture in a photo.

Ilona could tell he was trying to change the subject, but Melissa was interested.

'So Emil, did I marry an a-rist-o-cat?' Melissa asked.

Emil turned around to look at her in the back seat and winked. 'Stick with me, honey.'

'What are you? A lord? A count, perhaps?'

Ilona glared at her son, then smiled sweetly at Melissa.

'Well, the Pálffy family were awarded the title of baron. I am a baroness, and Emil is a baron, but of course titles were abolished when I was seventeen.'

Ilona paused for emphasis, then added: 'I believe many people would like to see titles restored.'

Emil laughed. Ilona, annoyed, went on: 'Before the war, there were the fairy-tale summers. Always something to do. Our family were major exporters of fruit and grain. My grandfather and his father had the foresight to make sure there was always some crop to harvest from early spring to late autumn. First came the sour cherries, then the sweet variety. Apricots and plums ripened in the summer; apples and pears in the autumn. Peaches didn't do well for papa. I remember when he was so frustrated with all the bruises — you know one small bruise means the fruit can't be sold. He ordered the trees to be dug up and rapeseed planted instead to make oil.'

'That does sound like a fairy tale,' Melissa said, still using her polite voice.

Ilona, pleased, took this as encouragement.

'The orchards seemed to be always in bloom; bees were forever buzzing around. And we ate so well with what the farm produced and animals we reared. Plum dumplings, smoked meat, pork, churned butter, cheese and milk fresh from our five cows. The foreman kept the beehives, and we had the best honey in the country, I think. Full of flavour from all the different fruit trees.'

Ilona's cheeks were aglow; her eyes sparkled. She wasn't shoe-horned into the back of a Lada skirting potholes, her mind was back at Tura, when she was a young girl.

'During the war, my father and the foreman hoarded a generous supply of food so we wouldn't starve. Of course, my father was a great patriot, so he never would have been under suspicion by the *Hungarian* government at the time. Naturally the Germans tried to find it all, the soldiers were nasty that way. Imagine not caring if we starved —'

Emil snorted. 'Yeah, imagine wanting to feed the towns-people, too!'

Melissa playfully slapped her husband on the shoulder. 'Ilona, ignore him. I think these stories are great. You should write them down.'

Ilona continued, '— my father knew all the places the soldiers would never even think to look. My brother thought this was very funny.'

'So what happened to the orchards?' Melissa asked.

Ilona sighed and her face seemed to collapse.

'They were nationalised when the socialists took over. A

collective now runs them.'

Then an idea struck her. 'I suppose they, too, will be privatised under this new government.'

She let that last sentence sink in. The socialists had taken everything away from her, but they could not take away her desire to prove their system wrong. It all came down to Emil. She didn't understand why he came back claiming to be *penniless*; she could help him realise that no American was truly without means.

'Surely with a bit of work, you could wrestle the orchards back into the hands of the family too, Emil,' she said, casually. 'By the way, István, how are your businesses coming along?'

István glanced sideways at Emil.

'Good.'

'Always finding ways to improve me, eh, *Anyu*?' Emil didn't bother to turn around when he spoke.

'Isn't that my job, son? The job of any mother?' Ilona said. 'To help their children be their best?'

'Hey Melissa,' Emil said. 'Did you ever consider that you married a farmer? We could be the living version of "Green Acres". You can be Eva Gabor.'

'Darling, I love you but give me Park Avenue,' Melissa sang in her best Hungarian accent, which, considering they were in Hungary, was bad. 'I didn't know you watched that show.'

'Yeah, the Molnars loved the reruns. They thought Eva was hilarious,' Emil said, clearly pleased to have changed the subject.

Ilona scowled. She had no clue that Emil and Melissa were talking about an old US television show.

'It's important Emil that you understand your heritage, and pass it down to the *kisbaba*,' Ilona said. Then, leaning toward the front seat, she asked her son, 'Why are you so flippant?'

Emil didn't answer.

'My grandfather purchased the land from the Eszterhàzys, shortly after Emperor Franz Josef bestowed the title of baron. He asked Miklós Ybl — the famous architect — to design it, but Miklós Ybl was too busy, so one of his students, Gyula Bukovics, was hired. He also designed many of the *kastély* on *Népköztársaság út* in Budapest.'

István's head jerked up as he looked back at the women from his rear-view mirror.

'It's *Andrássy út* now, Ilona.'

'Oh yes, of course.' Ilona bobbed her head in agreement, then she turned to Melissa to explain. 'The Soviets changed many of the main street names, so our new government is changing them back. *Andrássy út* was its original name, but the whole time I have lived in Budapest, I've known the street as *Népköztársaság út*.'

Melissa laughed. 'Nehpkurse — what?'

'It means People's Republic,' Emil said, turning around to look at his wife. '*Népköztársaság út*. I was really confused when I first got here. So many streets have been renamed!'

Melissa tried again. 'Nehpcursetarblahblah.' She laughed. 'What a hellish language. I'm glad it's called *Andrássy* now. I love that boulevard. That's where the opera house is, right, Ilona? Where my appointment is? It's an absolutely beautiful area. Gorgeous.'

'AndráSHy,' Ilona tried to correct her daughter-in-law's pronunciation. 'And, yes. That's where your appointment is.'

'Wait. So let me get my head around this. Your palace was designed by the same guy who built the Opera House?'

'Well,' Ilona was pleased Melissa got the message. 'One of his students.'

Melissa's eyes widened.

'Oh my God, Emil.'

Ilona could see Tünde was getting heavy in Melissa's lap, as if she were starting to nod off.

'We're getting off the subject!' Ilona reminded the people in the car cheerfully. She was so pleased that Melissa took an interest in this.

'The Pálffy was built in a neo-renaissance style; to express a new life, renewal, beauty.' Ilona paused for a moment to think.

'Renewal,' she said the word again, letting the meaning drift to the front seat of the car, hoping the idea of a new life in Hungary would sink in.

Emil said nothing. He was staring out the window and Ilona wondered if the message was sinking in. Tünde's chin had fallen onto her chest. Erzsi's head, too, had rolled forward — Ilona was expecting to hear snoring at any moment — but she saw that Melissa looked fascinated. Maybe Ilona could get through to Emil via his wife, she thought.

'When I was a girl, I used to spend entire winter days up in the turret huddled under a thick goose down duvet. I'd read a book or just watch the clouds float past. I was as high as the geese who were flying away from us. I felt I could look them in the eyes if they dared to look at me. I loved watching snow blanket the leafless trees. It was so idyllic listening to the tick-tock from the clock tower when everything was so quiet.'

Ilona imagined her granddaughter doing the same when she got older. She hoped at least some of the books from her family's library were still on the shelves even though it had been nearly fifty years since her family had left. It was quiet in the car and a bit stuffy, but in a comforting way, as it calmly jostled its inhabitant. Outside, leaves on the trees were turning golden; the deep purple and rust reds of the asters off-set them nicely.

Ilona's mind was back to a time before the war, before German troops ransacked the grounds; before the Soviet soldiers came after them and stole her youth. In the car, her mind had returned to a time before all that. When she was secure, innocent and loved. She felt giddy, excited and happy. Warm and safe; surrounded by the people she cherished.

István turned down the rutted driveway leading to the Pálffy. He was an expert at skirting potholes deeply embedded in dirt roads. Emil placed an arm against the dashboard to steady himself. The women in the back bumped shoulders. Erzsi woke up and dabbed at a bit of saliva from her chin. Ilona leaned forward and strained her neck from the back seat to get a look. Emil and István, in the front, saw it first.

'Ladies and gentlemen, the great Pálffy *kastély*,' Emil said, his voice full of sarcasm.

The *kastély*'s roof sagged. Portions of the stucco had fallen off, exposing a raw brick façade in the middle of the building. Stone cornices were deteriorating. Half of an upstairs balcony had collapsed. A branch of a bush — elderberry? — had taken root in a corner. The wooden window frames had peeled and were nearly colourless and rotting. A few shutters hung crookedly from their hinges, slats broken. Some cellar windows were cracked.

'There it is,' Ilona said proudly, as István pulled the handbrake on the car. Ilona opened the door before he even turned off the ignition. She was anxious to get everyone out of the Lada with as little fanfare as possible.

'God,' Emil said in a low voice, to himself. 'This thing looks like it will collapse in the next big storm. People live here? Is it even safe to go inside?'

Melissa heard him, though, and gave him a playful slap on the shoulder.

'This is amazing. I can't believe your family once owned this. Emil, it's almost a castle for God's sake. It even has its own clock tower! I had no idea you were an aristocrat. I think my family were a bunch of horse thieves back in Ireland before they got to Ellis Island. Why didn't you say anything?'

Emil shrugged.

No one spoke as they concentrated on climbing up the once-grand staircase that led to the entrance. Cracks and missing pieces of marble made the ascent difficult. Emil kept a firm grip on Tünde. István escorted Erzsi, gripping her elbow. Ilona nearly skipped up the stairs, as if they were in the same condition as they had been in 1946 and she was a happy teenager who was relieved the war was finally over and the Soviets had not yet arrived.

THE PÁLFFY *DE TURA* KASTÉLY

The Pálffy *kastély* had gone through hard times, to be sure. The Soviet captain who confiscated the *kastély* lived in it with other officers until they were sent back to Moscow. Along with the livestock they hadn't already eaten, they took a few pieces of choice furniture with them: a Biedermeier secretary with walnut inlay, a book display case from the same era, a Florentine mirror that had hung for nearly a century over a fireplace, two dressing tables and matching wardrobes, several crystal chandeliers, the Herendi china set for twelve, Bohemian crystal water glasses and matching goblets for both red and white wines, several Transylvanian rugs and various paintings from nationally and internationally recognised artists.

The jewellery from Ilona's mother and grandmother had already been taken by German soldiers soon after their arrival at the *kastély*. Then Soviet soldiers took their clothes and shoes and any they didn't want they gave to the peasants in the locality, showing themselves good communists.

The Soviet captain would have taken the Pálffy extendable dining table and twenty chairs but they were needed for the estate's next purpose. The Hungarian army hastily lined up beds along the walls of the eleven bedrooms and their ante-chambers and turned the house into a convalescent home for wounded and shell-shocked soldiers. One Hungarian administrator decided the carpets would cause a problem for soldiers with crutches so he had them removed and sent them to his home, along with a painting he liked. It was of a family picnicking at a lake he knew well; as a kid he had climbed over the wall into the Pálffy grounds to go swimming in that lake.

Some of the nurses liked the remaining candleholders and mirrors. An electrician brought in to update the wiring decided the sconces were in the way, so he took them home. The missing mirrors and paintings for a while created a two-toned effect on the walls. Ghosts of a family past. None of the locals felt any sympathy for the Pálffy family as they were not seen as good masters and had a reputation for meanness.

Once the last soldiers left, it was clear the building would make a suitable retirement home. The beds were upgraded; the ante-chambers were converted to bedrooms; the remaining antiques in the salon were replaced in the 1960s with bright modern settees and chairs with a cheerful red and orange pattern where guilty adult children could visit their parents. The wallpaper was painted over in an institutional cream. Since then, little had changed; except the paint was now peeling off. The wide hallways and large windows were a reminder of its former glories. For forty residents it became their home.

Ilona welcomed her family and friends into the *kastély* with a flourish. She knew where hooks had been installed along the foyer wall for jackets — a Biedermeier wardrobe had been there once, used for the same purpose.

'This is the foyer,' she said.

'I love the polished marble,' Melissa commented.

'It's so light and airy,' Erzsébet said.

Melissa craned her neck around. 'Look,' she said, pointing to the fanlight windows above the entrance. 'Those windows and those...' Melissa walked in a circle around the foyer pointing to mirrors around the ceiling, 'create enough natural light that they don't need to turn on lights. Amazing. Why don't we do that in modern buildings?'

Ilona beamed as she ushered the group into the main sitting room, where a few of the residents were relaxing. A middle-aged woman, probably a visitor, looked up at the group.

'Should we wait for someone? Are we allowed to just walk in?' Emil asked his mother. He had to speak loudly because the volume of the TV set in the corner of the lounge was turned up too high.

Before Ilona could answer the director of the home raced to catch up to them. '*Jó napot kívánok,*' she said, attempting to hide her nervousness. She smiled at each member of the party as she shook their hand.

Ilona gave the director her hand, but she didn't squeeze.

Erzsébet nodded at the jungle of *dieffenbachia*, snake plants and peace lilies that grew in clusters throughout the large, bright, clean lounge. Philodendrons, decades old, climbed around the two-metre-high window frames.

'Such a bright, cheery home for the elderly! You have to tell me your secret about how to care for these African violets,' she said, nodding at the purple flowers on the side tables. 'Mine all seem to die.'

'The residents love to tend to the plants,' the director said. 'That philodendron has been here longer than I have. If you'd like, I can get you a clipping.'

Erzsi nodded enthusiastically.

Melissa piped up in her broken Hungarian. 'Everything nice and clean. Its a beautiful place.'

The director looked rattled when she realised a foreigner was in the group.

'Of course it is,' Ilona said sharply in Hungarian so the director would understand. 'Why would it not?'

Ilona nodded to one wall in an alcove. 'My mother chose that wallpaper, I remember it.'

No one mentioned it was faded and torn in places, where some obviously bored person had taken to peeling it off. To cover the largest blank spaces, the staff had placed reproductions of idyllic countryside landscapes and sweeping vistas of Lake Balaton by famous Hungarian artists, reminders of a time and a glory long past: golden haystacks, peasants taking a noonday nap among mown grain, a wizened boatman staring directly at the viewer, oar in his hand. There was quite an art collection on the wall.

Emil wandered over to examine a picture of a girl in a red skirt and blue apron, holding a wicker basket, yarrow plants in the foreground so distinctly defined, he thought at first glance it was a photograph.

'Édes,' Ilona said in her best mother's voice. 'All the original art was taken long ago. *These…*' she said, switching to English with exaggerated disdain, 'are just reproductions.'

What held Emil's attention, though, wasn't the art. He leaned into Melissa's ear.

'Look at the deep crevice hidden behind the frames. They run from the top of the wall down nearly to the floor,' he said.

Melissa nodded, pursing her lips. Her hands were clasped behind her back. She assumed the same posture as she affected when she walked around a museum.

'Look at the stucco ceilings, they're beautiful. You can see remains of flowers and garlands in that corner. The stone carvings around the windows! And I love the marble floors.'

'Wait until you see the next room,' Ilona said.

She led the group into the one room that had remained almost unchanged in more than forty-five years since Ilona had lived there. In the smoking room, the billiards table, too heavy and too large to be easily removed, took pride of place. The green felt was worn, the leather pockets had stretched under the weight of the balls — all of which were still neatly lined up waiting for the next break; the wood on the cue sticks, lined against a built-in bookcase, had been regularly oiled and cleaned, their tips carefully re-glued.

István and Emil looked at each other, wide-eyed.

'Wow. I'd love to get that into the new club,' Isi said, running his fingers down the length of the table. Not a speck of dust.

Emil picked up a ball. 'Are these ivory?'

'Yes,' Ilona said, pleased he noticed.

'The wainscotting will need some new varnish. The wall new paint, of course,' Ilona said over her shoulder, as if someone behind her was jotting down a list of 'to dos'. 'Otherwise, this room is in excellent condition.'

The director hurried the group on, attempting to prevent Emil from turning on the lights to get a better look at the billiards table less he be electrocuted. Emil glanced curiously at her, but said nothing.

Ilona marched like an environmental health inspector through each room; they stopped briefly in the smaller sitting room, where Erzsi admired the pink damask on the sofa. The kitchen had been modernised and adapted so that it could provide meals for the forty residents, stainless steel countertops and an oversized gas oven. A steel refrigerator stood next to the larder where Ilona's family used to store their harvest every autumn.

As they walked back toward the foyer, preparing to attack the upstairs, Ilona was convinced the *kastély* was in an acceptable condition.

'The bathrooms and the kitchen will need a complete overhaul,' she conceded to Melissa in English. 'Well, with all the new appliances on the market these days, you'd want to do that anyway, right? You could get a microwave!'

Ilona slowed her walk so Melissa could catch up. She squeezed her daughter-in-law's arm conspiratorially.

'My grandfather built this *kastély*, before I was born. You two can refurbish it to its original glory,' she said. 'Think how much fun that would be!'

Melissa opened her mouth, but Erzsi quickly stepped in.

'Shall we look upstairs?'

Emil nudged István, who was dying for a cigarette, and the two of them slipped out the back way.

The herb garden at the foot of the path was tidy even in early October. István and Emil nodded hello to an elderly gentleman wearing a tattered suit who sat on a stool cleaning a hoe with a dirty white rag. A few steps beyond him, though, the once perfectly landscaped garden and park had become overgrown.

The two men stepped over the tall grass to a side of the old stables away from the gardener's attention. Isi pried open a boarded-up window and climbed through. Emil followed. Both coughed because of the dust, blinked to adjust to the light and peered into empty stalls.

'This would make a great studio space,' Emil said.

He imagined huge windows — what once were horse's stalls — creating natural light on a freshly waxed wooden floor that might be used as a dance studio or gallery space. In his mind he built a darkroom along the far north-facing wall not far from where he had seen a well still bubbling water into a trough just outside the building.

István lit a cigarette and leaned against a wall.

'You'd really move here?' He asked. He picked up a stick that looked like it might make a good cane and began drawing circles in the ground.

'God, no.'

Emil ran his fingers through old straw and was surprised that it still seemed fresh, or, at least not mildewed. 'It was just a thought.'

'Yeah. We all have dreams.'

'Oh. Right. How's your business going anyway?'

'I got that investor I told you about. The guy who lent me that money? We had another meeting. He had some insane ideas about how to move forward,' István said, shaking his head for emphasis.

'Yeah?'

'We're making plans to open a whole string of nightclubs

all over the country. And fast, too, before anyone else buys them. They'll all look basically the same. That's what you do to minimise the refit costs. They'll be really nice and classy.'

Isi looked at Emil for a moment. Emil seemed to be staring at the dust particles floating in the sunbeam. He didn't appear to notice István had stopped talking.

Isi grunted, then ground out his cigarette with the toe of his foot. He tapped Emil on the head with his cane. 'Shall we go back?'

They climbed back out and walked slowly around the *kastély*. It was larger than Emil had thought. There was an entire wing that couldn't be seen from the front.

'Jesus this place is enormous,' he said.

They slipped back into the *kastély* from the front door and the pair slouched by a corner in the foyer to wait for the women.

István, still carrying his makeshift cane, examined the wood. No bark was left on the stick; it was smoothed not from sandpaper or a file, but perhaps from a hand that had worn down the sharp edges through years of holding it. The wood was dark from a plum tree.

'That's really beautiful,' Emil said, looking at the stick.

'What do you think this had been used for?' Isi asked Emil.

István held up an end for his friend to examine just as the women walked to the top of the main staircase.

The men standing in the foyer looked odd, as if they were little boys again. István was pointing a stick at his friend, and Emil, standing erect, stared down the long end of the cane in all seriousness. To an outsider, perhaps, one would expect Emil to raise his hands any second in a game of cops and robbers. What Ilona saw was not her son and a friend holding a stick, but a Soviet captain who had arrived in the spring of 1946 to ask her father to 'voluntarily' sign over the orchards to the government. She gasped.

'What is it?' Erzsi asked, when she saw Ilona go pale, looking down the stairs at Emil and István with a shocked expression on her face.

Ilona couldn't answer; she stood erect: a statue of memories stored for a lifetime in stone.

'Ilona?' Melissa said.

The two men looked up to see the colour had drained from Ilona's cheeks, her hands shaking. Emil thought Ilona's knees were about to buckle.

'*Anyu*?' Emil said. He ran up the stairs, took his mother's arm and helped her navigate the stairs. 'You OK?'

Erzsi asked the director for a glass of water.

'She's overwhelmed by the excitement,' Erzsi said.

By the time Emil had guided her to a chair in the lounge Ilona had recovered her composure. She took a long breath.

'Oh my, it's warm,' she said, smiling weakly at her son. She kept hold of his forearm making sure he was still alive. She blinked again to ensure it was István, and not a Soviet captain, by his side. Then, staring at the group that had crowded around her, Ilona reddened a little.

'I believe I've seen enough today. Shall we go and have our picnic?'

Down by the lake, Melissa spread the blanket. Erzsi and Ilona unpacked the food, while István sauntered over to water a tree.

He lit a cigarette on his way back. Ilona was dismayed to see that Emil changed Tünde's nappy in full view of the others.

Ilona, her legs folded underneath her skirt, ignored her son and smiled warmly at Isi as he walked back to the group.

'So, István!' She said, perhaps too enthusiastically. 'When are we going to visit your new nightclub?'

István smiled back. 'It's all going really well.'

'See, son? With a bit of work, you could start a business in Budapest, too.'

Emil did not reply.

'I'll bet Isi would help you, right, Isi?'

Isi looked away and shrugged.

Emil chose a devilled egg to share with Tünde.

Melissa, who could not follow the conversation, lay down on the blanket to soak in the last warm sunshine of the season. As she closed her eyes, she was aware of the melodious sound of birdsong, something she now realised she rarely heard in Budapest. It was calming.

Ilona smiled at her son. 'I can help you get started reclaiming this estate, even!'

Emil nodded at his mother; his lips were tight.

'Hey, Tünde, wanna come with me?' He took his daughter's hand and walked back toward the old people's home, his camera strap weighing heavily around his neck. Ilona could see him aiming his lens at the *kastély*, like he had done all those years ago. Tünde examined a dandelion.

Ilona was tired. The day had been exhausting; she tried so hard to make it perfect. Why was Emil so difficult and stubborn? She closed her eyes and breathed in the fresh country air.

After a few photo shots, Emil walked back to the blanket and sat quietly next to his mother. He gave his daughter her sippy cup and popped another devilled egg into his mouth. He hadn't had any in years.

'*Anyu*,' he asked, in gentle tones. Ilona opened her eyes and smiled at him. 'What happened on the stairs? What were you thinking? Remembering?'

The corners of Ilona's mouth dropped. Her eyes went vacant.

'Oh my,' she said vaguely. 'It was so warm in there.'

She handed a piece of cucumber to her granddaughter and looked up at Emil.

'Would you like one?'

'You are impenetrable.'

'What?'

'Nothing.'

'I didn't hear what you said.'

Ilona took another sip of tea Erzsi had poured from the thermos, but she could feel her hand quivering slightly as she lifted the cup to her lips. She tried to take a deep breath, then looked over at her son and smiled. The colour still hadn't come completely back into her cheeks.

'*Anyu*,' he said, almost in a whisper. Ilona leaned in to hear him better. For a brief moment, he almost sounded like his father. 'I'm here to learn more about my home country. That also means I want to learn all about what you have experienced in your lifetime, not those old stories from grandma. What happened to you and grandma after the war? How did grandpa and Uncle Béla die?'

She stared at her son as if paralysed.

He continued in a slow, low tone. 'What was papa like? Did my escape bring you any pain? You've never mentioned anything. You didn't even tell me you moved flats,' he said. 'There's so much I don't know about your life.'

Ilona considered Emil. He seemed so concerned, so earnest. Like his father once had been. Ilona didn't like being asked questions. She had been forced to answer too many in her life. Through the decades she had become adept at learning how to deftly turn conversations; how to deflect; ask questions back, feign interest, store information that she could use later. She memorised personal details that might be useful in some undetermined time in the future. *Always move forward*, her mother had told her. *Never look back. We don't talk about these things*.

'Emil, enough…' she said, turning to her daughter-in-law with a smile and switching to English.

'Melissa, tell me, how did you like the Pálffy?'

Emil groaned and rubbed his forehead.

Melissa, oblivious to Emil's pleas to his mother, opened her eyes, propped herself up on her elbows and considered the question.

'Oh my God, that place must have been amazing once,' Melissa said. 'The artistry, the craftsmanship, the stone work! It took my breath away. I loved that ceramic fireplace with flowered tiles. The one in that bedroom? Emil, you didn't see it but it was gorgeous. The colours were so vibrant!'

Emil nodded.

'And the master bathroom upstairs — it must have been installed in the 1930s, before the war. I loved the white and black tiles, that claw bathtub. It's great they never took that away,' she added.

Ilona watched as Melissa became more animated.

'And the billiards room! I've only seen those in films.'

'Yeah,' Emil agreed. 'That was my favourite room too. They really took care of it.'

Melissa scrunched her eyes, like she was calculating something.

'Does Hungary have laws to protect historic buildings? Like, do you have to abide by strict guidelines when you make repairs?'

Emil practically snorted. 'They certainly didn't used to. Did you see what they did to the kitchen?'

'You didn't see the upstairs, the way they split up the bedrooms.'

'Bad?'

'Criminal. That's my point. If you're going to renovate a place like that, you have to do it right.'

'— which means expensive,' Emil said.

'I mean, those bevelled windows are beautiful, but I'll bet they rattle like crazy in the winter. And the roof definitely needs replacing.'

'Not to mention insulation,' Emil added. 'I wonder how the place is heated? Oil furnace, I'd bet.'

'Oh God.'

'Well,' Ilona said, 'these things will take time. Clearly it's habitable the way it is, otherwise they wouldn't be using it.'

'I dunno. I'm not sure how long those people will be able to stay there,' Melissa said. 'And to renovate a place like that. To really do it justice would take millions of dollars.'

'Vhich nobody has, right, Ilona?' Erzsi stared at her

friend. Ilona tightened her lips.

Isi stood up and stretched his arms over his head.

'Hey, that picnic was delicious. Are we ready to head back?' Isi asked Ilona in Hungarian.

Tired, the group drove back in silence. Tünde fell asleep almost immediately. Emil stared out of the window, framing the countryside in his imagined lens. Melissa couldn't wait to write to friends back home to tell them Emil was a baron with an ancestral castle. She didn't understand why he had never told her. Erzsi wished Ilona would be content with what she had: a son, a lovely daughter-in-law and a sweet grandchild.

Ilona had thinking to do. Emil and Melissa hadn't said no, exactly. They only said that the *kastély* would be expensive to renovate.

'You know,' she said, breaking the silence. 'I'll bet if you wrote to the Molnars, they'd be interested in helping you out with the renovation…'

'…*Anyu* no, stop.' Emil inerrupted.

'Or maybe your parents, Melissa.'

Melissa laughed. 'Hardly.'

'*Anyu*, enough!'

'Well, if István could find an investor and build a business, you can too, Emil.'

Emil didn't reply.

'Melissa, you liked the Pálffy, right?'

Melissa nodded her head and shrugged her shoulders.

Ilona patted Melissa's knee and gave her a quick smile.

Well good. Ilona thought to herself. These things take time. She had planted a seed. It seemed to find fertile ground with Melissa at least. Emil had simply been away too long. He needed to learn his place. She needed to formulate the right strategy.

'You know, this is an opportune time. Companies, land, real estate — anything you want — is up for grabs. The country is bankrupt and the government is selling off everything the Soviets had confiscated. It just takes a bit of negotiation, right, Isi?'

'Yeah,' Isi said.

'And oomph,' Ilona added. 'Like István has.'

Ilona could see that Emil's neck was reddening. That was the problem, of course. No oomph. Emil lost his initiative in America. Once, he fought hard and viciously to win competitions. She would hug and kiss him when he won, so proud of everything he had accomplished. He'd sulk when he came second, even though his teammates would pile on him, slapping his back that he'd reached the podium.

Sitting in the back of Isi's Lada, Ilona stared at the back of Emil's head. She could see grey hairs. Those years in the States had made him soft. He was not ambitious anymore. The oomph was gone. Nowadays it seems he would rather play on the floor with his toddler than do any real work.

SWIMMING

Emil didn't take Melissa or Tünde to the swimming pool where he used to train — he wanted to visit there by himself — and realised as soon as he got there it was the right decision. The place hit him like an acid flashback: heavy chlorine masked all other smells, echoes at even the least movement; the humidity that clogged his pores; the sensory deprivation when he swam underwater, the grunt and pain as he practised his flips and turns, his muscles groaning as he willed them on to finish the last laps. The rush he felt when he heard his name called to pick up a medal; the cheers from the stands that echoed from the ceramic walls that made it sound like there were hundreds of people when there probably were only a few dozen. On the surface the smells and sounds were no different from any other swimming pool, but somehow this one felt more intense. Those sensations would have been hard to explain to Melissa.

It didn't seem like his life; as if it was another existence led by a wholly separate person, it was so unconnected from who he was now. As if with his escape, he had been able to fashion a completely different person even though at the time, he hadn't even been aware that he had wanted to. Up until he had met Melissa, he had lived his life reactively, going along with what his mother, his coaches, even his grandmother had wanted for him.

When he walked into that swimming pool, he was both embarrassed and almost proud that the attendant had to remind him to take off his street shoes. Of course, no one there knew him, but the coach said he had heard of him.

'Have you been in touch with your old teammates?'

'Not yet.'

'Don't.' The coach's soft belly jiggled under the white polo shirt and shorts he wore as he shuffled around on blue plastic sandals collecting towels that had been left behind after the morning practice. He didn't look Emil in the eyes.

Emil squinted and cocked his head, waiting for an explanation. He thought the man wasn't very friendly, unusual for Hungarians, who'd usually talk your ear off.

'They'd probably punch you in the face. The secret police went hard on them, especially the coach.'

'Oh my God, I hadn't thought of that. I left in a strop,' Emil said. 'I guess it hadn't occurred to me what would happen to anyone else.'

The coach shrugged. It wasn't a friendly gesture, or even a hostile one; just a reaction.

'I remember how frustrating it was watching the Montreal Olympics from Ohio. That East German who came in fourth? I had beaten him twice in the 200 Metre Butterfly during trials when we were kids.'

The coach just smiled impassively and shrugged his shoulders again. Then he looked at his watch and nodded a curt goodbye as he rolled his cart full of towels into the back room.

The day after the 1976 Olympic swimming finals, Emil dived into in the Ohio State University pool. For hours, he swam laps. Hearing the voice of his Hungarian coach in his head, he checked his style and his kick. Hearing the voice of his new college instructor, he checked his timings; his strategy. For days, he spoke only to his coaches and teammates. When school started, he barely attended classes. He only met a few people; one had been Melissa, whose brother was also a member of the swimming team. He had noticed that she watched him, but he had been too shy to talk much to her.

In the winter season, Emil matched the second-place Olympic time. It was a college record and made the university paper. The Columbus Dispatch wrote about it too. Associated Press picked it up. That night and the next day, there were knocks on his dormitory room door.

'Kovács, phone!' Some anonymous voice would yell on the opposite side of the door.

Journalists from out of state wanted to talk to him about the record; a national television station was interested in doing a piece about his escape. A scout for the national team asked to meet him. Emil turned down all the requests. He stopped answering the door. Instead, he slept. He was exhausted mentally and physically and had nothing left to give.

Back in 1974, when he swam to Trieste the night before a race in Yugoslavia, he was exhilarated. When he broke that swimming record at Ohio State, he just felt empty. That was the day he realised that he hated swimming.

He slept, avoiding the obvious next question. He was surprised when Melissa knocked at midnight a few days into his hibernation.

'Special delivery!' She held a pizza box in her hands, and had squeezed a bottle of Zinfandel under her arm. Her brother had told Melissa that Emil had disappeared and had sent her to investigate, but Emil only learned that months later.

Emil opened the door a crack.

'So why are you incognito? Avoiding the paparazzi?'

Emil wasn't sure why he opened the door wider so she could walk in. She plopped down on the unmade bed and sat crossed-legged near the pillow. He liked the way she whipped her hair over her shoulder to keep it out of the food. The pizza box balanced between them. From her rear jeans' pocket, she pulled out a corkscrew. Emil looked around the room for two glasses and was embarrassed when he only found one.

'That's OK,' she said. 'We'll share.'

She waited for him to explain why he hadn't been answering the door, but Emil wasn't used to talking about his feelings.

'I guess I decided I don't like swimming.' He shrugged like it was no big deal.

She narrowed her eyes like she was trying to understand the concept of devoting your life to something you didn't like. She took a swig of Zinfandel from the bottle. A drop lingered on the edge of her lip, which she wiped away with the back of her hand.

'So what do you like to do?'

The question stung him like chlorine hitting his sinuses. When he was ten his school noticed he was an exceptional swimmer and had the right physique. It was assumed he wanted to put in five hours a day swimming. His mother regarded each of his victories as a step to redemption — from what, he hadn't been sure. He found it easy to follow his mother's certainty. His grandmother made special dinners when he reached the podium. Péter, István's dad, slapped him on the back and told him how he was making his family proud. Erzsi hugged him. István grinned. In America, he swam for his High School to get a scholarship. He swam at college to keep it.

'No one has ever asked me that.' Emil could feel a lump in his throat, he found swallowing difficult.

Melissa knitted her brow, averted her eyes, choosing to concentrate on the pizza slice in her hand.

'Charlie has always been a water rat, so it was clear he'd be a great swimmer. No one ever asked me if I *liked* to dance, I just always felt like I *had* to dance.'

Since he couldn't think of anything to say, he jumped up from the bed and turned on a homemade Steely Dan tape.

'What do you like to do?' Melissa asked again, absent-mindedly bobbing to '*Reelin' in the years… stowing away the time…*' She looked directly at him and he felt his heart jump.

He wanted to say something profound, or at least truthful. He racked his brain: maybe something pithy would suffice. He managed a shrug.

He was equally tongue-tied when Mrs. Molnar asked him how he was settling in America or whether he missed Hungary. In his family, his mother and grandmother never talked about their feelings. Emotions weren't his thing. If they were, he'd have told his sponsors that he missed his mum, that everything seemed too big and artificial, that he wasn't used to sleeping in a bed of his own let alone his own bedroom. It would have sounded silly or even weird to an American, but he missed sharing the bathroom, the bed, the TV. He couldn't believe the Molnars had a television in their kitchen. Admittedly there had been days in Hungary when he wished he could get away from his mother and just be alone. Those early days in Ohio, sitting in his own bedroom, he was lonely. Literally too lonely for words. Maybe it was the language, but he just didn't have the words to talk about feelings. Now though, he had the words and barely an accent but he still couldn't answer Melissa's question.

'Woah, it's one thirty,' Emil pretended to yawn. He wasn't really tired; he had slept all day. He just didn't want to talk anymore.

Melissa nodded, but didn't take the hint. She took another swig from the bottle and handed it to him. When she did, she looked deep into his brown eyes. He wanted to kiss her but didn't. Why would such a beautiful, open girl be interested in a loser like him, someone who couldn't even answer a simple question? With his free hand, he picked up the last piece of pizza, only he held it wrong, so that the cheese slid off the crust, leaving him with a limp wet triangle. She laughed.

After they had polished off the wine, Melissa stood and stretched, her arms reaching to the ceiling. He stared at the exposed skin between her jeans and T-shirt and wanted to touch her hip bone. He quickly averted his eyes, so she wouldn't see him looking at her. She promised to check in on him the next day. They nodded goodbyes.

Emil climbed back into bed. And he dreamt of his father.

Emil knew it was his father because he looked like the

man in the framed photo his mother kept on her dresser: a tall lanky guy with his light trousers belted at the waist, hands on his hips, his feet spread apart, his shoes oddly mismatched.

Actually, there were two photos on his mother's dresser in identical gold gilt frames held together by a hinge so that they could stand in a V-form without support. The photos were taken the same day. On the left was a shot of his mother sitting on a picnic blanket just so, to show off a slightly swollen belly, smiling coquettishly, almost like she was flirting with the cameraman. Her hair was redder then, and it seemed to Emil, her eyes a deeper hazel. The other was the photo in his dream; his father, grinning on a summer day, months before shrapnel would rip off his face, three months before Emil was born.

As a kid Emil had loved an old Zorki camera that had belonged to his dad. Each Christmas, his mother would put in a fresh roll of Fortepan film. Those thirty-six prints would record New Year, his birthday, her birthday, grandma's birthday, summer at Lake Balaton and later, important swimming races. He loved being able to turn the spool to advance the film, peer through the viewfinder, carefully holding the camera steady like he had been taught: his hands almost white from holding it tightly.

It could take several minutes before he pressed the tall pin at the top and felt the weight of science and magic combine as the metal shutter snapped in a fraction of a second with a heavy, loud *click*. He felt like he was performing an important and mysterious trick.

In the autumn, he and his mother would take the camera to the shop, where the man behind the counter would place the whole device into a large black bag with two holes for his arms.

With his hands in the armholes and after a few contortions of his face — eyebrows furrowed in concentration, mouth pulled to one side then another — he would adeptly manoeuvre the thick black ribbon from the camera to a spool which he would use to develop the film into pictures. A week later, Emil and his mother could relive the happy memories of the year.

As a little boy, Emil had wanted to be that film developer. He wanted to know what went on inside that black bag. How did it work? How did that pin on the top of the Zorki transform into a piece of paper with his grandmother blowing out candles?

When Emil woke up in his dormitory room, hungry and groggy from the Zinfandel, he decided to take a photography class. It was a daring move; frivolous, against everything he had learned from his mother and the Molnars. That voice in his head told him it was a waste of money. Hungarians studied maths and science. He had chosen engineering as his major and found all the classes boring.

He couldn't just begin a course in photography, though. The university insisted he first take an Introductory Art Course. The class was a struggle: in Hungary, you had to do things *right*; follow instructions. Here he had to develop a vocabulary to explain why he liked or didn't like a work of art. He had to think, defend, justify, feel, analyse.

His first assignment in the art class had been to draw a bicycle in ten different ways. He had three days to complete the task. Emil was despondent as he wasn't sure what he was supposed to do.

On Friday afternoon, he walked out onto the quad with

a brand new sketchbook and some charcoals he had just purchased at the university shop. While other students sat cross-legged on the grass reading or playing frisbee, he sat on a bench and stared at a bike rack. He felt stupid, embarrassed.

One, a blue battered Schwinn, leaned against a black guard rail that protected some hedging. Emil decided to draw it. He thought of his instructor's words: 'draw what you see, not what you think you see'.

Emil stared down at the bike. *I think I see a bike*, he told himself. He thought of his swimming teammates: the jokes they'd tell each other. An errant frisbee hit his elbow and Emil briefly considered joining the game.

After probably an hour of staring intensely at bicycles he thought he understood the challenge. It was far more difficult and satisfying than beating the East German's time. It was the most liberating task he had ever been given, no longer bound by the idea that there was a right way to do something.

Emil began sketching. A charcoal sketch of bicycle spokes, the fifth or sixth of his series, was among his favourites. In another he sketched with his right hand and not his left using a crayon to make a flat picture of a bike as a kid would have drawn it; like a cartoon with no perspective, just whimsical. The last drawing, though, was heavy, gloomy and foreboding. He drew it in the small hours between Sunday and Monday while it was raining. His Dylan tape was playing in his clock radio and Emil had turned off his desk light and looked out of his dormitory window. He saw it. A colourless bicycle gleaming under a lamplight on a rainy night. It looked sinister, like it might take the rider down a wrong path, but Emil wasn't afraid. Maybe it just took the rider a different way. It took him four attempts to catch the right mood.

The next morning, with his ten drawings under his arm, Emil walked into the class full of adrenaline even though he had barely slept in the last thirty-six hours. He got a C, which to him, felt like a success. He had never drawn anything since he was about eight years old, aside from an occasional doodle on a napkin. Now, he felt like he needed to make up for lost time. He called time on swimming and gave up his scholarship. He got a job washing dishes. Only then did he dare tell the Molnars of his decision.

'Are you sure this is what you want?' Mrs. Molnar had asked.

Mr. Molnar only sighed. Tom was going for a business degree. Sandy was applying for a master's programme in engineering. Useful fields of study that led to high-paying jobs.

Art, then later, photography, was all that now mattered to Emil in the same way that swimming once had. While training had taught him self-discipline, art showed him that work needn't be a chore. His day was challenging because he loved what he did.

Success had nothing to do with being faster than the person in the next lane. He had spent too much time trying to please his mother and his coaches. At twenty, for the first time in his life, he understood that success was something personal, feeding his compulsion for perfection, being proud of himself. Practice will never make him a perfect photographer and he will never take the perfect photograph. He will never have an ideal; the paragon of success will not likely come to him, it's the striving that makes him wake up in the morning. Always a new idea; a new technique to try. Something more to master.

He had never been completely satisfied with any of his work. If one of his teachers, or later a buyer, admired his work, he would shrug. 'It's the best I can do at the moment.'

A day or two later, he realised his photographs were shit. He learned he had to stop looking at what he had done. He was constantly analysing, evaluating, picking apart not only his work, but those of others. He loved it.

The Ballet

That evening when Ilona got home from work she beamed expectantly at Melissa.

'Did you meet the artistic director? How did it go?' she asked her daughter-in-law.

'The artistic director? Is that who you thought I wanted to meet for a coffee?' Melissa's eyes blazed. She turned on her heels and slammed the bedroom door behind her, refusing to eat dinner with her mother-in-law.

Ilona did not understand why Melissa would not come out of the bedroom. Melissa could hear Ilona and Emil talking during dinner and it took all her willpower to stay away.

'It took a lot of work setting up that interview, Emil,' she could hear Ilona saying. 'The least Melinda could do is thank me. The least.'

'Her name is Melissa.'

'Well, I thought *Melissa* was a dancer. She didn't even try to impress them at the National Ballet: she didn't even wear a leotard. Or a tutu.'

That night, Melissa cried in Emil's arms.

'I'm not sure what your mother told them,' she said. 'It was so embarrassing, Emil.'

Emil patted her back.

'Why can't she leave things alone? Why does she always have to make things bigger than they're supposed to be?'

'She's always been like that. I remember one time, instead of asking my coach a question about an event I was to take part in, she went to the head of the swimming programme.'

'I just wanted to meet a friend, Emil. Did she really think I could just waltz in and become a principal ballerina overnight? Like, what kind of fairy-tale universe does she live in? That takes a lifetime of work.'

Emil nodded sympathetically.

'A prima ballerina who lives in a castle. Does your mother live in la-la land?' Melissa was just warming up. 'A *baroness* prima ballerina who lives in a castle.'

Emil stayed quiet. Melissa hated it when he did that. She would have continued with her rant, but she could see that Tünde was getting upset.

'Girl, you are going to suck those fingers off your hand,' Melissa gently pulled Tünde to her. She fell asleep cuddling her toddler the way she once did her stuffed bunny, leaving Emil to deal with his mother.

EMIL

About a month after they arrived, Emil took the tram to *Moszkva tér*, where he and his mother went shopping on Saturdays when he was a boy. She probably still did occasionally, he guessed. He made a mental note to ask. In the autumn, he remembered, the square was paradise. As part of his project, 'Hungary in Transition', Emil wanted to see how that was changing. The way Emil remembered it, *Moszkva tér* in autumn was idyllic, out of a children's film, smiling people carrying wicker shopping baskets on their arms or pulling shopping trolleys behind them. *It was the perfect place to start documenting the country*, he thought. While he was taking photos in the main square his mind went back to his childhood and the times every autumn when József bácsi, Uncle Joseph, brought his mother a large sack of potatoes. Sometimes he'd throw in fruit and a bottle of homemade schnapps. József had worked on Ilona's family farm his whole life. Somehow, the two had remained friends; only after Ilona's family lost the farm, it was József who controlled the food. His mother once told Emil that József's father saved her life, but she never explained how.

The day after their trip to the *kastély*, Emil had asked his mother once again about the farm. About Józsi's father.

'What were you remembering when you were at the top of the stairs?'

'I was just thinking how wonderful it would be if we could live there again!'

Emil sighed. It was the same when he asked her about his father.

'You know, you look just like him,' she said. She never let her guard down.

Emil shot a few frames of the potato farmers, but then the younger one started posing for the camera, attempting to show off his barely observable sixpack. The other guy — his father, maybe? — laughed. Emil waved them off. On a normal day, he'd joke with them, put them at ease so he could capture just the right scene. This day, he wasn't in the right mood to record *Moszkva tér*. It was all wrong. He just wasn't getting anything.

The wide streets encircling *Moszkva tér* were like the other streets and squares he'd been visiting: tired looking and resigned. He could barely breathe walking down *Rákóczi út*, which was choked with the toxic black smoke of lorries and cars; the streets were noisy because the silencers and shock absorbers could no longer be replaced, so the parts were just cleaned up and put back in as best as possible. This wasn't the Budapest he remembered at all.

The acrid stench from the streets — a cocktail of diesel from cars, sulphur and coal from the chimneys — clung to his clothes and stung his eyes when he walked for too long. Smoke blackened the once elegant buildings constructed at the heyday of the Austro-Hungarian empire. *Andrássy út* near his studio was an eclectic mix of Baroque, Renaissance, Secessionist and Art Nouveau beautiful buildings, with their waves and curlicues pin-curled along the window frames. But now their stained-glass windows, green-tiled roofs and gargoyles were buried in layers of grime and exhaust fumes. It was as if Soviet-era pollution covered the opulent excesses of the Austro-Hungarian empire with shame.

Pieces of the façades had fallen off, sides of buildings had pockmarks. Emil noticed the distinctive holes in buildings in various places about town. When he was a kid, he hadn't noticed them. Now Emil knew they were bullet holes left defiantly by street workers and repairmen so that the people would never forget the Soviet betrayal. Like a wounded soldier unabashedly showing off his scars. Never forget, never forgive.

The pavements were buckled and broken throughout the city. Black tar oozed from the cracks in between the pavement slabs. Emil could hear the grit under his shoes, although the path itself used to be tidy, swept regularly in the socialist days that ensured full employment. Now he found that if he didn't constantly look down, he would stumble. That's likely why pedestrians kept their heads bowed. Hungarians weren't shy or downcast like you think when you first arrived; they were simply being sensible, concerned with their safety.

Emil had come to *Moszkva tér* hoping for something different. The liveliness that comes from a market. That feeling of excitement to see what the farmers or butchers were offering that week. Expectations, cravings, hope. That was what he had in mind for his exhibition, 'Hungary in Transition'.

Instead, *Moszkva tér*, like the rest of the city, seemed to be sagging. Irritated, Emil threw his camera bag on his shoulder and began walking. He remembered from his childhood the steep path up to Castle Hill, maybe a bit more than a mile away. Back then, the walk had been worth it: the view of Pest on the opposite side of the Danube was stunning. The bridges, each with their own style, vying to be noticed. The parliament, so grand and imposing, perched next to the river.

Castle Hill was a refuge high above the city. It was quiet where most of the capital was chaotic, and clean where the rest was dirty. It retained its classiness while most of Budapest had succumbed to years of neglect. He remembered the anticipation he felt as his mother picked out coins from her purse and handed them one by one to the ice cream vendor with the red and white awning shielding the silver wagon from the heat of the day. Maybe Castle Hill would get Emil the photos he was looking for.

Though it was late autumn it was still hot in the sun. In spite of the breeze, Emil's back began to drip with sweat as he waited to cross the tram tracks, diesel exhaust from lorries rumbling on the busy street burned his eyes.

He was feeling every ounce of his bag's weight but he didn't mind, as his walk led him into a quiet neighbourhood, tidy narrow flats with mediaeval frontages, leading to the castle. He looked up at the tree-lined streets; at least they had not changed. The shade was welcoming. On he walked. He took deep breaths, grateful for the oxygen; the quiet. Away from the traffic he could feel his body relax.

The next neighbourhood was entirely different. Breeze-block flats separated small turn-of-the-century art deco apartments. Drying laundry waved like flags from narrow balconies with black wrought iron railings. He didn't remember it being this long of a walk. *Wow*, he thought, *I'm getting out of shape*. And on he went. He was back to a busy street. One without trees. More loud, stinking Lada and Moskvich cars sped past him. This can't be right, he thought. He trudged further. He passed a run-down *csemege,* a small corner store. Then he was back to the breeze-block flats.

He was lost. Emil felt a slight twinge of embarrassment. How could this happen? This was his town. His sour mood had returned. Emil asked for directions in English, surprised that the young woman walking by in stylish clothes could answer him, although in very broken phrases. Emil let her struggle.

As he finally reached the top of Castle Hill, Emil noticed a group of, oh, ten or so guys standing around with their hands stuffed in their black jackets, a few taking drags from their cigarettes. It had become a joke between Melissa and him that apparently every Hungarian man owned a black jacket.

'Gotta get you one quick,' Melissa had said with a twinkle in her eye. 'Otherwise they'll never give you back your passport.'

The men were gathered near Buda Castle, where a Hilton had opened a few years back, next to St. Stephen's Basilica. At least the *lángos* stand selling greasy fried flatbread and the ice cream van were still there. So was the Ruszwurm pastry shop, where his grandmother took him for his twelfth birthday. Emil's mood lightened. Little had changed up here.

There was a reason tourists liked it up here. The view was stunning. The tops of trees in their lime greens, golden yellows and rusty browns billowed like clouds down to the river, where you could catch a spectacular angle of the Chain Bridge. A barge floated under it as Emil aimed his lens. He switched cameras, so he could get some black and white images that would capture the sharp contrasts of the buildings on the Pest side of the city. He worked slowly to compose the picture. He centred the bridge in the middle of the frame so it pointed at the stark Soviet style office buildings on the other side. The cupola of a church peeked out beyond as if it was poking fun at the modern buildings.

Next, Emil steadied for a wide angle shot of the *Halászbástya*, Fisherman's Bastion that bordered the castle district. He stayed with his black and white images; the afternoon shadows were creating some great opportunities reminiscent of André Kertész's work. He wondered if he could get Lady Liberty from a better angle from up here.

When he was in college he had studied every photograph by Kertész that he could: dissected them, analysed them and then went back months later and looked again. What made them great? Though everyone else at art school owned Nikons, Emil chose a Leica because Kertész had used one.

Emil spent the rest of the afternoon shooting the sharp angles of the bastion, its stairs, the curves. This was beautiful. It was as if he was back at art school and focused on form and shapes, not the documentation of 'Hungary in Transition'.

He stopped to order a drink from the ice cream vendor and noticed the men were still huddled in their group. He studied them for a moment, then he realised they were taxi drivers. Were there really so many tourists these days? Emil put away his Leica and strolled over for a chat.

Only a couple of them had been driving taxis before the wall came down, they told him. One man, a short squat guy with a moustache in his mid-forties named Bálint, said he had worked in the import/export office. It was a great life; his Russian served him well. Then trade between the Soviet nations collapsed.

'They made me redundant!' Bálint said, nearly spitting. 'That's an affront; I'm not useless.'

After six months of not finding a job, Bálint said, he needed money to pay for the rising rent and the cost of food, which was almost a luxury these days. That's why he started working as a taxi driver. A second man said he was giving tours at the cathedral, next to the castle. He used to teach.

'You used to be a history professor?'

The man nodded. 'The universities don't have so many people now.'

Bálint piped up. 'My wife used to be a physicist but now is a nanny for a British family who've just moved to Budapest.

Emil stared at him. 'A physicist is now a nanny?'

Bálint nodded. 'They are investors so, very wealthy. She makes twice the money she used to make. It's a little boring though, she says.'

'She can't get a job as a physicist anymore?'

'All these changes,' he shook his head no. 'The government says we are supposed to "adapt" but I'm thirty-eight years old. What am I supposed to do?'

The other men nodded.

'They need to go back to the old ways. I mean, this "market economy" is bullshit. Wasn't the price whatever the market demanded?' Bálint said, crushing out a cigarette with his shoe. 'Don't we demand that prices be lowered?'

The others laughed.

'The problem is, no one can spare the money for taxis anymore either. What are we supposed to do? It was better in the old days,' Bálint said.

The other men nodded their heads.

Emil just listened.

'*Háát*. What can you do?' another guy answered. The rest of the taxi drivers nodded in agreement; their fists still firmly rammed in their jacket pockets.

There it was again, Emil thought. *Háát*. Most people just accepted their lot, assuming life would just get worse.

'Why are you giving up?' he asked them. 'Isn't this supposed to be a big chance now?'

'A chance for whom?' the history professor asked. 'What am I supposed to do now?'

The other men looked down. One guy began digging his toe into the gravel. *Háát*.

Emil wanted to understand. Why had they lost hope? István was doing something. He seemed to be the only one able to accept the past and move on. These guys, standing outside the Buda Castle smoking cigarettes, were just waiting for someone to make life better for them. His swimming coach used to tell the team that you only lose if you give up hope — and if you give up hope, you deserve to lose.

The country should be on the brink of something momentous the way Castle Hill had been given a face lift for tourists. That's the direction the country should be headed. Why weren't they ebullient that the communists were gone?

Instead everything seemed drained of energy; weary, beaten down, like *Moszkva tér*. As he trudged home, Emil thought that maybe he should change the subject of his exhibition. He was here to document change, but instead his new title should be *Hungary, Defeated Again*! No wonder a Hungarian, Rezsö Keress wrote *Szomorú Vasárnap, Gloomy Sunday*, a song that drove people to suicide. It's a national pastime, feeling deflated. The past is always present. Emil couldn't put his finger on why. He just knew that he was getting annoyed with people shrugging their shoulders. *Háát*.

Emil hitched up his camera bag, unaware that he was marching down the hill swinging his free arm frantically.

The Hungarians in Cleveland, he thought, got stuck in the past, too. They re-lived it; spent their days reflecting on what happened; asking if they had been foolish in not seeing the double cross in the first place. They remained paralysed, forever playing the tape in their heads; rewind, press play; rewind, play. Hoping to change what they had said or done. Rewind, play. The noise was loudest when they had too much to drink.

Even now, Mrs. Molnar constantly relived the Soviet intervention, as if she could have changed anything and kept repeating the same story.

'We had only a few hours to pack before the secret police, the ÁVH, would sweep in and arrest us. I was frantic. I looked around the flat: at the sofa, the side tables, the bed. None of it was important. I could only think of my boy Sandór. He was only a baby. He wouldn't be able to grow up in his homeland, and only the Lord knew what was waiting for us. Would we be killed before we crossed the border? Would Sandór end up growing up in a refugee camp? Would he forget his heritage, his language? I knew what was happening, but he was so innocent.'

Her eyes would start to redden.

'So I packed both our suitcases with everything for him: his clothes, toys and books. Everything he owned. I added only a set of fresh clothes for my husband and myself.'

Then, Emil knew, Mrs. Molnar's eyes would flood with tears, as if she had packed those bags last week. Her voice would grow weak.

'He grew out of it all in months. We had no photographs, no marriage certificate, no birth certificate, no silver, no jewellery. Nothing.'

At first, Emil was moved by these stories; each refugee had their own, sad, tender tale. They were heartbreaking. After a while he had become as tired of hearing them repeated endlessly as he was of the defeatism he saw now, here in Hungary.

The day before he had escaped, he had realised that once his swimming days were over, he'd no longer be useful to the state. Then what would he do? Would he spend his days in the same bland concrete breeze-block flats as everyone else, working in a grey office at a forgettable job?

Emil turned right onto *Fö utca*. He slowed his pace as he looked out on the river. *There's something calming about the water*, he thought. Then another notion hit him. If he had stayed seventeen years ago, would he now be standing around with his hands rammed in the pockets of his black jacket like these taxi drivers who used to be history teachers or would he be more like István?

Back in the States, Emil had always felt he was moving in the right direction; progressing towards a new era. That is what he thought he'd find when he got to Budapest. It was a monumental time in history. A turn of fortune that few people thought would happen, especially without bloodshed. No one considered the socialists would just turn off the lights and leave the building, but it did happen. Almost as easy as that. It was a new day, a new dawn, a chance to make a new country. And these guys are standing with their hands jammed into their jackets. Emil felt that same dreariness he had encountered as a teenager was creeping back and he didn't understand why.

MELISSA

While Emil was working, Melissa liked to explore Budapest on her own. She hoisted Tünde on to her back, adeptly crossed her handwoven cloth around her front then tied a large knot behind her, just below her daughter's bottom. The knot also acted as a little seat for the toddler. Melissa got the impression that Tünde liked peering out of her perch on her mother's back; Melissa couldn't imagine mothering without her baby sling. A friend wove it for her from her massive loom when Melissa was pregnant. They got the idea to weave it after Melissa's friend had returned from a trip to Botswana, where all babies spent their days swaddled in slings. When Melissa wore it she felt a kinship to mothers all over the world.

'Do you need a pushchair dear?' Melissa's mother had asked. Melissa had said no. Babies needed to feel the warmth of their mums, not be ensconced in a pushchair. Now, two years later, Melissa still felt that way. There was no better way to travel than with a kid in a backpack.

With Emil gone with his camera and Ilona off to work, Melissa threw a nappy and a packet of wipes in her bag. In case they were gone long, she added a banana for Tünde and a cheese sandwich for herself. She had read that the flea market was cool.

Though Emil never said a word, Melissa was aware that she and Tünde were a financial drag, so she knew in advance she wasn't going to buy anything. The grant money was meant to support a single artist working alone in an Eastern European country. Emil needed access to a developing room and video editing equipment, so Fulbright connections and his college at home where he worked had introduced him to the ETLE University in Budapest. Even so, without extra income, it wasn't at all certain whether the whole family could last the whole year. If they were going to stay — and Melissa wanted to stay — she needed to find an income or be useful somehow.

Now here, she, Melissa, was alone. Still bitter that she had not been able to meet dancers. It would have been nice to meet artists other than Emil's friends. Women friends, Melissa thought. Preferably with children. So Melissa spent her days exploring. It was only for a year. She would concentrate on learning some Hungarian; immersing herself in another culture.

The best part of Budapest was its public transportation system, Melissa noted, as if she were writing a column for the Cleveland paper. Why couldn't Cleveland learn something from Europe?

Maybe she could write about these things, Melissa mused. She thought about what she would write: *children, of course, ride for free*, but Melissa's ticket was so cheap it might as well be given away too. And everyone gave up their seats for her, they were so polite, friendly.

They even offered Tünde sweets, something Melissa was getting used to. Apparently Hungarians never learned that they weren't supposed to give sweets to children. When she could, Melissa would politely intercept them despite her daughter's wails of protest, but now she was used to it. Melissa loved the strangeness of it all.

Getting to the flea market from Ilona's flat required a trolley ride, a few stops on the rickety metro, (*Europe's oldest*, Melissa pretended to write in her newspaper column), then a transfer to a bus. It took an hour, but Melissa had time.

Melissa loved flea markets anyway, and she knew she had to stagger her visits to museums with outdoor jaunts to keep her daughter amused. Tünde seemed to enjoy watching the other passengers from her high perch. Melissa noticed that her toddler seemed to even understand the coos from the other passengers. Or was that her imagination? Would Tünde learn Hungarian before English? Melissa kinda hoped she did. She pictured herself back in Cleveland speaking to Tünde in Hungarian like it was their secret language. What a snob, she could be!

The *Ecseri Piac*, Budapest's flea market, was more fantastic than Melissa had heard or even imagined. She had to stand at the entrance and catch her breath for a minute just to take it in. There was so much going on she didn't know where to look. The *kolbász* stand was open too early for customers but its barbeque smoke wafted up and mingled with the smell of the deep fried vat of *lángos* flatbread dough from the next grimy stand. The stench of over-boiled coffee overpowered it all.

'Hey Tünde, maybe we'll come back here for lunch?'

Melissa said.

Beyond the food stands, were rows upon rows of small booths each seemingly selling something different. Dust permeated everything. After the permanent places came outdoor spots for the day traders. She could hear the low murmur of the swarm of people who made up the colony of visitors. Here, midday on a slow Tuesday, she felt like she was at a Fourth of July garage sale back home, only on a grander scale.

Back in Cleveland, they sold junk. Here, at this flea market, there were real bargains. Only a few steps in from the entrance she already could see antique furniture, everything from walnut cabinets to trestle tables easily more than one hundred years old gathering dust under sagging awnings. Melissa decided she would walk around first before diving in.

Behind the stands with chipped green paint and thin glass, people had plopped down blankets or old card tables and displayed, well, everything. Melissa was overwhelmed. She didn't know where to look.

Rows of worn-out men's leather shoes, cleaned and polished, lined neatly next to a table of Herend Porcelain. She didn't have to look at the back to verify the manufacturer. She knew all fine china sold in Hungary was made by Herend, which, according to Ilona — who was shocked Melissa had never heard of it before — was the finest porcelain in the world.

They made an adorable bunny in a powder blue fishnet pattern with gold-tipped nose and toes, which Melissa hoped she could find second-hand to send to her mum for Christmas. She nosed around the table seeing if she could find one.

'Bunny rabbit?' Melissa asked the woman sitting at the

table. Melissa put her fingers to her head to demonstrate two ears.

The woman knitted her eyebrows together and shook her head. She pointed to the delicate green pattern on the dinner plates; picked one up and tried to press it into Melissa's hands.

'*Nem köszönöm*, no thank you.' Melissa waved her off and continued down the aisle.

Antique side tables, silverware, old Soviet medals and pins — clearly for tourists — hats, kitchen appliances that looked like they came from the 1950s, all in perfect condition, were to be had.

One stand was filled with every kind of lamp imaginable: desk lamps, reading lamps, crystal chandeliers in a variety of sizes and periods, ceramic kitchen lamps, ceiling lamps, brass lamps, wooden lamps, wall sconces. Melissa, with Tünde on her back, inched along the narrow passageways unsure where to look next.

God I wish we could bring some of this back, she thought.

Another stand seemed to corner the audio market: radios from the 1940s to modern day turntables, Victrolas, speakers, amplifiers and radios were stacked floor to ceiling. A scratchy record blared out classical music, Liszt, maybe? Melissa smiled at the man next to the speakers.

One table had what appeared to be used auto parts: mufflers, brake pads, belts, tubes, tyres, spark plugs, distributor caps for the Trabants, Ladas and Dacias clogging the streets and her lungs. The man sitting behind the table held a cloth, which he was using to clean the parts. It smelled of oil and petrol.

The table next to him was filled with nails and screws of every size, along with a few aged hammers, files, awls and screwdrivers.

'Unbelievable,' Melissa said to Tünde.

Tünde made 'oooohh' noises when they passed a stand with old toys; really old, like a spinning top, metal chickens and wooden farm animals whose paint was fading.

Melissa was astonished at how cheap the animals were — pennies really. She didn't bother to haggle. She bought the horse and handed it to Tünde.

Next to the toys was a space with a lamp, a rug, and a makeshift rack that held clothes, a few dresses, blouses and sweaters; a woman sitting on the ground next to it smiled hopefully as Melissa walked past.

'Cloth-hes?' She said, pointing to a pair of jeans folded neatly on a hanger. The woman was the same age as Melissa; Melissa longed to be able to speak to her; have a friend. Instead she shook her head.

'No thank you.'

Next was a short, squat man probably in his mid-forties with thick black hair. He stood next to a wooden wardrobe with flower arrangements of deep reds and blues painted on the front panels. At the bottom was the date, 1900, inscribed with initials — the artist? the owner? Melissa wasn't sure.

The man nodded to Melissa and pointed to the wardrobe.

She nodded her head back to be polite and tried to walk on, but he stood in her way.

Startled, Melissa tried to walk around him, but the man put his hand on her shoulder and showed her the wardrobe, opening the door so Melissa could see the wide, clean shelving inside along with a tiny drawer hanging from the top shelf. He spoke in gentle tones as he lifted the hook and opened the door on the left side. He pointed to the three hand-carved hooks on both sides of a central pole — all in perfect condition.

Melissa bobbed her head again. She didn't like his hand on her shoulder. She stood stiffly and said politely one of the few words she knew in Hungarian.

'*Szép*.' Beautiful.

She tried to walk past again, yet he still blocked her path, staring into her eyes, keeping up the patter, though it sounded more insistent. Melissa felt the hairs in the back of her neck start to rise. Was he somehow trying to pawn off a stolen wardrobe? In broad daylight? The thought was absurd, yet it also frightened her a bit. The mixed emotions gave her the courage to refuse him.

'Sorry,' she said as politely as she could in English, raising the volume of her voice. She shrugged her shoulders to emphasise her body language. 'We're too poor to buy anything this time.'

The man looked sad and insistent. He still wouldn't let her pass. He spoke again in the same lilting tones that seemed to Melissa to sound increasingly desperate. Melissa looked around for help.

The woman with the jeans sitting on the blanket said loudly to Melissa: 'You not poor. You American, no? This man telling you needs to sell closet today. He lost job. You must to buy.'

Melissa looked at the woman anew. She realised the clothes on the makeshift rack were all women's clothes, probably the same size as the seller. The lamp and rug were likely hers, too. The shoe display, the porcelain — were they also from impoverished families?

She felt her pulse racing; her face reddened. This wasn't a garage sale. It was a sale of woe.

'I'm sorry.'

She didn't want to be there anymore. Didn't want to look at the man, who continued to speak in low tones. Tünde dropped the wooden horse; the man picked it up and handed it back to Melissa and pointed to Tünde, closing his eyes and making a gesture indicating she must be asleep. He seemed sweet, but he still wouldn't let her pass.

Melissa didn't have many more *forints* with her, but she knew she had a few ten-dollar notes in the back of her wallet. Money she hadn't yet exchanged. She pulled them out of her bag and held them out to the man. Did he have a wife? Children? Or was he a con artist? She didn't think he was.

The man looked at the dollars and then back at her. His eyes burned into her; then his upper lip curled and he slapped her hand, the dollars went flying. He began to yell at her; his cadence quickened. Spit arched from his mouth.

'I'm sorry. I'm sorry,' Melissa said, as she lowered her head and turned around.

The woman with the lamp and clothes rack tutted loudly in disgust. Melissa could still hear the man yelling at her as she raced down the row of blankets; feeling the heat of the eyes of the people she passed. Had they stopped to watch the scene?

Melissa went inside the first stand she came to, too nervous at first to take in where she was. It was quiet and darker than outside and that was all that mattered. Once her eyes adjusted to the light, Melissa saw she had run into what she could only describe as a small art gallery.

Landscapes, portraits, naïve paintings — all in ornate

frames covered the walls; oils, acrylics, mostly, but she could see in one corner there were lovely watercolours; inks; chalks.

One oil painting in particular caught her eye at the far side of the wall. It depicted a 19th-century woman wearing a white dress with a bustle and a wide hat adorned with pale pink roses. She was sitting under a wide linden tree that was shading her as if she had a wide green, full parasol. A bright red blanket had been spread out for her, so her white frock would not be spoiled. She peered down unabashed into the face of a young man who was resting his head in her lap, his knees pulled up. His own hat fallen off to the side.

Melissa instantly loved the scene because, unlike a French painting, there was no wine; no baguette, no food even. Just two lovers who stopped on a sunny day to rest under a giant, ancient tree that protected them from prying eyes. Sparse but filled with love. The painting and the stand calmed her nerves.

A slightly balding man wearing a baggy grey suit greeted her absentmindedly, but politely. '*Kezét Csókolom*,' I kiss your hand.

Melissa almost rolled her eyes. He wouldn't have wanted to kiss her hand if he knew what had just happened.

But the gallery owner wasn't interested in her; he was standing next to a big, large man with a fake tan and red jeans. A navy blue cable sweater was tossed over his shoulders; the arms of the sweater folded like socks draped his chest. His button-down chequered shirt had a discreet Hugo Boss insignia on his left breast. The man slouched a bit; his left hand tucked casually in his trouser pocket, his right hip jutted out, his left knee shook impatiently as he flipped skilfully through a rack of paintings. He seemed so out of place.

The man rarely stopped to regard the works. *Click, click, click* as each painting was tipped forward.

Like the man outside, the stand owner kept up a steady monologue about the paintings, Melissa guessed. Next to the tall man, a smaller, stocky man translated into German. She could understand a bit of what he was saying. The paintings were from the collections of important and lesser Hungarian aristocracy. One portrait of a woman, he pointed out as the tall man flipped past it, was once the lover of Klimt, he believed. A muse, an important Hungarian patron of the arts at the turn of the century.

Another, he said, is thought to be a work of a minor Hungarian female artist who was active in the Blaue Reiter movement. They were still working on the provenance of it. The tall man said nothing. He moved to the next rack — *click, click, click* — whipping through the paintings the same way she perused racks of CDs back home.

Fascinated, Melissa didn't bother to hide the fact that she was staring at them.

The proprietor pointed to the landscape that Melissa had noticed as she entered. That too was by an early Secessionist, he said. The German didn't look up, he appeared engrossed with the paintings he flicked through.

Melissa wondered what he was looking for. An old portrait that once belonged to his family? Some esoteric masterpiece? He wasn't saying, but by this time, it didn't matter. Melissa was mesmerised by the rhythmic *click, click, click*. One by one, rack after rack, the German looked at each painting without saying a word.

At each rack the proprietor told a story about at least one

of the works. Whose collection it had been a part of; what they knew about an artist; who they believed might be in the painting. Melissa could see a few gorgeous works of naïve art flash past the German's glance.

She wondered what they cost, astonished by the works in this small stand in the middle of a flea market. Why wasn't he in a proper gallery? Was this guy legit? She would have to ask Ilona or Erzsi. Melissa pretended to be interested in a rack full of charcoal drawings. Dark, brooding etchings with sharp lines; some with a distinctive Soviet fatalism to them.

Finally, the German spoke to the translator. His voice was surprisingly loud after the quiet tones of the proprietor. She could feel Tünde stir at the sudden noise. He pointed to one of the racks with the older oil paintings in them.

'I'll take all of the frames in this rack,' he said. 'How much does he want?'

The translator didn't seem to understand.

'Frames? You want all of the paintings in that rack?'

'No. Just the frames. They are exquisite,' he said. 'I don't care for portraits of lesser Hungarian aristocrats.' He emphasised the word lesser.

Melissa looked anew at what the German saw. Some portraits had distinct ornate frames with family crests and emblems. One dark wood frame had what appeared to be inlaid tortoise shell. The frame on that possible Blaue Reiter oil, on the other hand, had stripped-down geometric lines. A beautiful art nouveau frame was almost jarringly asymmetrical. In Germany, these would be treasures.

Embarrassed, the translator asked the proprietor what he wanted just for the frames. The proprietor's face reddened.

The two Hungarians spoke rapidly for a few minutes, and although Melissa didn't understand the words, she clearly could perceive their meaning.

Impatient, the German pulled out a wad of Deutsche Marks, making sure the proprietor could see.

'I'll pay cash.'

It was then that Melissa noticed a pile of canvases in a corner behind the proprietor's desk. Each was naked, exposed and stripped of what were works of art in their own right. This had happened before.

Melissa felt her stomach churn.

Tünde was waking so Melissa left the stand. She had seen enough for the day. People were selling their furniture; their clothing; their shoes, even. Car parts! And the wealthy were buying frames, not the paintings themselves, only frames.

Melissa felt dirty as if she was somehow complicit in all this. She felt sorry for that woman sitting on a rug; they were probably the same age, and here was Melissa, spending a year in a foreign country and there she was, selling her clothes and furniture. Melissa wondered, *what could that woman get in exchange for a lamp or a dress? Pay her electricity bill for that month?*

Tünde was getting fidgety; Melissa plopped her bag down under a leafless tree not far from the stands selling coffee, greasy *lángos* flatbread and spicy wursts. She sat on a broken chair which she had dragged over and changed her daughter's nappy on her lap. She breastfed Tünde, grateful to have a moment to calm her nerves. She pulled out her cheese sandwich and took her first bite when she heard an English voice.

'Mummy, mummy. Look at me, mummy,' a little girl, probably five years old, with her fringe hanging over her eyes, said. She wore a bulky jacket and red corduroy trousers.

She wasn't loud, but because she spoke English, her voice stood out. She twirled on her tiptoes with her hands over her head. She didn't make it around. Didn't matter anyway. The mother had her head turned away as she chatted with a friend who was absentmindedly rocking a pushchair, jostling its occupant to sleep.

'Mummy, Mummy, look.' She pushed the hair from her eyes before setting her arms over her head once more. Melissa thought her British accent was adorable.

Tünde watched as the little girl made a full circle in two pushes, her jacket billowing out slightly.

'Very good,' Melissa said, using her best teacher voice. 'Keep your head high. Don't look down; straight back. Yeah, like that. Now. Try again.'

The girl made it nearly around in the first go.

'Excellent!' Melissa said.

The girl smiled coquettishly and inched closer to Melissa.

'Do you want to see me do it again?'

'Imogen, darling, come back. Don't bother the poor woman,' the little girl's mother said in a stage voice so Melissa would hear. Her voice was slightly raspy, the way a smoker sounded.

'No bother,' Melissa answered back. 'I used to teach dance back in the States before we moved here. We were a dance troupe with a school attached.'

The two mothers' eyes widened.

'Oh my God. That's heaven to our ears,' Imogen's mother

said, stubbing out a cigarette.

'Where did you work? Who for?' her friend asked. Her voice was crisper than Imogen's mum.

'I was a member of a dance troupe called *Jump!* and I taught modern dance on the side. Some friends and I run a dance studio. I'm, like, on a sabbatical.' Melissa assumed a professional tone of voice, enunciating her words. She loved speaking English to someone. She'd chat with them all afternoon, if she could.

The two women looked at each other, smiling.

'Would you be interested in doing it here, too? Our older daughters are dying for after-school activities,' her friend asked.

'Just like that? Where would I teach?' Melissa had hoped the women would ask.

'We can ask the school if you can use their gym,' Imogen's mother said.

'School?'

'The international school. It's for expats,' she said. 'It's small, and so many people are arriving now. Nothing's set up. If you can do it, I'm sure the school will be happy to lend you the space.'

'Of course,' Melissa smiled. 'Let me give you the telephone number of where we are staying.' She reached into her bag for a piece of paper.

On the way home, Melissa wondered how much to charge these 'expat' women. They looked rich, with expensive jackets and shoes. She had seen a few around town, but hadn't met any. They lived in the upmarket side of the Buda Hills and tended to drive Land Rovers. Not Cleveland types at all. Could she set up more than one class? Charge Deutsche Marks, dollars, pounds?

Melissa's mind was racing ahead — she'd contact the school the next day. She'd put up some posters around the school to advertise. Of one thing she was certain, she wouldn't tell Ilona a thing about her plan.

On her way out of the flea market, Melissa noticed the man with the painted wardrobe and the woman with the lamp and clothes out of the corner of her eye. Neither looked like they had sold enough goods to pay for their heating bill or rent.

For Melissa though, the outing had paid off. She did some mental maths, reckoning with three classes a week and still having time to explore the country. If she could make money, maybe she and Emil could afford to find a place of their own. Move out of that flat; get away from Ilona.

JANUARY

It had taken months before Emil made his way to *Kossuth tér*. Avoiding it was a feat in itself: the Parliament, standing majestically on the riverbank, was the capital city's greatest landmark. The third largest in the world, yet barely in its life has it been useful. Anyone looking at the city from Buda, where he lived, couldn't escape seeing the imposing building, especially when it was lit up at night, casting its black shadows on the water.

Emil felt he needed time before he could go. He knew it was where his father had been murdered. He tried several times to bring up his father casually at dinner, but Ilona only brushed him off.

'He was a great man, Emil, but naïve.'

While the Hungarians in Ohio freely talked about their memories, the people who stayed behind seemed to keep their thoughts tucked away in the bottom drawer of the wardrobe. Ilona avoided mentioning the events that brought about his death, even when he said he was considering using that topic for his exhibition.

'What exhibition?'

'I told you, before I leave I want to hold an exhibition.'

'Are you still thinking of that? Let's get you lined up with István, dear,' she had said, patting his shoulder.

It was so easy for her to skirt round the subject Emil wanted to discuss, especially if she could steer it to that damn palace. Worse, if she could needle him about how he had failed her. He had missed his mother when he was away. Now she both annoyed and intrigued him. What lay beneath that hard skin of hers?

'What were you thinking about at the Pálffy, *Anyu*? Can we talk about that?'

'I was thinking about how I can convince you and Melissa to stay here,' Ilona replied. More than once, Emil had looked at his mother and sighed. She never asked him about his work. She didn't seem curious about his art, or his grant and the Hungarian project that had brought him here.

Unsurprisingly, the Hungarian library had only one book on the 1956 Uprising and it had been written by the victors, the Soviet-backed government in the mid-1960s. Emil had brought with him copies of old archival footage from Pathé, which he had obtained from the university in Ohio where he taught. The news agency where Ilona worked was allowing him to look through their archives. But he needed more, more eyewitness accounts; more original stories to make the photo montage he had in his head. It was difficult finding anyone to open up about the past.

He had decided to go on this grey winter day because he liked the light. It was bright enough to take some clear shots but not too sunny, so he could avoid shadows. He started across the river in *Batthyány tér*, where he could get a full view of the parliament building. He felt comfortable there. From the red brick market building, *vásárcsárnok*, with the gigantic socialist star beckoning everyone from afar to the fussy baroque St. Anne's Church, with its pink stone façade and green copper towers it was his. He knew it well, because of its central location. He had taken Melissa and Tünde there. It was where, as a kid, he would buy something to eat on the way back from early morning practice. Not at the market, which by the time he was a teenager, had turned into a tennis centre for party members, but from the small shop next to it that doubled as a *söröző*, a beer bar, where shabby men lingered even early in the morning. Batthyány square was also where he and his teammates hung out for as long as they could at night, just sitting under the one single tree, sipping beer and swinging on the thick black chain that separated them from the river. Their only light came from the dozens of spotlights that lit up the parliament across the wide Danube.

Even then, as a kid, he didn't like to acknowledge the parliament building. One of the few things he knew about his father was this: that he died outside the parliament building.

Emil found that his shoulders had tensed up as he boarded the underground to make the quick trip to *Kossuth tér* stop. Then he rode up the steep escalator and stood at the spot where his father had his face blown off.

Emil stood tall, his hand holding the strap of his camera bag, and breathed in. The winter air was crisp; it stung his nostrils. Parliament was not in session, so the square was still, there was a muffled silence, though he could hear the distant hum of cars. Not even the seagulls cawed.

Here, where the cobblestones were kept neatly swept and

the lawns even now were trim for tourists and members of parliament, Emil tried to imagine a bloodied body. That was one of the few things he knew about his dad, that he died with his face blown off during the 1956 uprising. His mother would only allude to it, whisper it. As a boy, he and István had murmured it, wide-eyed and hushed. The way they had discussed everything else off-limits to kids.

As the uprising receded through the decades, it couldn't leave a residue because under Soviet oppression, no one living in Hungary could filter it. Hungarians couldn't dissect it like the diaspora in Cleveland did.

Every American can tell you where they were when Kennedy was shot. Emil guessed that every Hungarian knew where they were during the uprising, but they wouldn't be eager to tell you. He could see that they still felt the pain of the loss of a friend, or a sister or a father. To name them would be to recognise and exult the people who were counter-revolutionaries in the governments' eyes. To name them would be to draw attention to yourself. Emil saw that people were still afraid. Like his mother was. As if in 1991 it still could happen again.

Emil blinked a few times and tried hard to imagine what had happened, but nothing in his experience gave him the material he needed to fully digest it. He could only see in his mind's eye a film version of the events, yet he could feel an eerie stillness. *Kossuth tér* on a January day might be without people, but it would never be devoid of sorrow.

Even after the reburial of leaders of the 1956 uprising, people seemed reluctant to mention it. That reburial, only a few years ago, was the beginning of the end for the communist government. It was then that opposition leaders dared to say the martyrs' names in public. The speech that caused the biggest storm was made by the youngest person on the dais, a student only twenty-six-years-old, who hadn't been born when the uprising happened. None of the older politicians was brave enough to do what that guy had done. Viktor someone, Emil couldn't remember his name. He dared to demand the withdrawal of the Soviet troops who had once fired at the people and into the buildings that still bear the scars.

'It was then, in 1956, that the Hungarian Socialist Workers' Party took our future away from us — today's youth. Therefore, in the sixth coffin in front of us lies not only an unknown murdered youth, but also our next twenty or who knows how many years,' he had said.

The Hungarians in Cleveland roared in ecstasy over those words. They were the words that ultimately helped mark the end of socialist rule. They were the words that even a year later are still quoted in Cleveland, and yet, they are words that people here in Hungary still found hard to repeat. The Soviet troops remained in place, seemingly at the ready in their barracks. It seemed to Emil that no one would breathe freely until they were gone for good.

Standing in the middle of *Kossuth tér* where his father died, Emil tried to process the event. Feel it, smell it. He walked around the perimeter. He ambled to the river in front of the parliament, the damp breeze wafting up chilled his bones. He bent down and touched the gravel of the path along the Danube where he sat. Had this same bench been here thirty years ago? He sat on it and brooded.

He was so lost in thought that he barely noticed the man

who sat next to him looking out at the Danube on a quay not far from the Parliament. He was an old guy with a big nose and side-combed thin hair, wearing a black jacket. Eventually, Emil did what he usually did when he came across an opportunity to meet people. He went slow, simply talked with the man about easy things like the weather and football. The man nodded and answered. He seemed amiable enough. It emboldened Emil.

'I'm Emil.'

'Gergő,' the man offered Emil a cigarette.

Emil declined.

'I'm visiting my mother. It's my first time back since I left in 1974.'

'How do you like it here?'

'It's changed a lot. It's more beautiful than I remembered.'

Gergő nodded.

Emil pointed to the parliament behind them to the right and told the man on the bench that his father had been killed over there in 1956. Emil thought telling his personal story would help put other people at ease. Get them to share their stories.

Like so many others, Gergő was silent when Emil brought up the subject of 1956. He only nodded an acknowledgement.

There it was again, a wall. A dyke, holding back memories. With nothing left to say, the pair sat once more in silence. It really was too cold to sit on a bench by the river in January. Emil sighed and decided it was time to walk around *Kossuth tér*. When he looked over at the man to nod his head goodbye, he noticed a subtle eye movement: *Gergő was looking around. Reflexive preservation*, Emil thought. As if the Iron Curtain had not fallen; as if the guy was still worried about the secret police. Emil leaned back on the bench and waited. After a while, the man huddled in close to Emil and said in his ear: 'It was a set-up.' He said it in a whisper.

Then Gergő leaned back on the bench. A thin lock of grey hair covered one eye, but he didn't wipe it back. Emil nodded encouragement, but Gergő stared out at the water and took his time.

'After Stalin died, we all hoped we could go back to living a normal life. We hated our leader, you know, Rákosi. I was still in Gymnasium then, but I remember the day he ordered the *Regnum Marianum* church to be blown up. My sweet mother, bless her soul, cried the whole week.'

Gergő crossed himself. Emil waited.

'We, my friend and I, ran down to the city park — that's where the chapel was — to watch it blow up. The chapel was a beautiful thing, all full of fancy swirls and curls. But Rákosi hated that church. It had been built just after World War I after we had kicked out the Bolshies. My father was one of the former soldiers who helped build it, too. He said he wasn't going to risk his neck in a war just to let some communists take over our country and steal our farms. In honour of all that, they built that church. Right there, in City Park, so everyone could see it.'

Emil was confused. He'd never heard about a church in City Park. He took out a notebook from his camera bag and jotted that down *Regnum Marianum*. Would the archives have any photos of it?

'Well twenty years later, Rákosi comes along and says that the church has to go. We weren't supposed to pray anymore either. My father almost had a heart attack hearing the news.

My mother cried and cried. But my friend and I, we ran down to watch the army blow it up. The older people weren't there. They all stayed away. The priests were there, though. So were some nuns. They were on their knees praying. A whole group of them, you couldn't hear their words, it sounded like they were humming, like bees.'

Gergő hummed, to demonstrate.

'So my friend and I stood our distance, to be respectful. The soldiers placed explosives inside the whole church and then the soldiers ordered us to leave. My friend and I just walked back a few steps. One of the older nuns started sobbing. It was getting dark and I knew my mother would be worried if I didn't get home, but I didn't want to leave without seeing the church blow up. There was a long pause. One of the soldiers talked for a while with one of the priests. Then the group said one more prayer, only loudly, and walked far away from the line. There was another long pause and then BOOM!'

Emil jumped. The man grinned. He had lovely laugh lines around his eyes. Emil hoped he would be able to photograph him. Now was not the time, though.

Initially, Emil thought Gergő was an old guy, but as he spoke, Emil realised he was probably his mother's age. As he recited his story, though, his voice had seemed younger, an octave higher. Emil saw that he was both delighted and repelled by the whole scene in his head.

This was too good to lose. At the risk of breaking the spell, Emil asked him if he could record it. Gergő shrugged. Emil took that as a yes and pulled a small tripod out of his bag, along with a portable video recorder. As Emil fiddled with the right angle to film, Gergő looked out at the Danube, as if the activity in front of him had nothing to do with him.

Emil pressed the red record button and settled in on his haunches, checking the viewfinder one more time.

'You were talking about *Regnum Marianum*. You said the uprising was a set-up? What did you mean?' Emil asked to get the conversation going again.

Gergő took out a cigarette and lit it. Emil knelt on the gravel, but it hurt his knees. He switched to squatting again. It was going to be a long story.

'The whole *templom* hit the sky, raining down rocks and dust and wood splinters from the pews and God knows what. I got dust in my hair. We all did. The nuns' black robes had turned grey; they looked like they were from a different order! My friend and I collected some stones and other things that had fallen near us. I thought I could sell them and make some money. Rákosi built a statue of Stalin with those stones from the *templom*. He banned religion, too. One by one those priests were sent to places outside the country. Reassigned. Stalin was now the new God to be worshiped. We were supposed to replace our crucifixes on the walls with portraits of the great almighty Stalin. In the end, no one wanted my rocks, my mementos. They were afraid of what might happen if we were caught with them, so I threw them into the Danube.'

Emil nodded, to encourage Gergő. But Gergő didn't see him. His eyes were back to a time long ago. He stared not into the camera, but out at the river.

'So what happened at the uprising?'

Gergő waved a paw at the camera, as if to say, 'All in good time.' Emil waited.

'Rákosi was thrown out after Stalin died. I was at

university by then, studying engineering. We all went out and got drunk, we were so happy. Imre Nagy was now our new Prime Minister. He promised reforms, made it easier to cross the border to go into Austria, if you had a passport. If you weren't class x, a dissident. I mean, if you had class x stamped on your papers, you couldn't do anything.'

Emil nodded. He knew about the different passports from when he was a swimmer.

'We students began talking about independence from Moscow. We didn't have riots like they did in Poland or East Germany or anything. We just talked about it. We were young. We didn't care who heard us. We talked; debated into the night, smoked a lot of cigarettes, drank a lot of *Bikavér*. You know *Bikavér*?'

Emil knew it. *Bikavér*, literally bull's blood, was considered the best red wine made in Eger. He made a mental note to buy some on his way home.

'This girl I liked, her name was Magda, she took to wearing those tight pants you could see in American films, not the drab socialist crap. She bought them in Austria. She looked hot. A friend of mine brought over records of Coltrane and Thelonious Monk, stolen from the *Amerika Haus* in Vienna. His father was in the government and he had a passport. I liked my copy of Gigi Gryce and Clifford Brown, 'ba-bah-dab-baah-baah-bap!' We saw pictures of people in the West wearing blue jeans and leather jackets. On Radio Free Europe we heard Elvis and Bill Haley. I mean, Stalin was dead and we had hopes but we still listened low volume, you know what I mean? The ÁVH made known that Western music wasn't appreciated.'

Gergő punctuated the word appreciated, to make sure Emil understood his meaning.

'You know ÁVH?' Gergő asked.

'Yeah, the secret police.'

'Now that Imre Nagy was in power, we thought we'd be free to listen to what we wanted; say what we wanted. We still played it at low volume, though. You catch my drift?'

Emil smiled. 'I get it.'

Gergő coughed a few times as if he was choking on a cigarette inhaled long ago. Emil wanted him to keep talking; wished he had water to give him.

'Nagy was arrested though, right?'

'Nah, that was later. You know things started going downhill after we lost to the Germans at the World Cup.' Gergő chuckled.

Emil didn't understand but didn't want to break the man's concentration. He smiled and nodded, pretending to chuckle too.

'You are right, you are right,' Gergő said, waving his hand at the camera again. This time, he too peeked at the lens. Emil thought he was warming up to the idea of speaking on camera.

'Nagy was thrown out by the Soviets. They brought in a friend of Rákosi. That made a few of us more than a little nervous. You ask yourself what you said, and to whom, you know what I mean? Those sorts of questions. We stopped talking about things. At least out loud. We had hoped that things were going to change.'

Emil kind of understood, at least the idea of that. So he nodded.

'Even he had to go. No one liked the guy; he was bad

news. Another Rákosi. And this time we thought we needed
to make sure his kind was gonna go for good. Enough of this
socialist crap. The discussions we had in the university canteen
turned into rallies. We had just come back from summer break,
so we were full of energy and fired up. We wanted Imre Nagy
back, our own political parties, free speech, and freedom of
movement. We wanted that Goddamn statute of Stalin torn
down. We wrote out sixteen demands.'

Gergő coughed, then he shook his head, looking straight
into the camera.

'Sixteen. I mean, we weren't happy with one or two
things. We wrote out sixteen demands!'

He shook his head in disgust.

'That's how Goddamn naïve we were.'

Gergő sat back on the bench, like he was remembering.
There was a long pause. Emil's knees were so still they ached
in the January cold, so he checked his video viewfinder to
make sure Gergő was lined up right, then Emil stood for a
minute, hoping he wouldn't break the momentum. He wanted
to look into Gergő's eyes rather than a camera. This was just
what he had been looking for; why he was here.

'Everything seemed to be happening at once. The rallies
were getting bigger; they weren't just at the university. That
made us all bolder. I felt a sense of freedom I had never felt
before when I went to those rallies. You could feel energy that
didn't exist when you just sat around smoking cigarettes and
listening to jazz. We weren't just a few students getting drunk
on *pálinka* or *Bikavér* and ideas. There were a lot of different
people at the rallies too. Farmers whose lands had been taken.
Families who had lost someone to a show trial. Bureaucrats

even, although I don't know why they were there. It's like the whole country had a problem with the government.'

Gergő chuckled again. Emil nodded.

'People made their own signs with their own complaints. Their own grudges. Everyone showed up for a different reason but for the same reason: we all hated the government. That was what we had in common. We hated the Soviets. We wanted them out, but it was all peaceful, you know?'

Gergő paused again, then his voice turned bitter.

'Then someone posted our list of sixteen demands.'

Emil knew a lot of what happened after that from hearing the old Hungarians in Cleveland, but he had never heard the tale told so raw. He was mesmerised. This was a recounting of his father's last days. Like Gergő, his father had been an engineering student. He almost wanted to ask him if he knew László Kovács. Would that have been too much of a stretch? Could Gergő have been a friend of his father's? He didn't want Gergő to stop talking, though.

'That's when the riots started, right?'

'A group of radicals decided to take over the radio station. That turned deadly and scared the hell out of us. I don't remember anymore, maybe two or three people died. I thought, 'well that's that.' We went back to university. I mean, I didn't want people to die.

'I was in class the next day when I heard there would be another rally and was surprised it would be so soon after the radio thing. The word was, this rally had to be peaceful; It was going to be in front of the parliament, but we were going to be cool. No rocks; no weapons. It couldn't be violent like at the radio station. 'Be cool, man,' I heard one guy say, in English, like he'd heard on Radio Free Europe. You know that radio station? It was good. Good music.'

Emil nodded, encouragingly.

'So on Thursday, we skipped classes and headed to *Kossuth tér*, right here —'

Gergő pointed off to his right.

'— I went with Magda. I made a sign that said "we aren't fascists". What I was trying to say was that they — the government — they were the fascists. I mean, they always talked about how they quashed the fascists in the war and anyone who opposed the Soviet Socialists were fascists. I wanted to let them know. We aren't the fascists in this fight. They couldn't call me a fascist. I wanted democracy. I wanted Imre Nagy back. Magda and some of the other women had cut out the communist symbol in the middle of our flag, so it was our Hungarian red, white and green flag again — with a big empty hole in the middle. She held it high and proud as we got on the metro to *Kossuth tér*. It was packed with other people. Way more than any other rally I had been to. I wasn't expecting that at all. People were pouring out of trams, the metro, walking in from town, from across the Danube. Every direction you could see, people were walking to the square. People were singing, chanting and happy. And no guns and no stones.'

Gergő's voice seemed louder, excited. Emil could almost see the crowds of giddy people marching toward the square in front of the parliament on a sunny October day.

'There were even people sitting on top of the Soviet tank that was parked on the edge of the square. A Soviet soldier was smoking a cigarette and talking casually to some girls sitting on his tank. I couldn't believe my eyes. He was smiling! Russkis never smile! Magda and I held hands. Our dream was coming true! I asked her half-jokingly if we could blow up the Stalin statue the next day. She laughed. 'Today we are peaceful. Tomorrow you can destroy the statue.' The square, it was packed. Thousands of people were there, maybe tens of thousands — it was the most I'd ever seen in my life! People were singing the national anthem. I was looking around to see who was going to speak. I mean, I didn't even see a stage set up. Where was Imre Nagy? Who had called the rally? Who had started singing the songs? It didn't look like anyone was leading us. We were all just there — and happy, joyous. No one was thinking.'

Gergő's speech slowed. Then, his voice lowered, he continued: 'That was the problem. No one was thinking. It was not long after that I realised why no one was there to speak to us… like I said, it was a set-up.'

He was silent for a while. He rested his elbows on his knees; back hunched forward. He was shivering. Was it because of the cold or the memories? His head bowed down. Emil could barely hear him. He hoped the video camera could pick up his voice.

'The Soviet soldier who we had passed? He casually climbed down into his tank. I turned and noticed for the first time there were tanks at each of the entrances to the square. Hungarian and Soviets soldiers were marching on foot toward the square. I dropped my sign and grabbed Magda's hand and told her to run. We ran for the Agricultural Ministry Building on the other side of the square opposite parliament —'

Gergő turned in the direction of the building and pointed

it out.

'The door was locked. What the hell? It was in the middle of the afternoon, why lock the front door of a government building?'

Emil shook his head.

'Other people were banging at the door too. Let us in! Let us in! Then I heard shots. Magda and I dropped to the ground by the front door of the ministry. I covered her head with my arms and could feel her shaking. That explosion I had heard years before when they blew up the *templom* was not as deafening as the bullets I could hear hitting the ministry building behind me. So much echo, so many screams, such terrified screams. When I heard the tanks firing into the crowds, I heard the screams. The screams I'll never forget. They were louder than the tanks. I thought about my mother, my father, Magda, who I could feel shaking but couldn't hear crying. The bullets kept coming and coming... it seemed like everything was in slow motion but fast too. I felt sweat pouring down my back and could feel Magda's body on mine. There were screams from everywhere'

Emil felt like he was there. Like he, too, could hear the endless bullets. Feel the betrayal. Wondered where his father was when the shooting started.

'Eventually the firing ended and I tried to get Magda to get up and make a run for it. That's when I saw that she had been hit in the leg. A pool of blood also was forming next to her and I couldn't tell where it was coming from. Then I saw it was me, I was bleeding, too. A bullet had grazed my back, but I didn't feel anything. Magda had fainted. I slapped her face, telling her we had to get out of there. It was urgent. I told her she needed to run with her one good leg, that I'd help her up. I was crying, telling her she had to get up. 'Magda get up, please get up.'

Gergő was on the verge of crying, Emil could tell. Still, Emil didn't want him to stop. He was mesmerised. Emil could feel the chill wind whipping up from the Danube. White caps on the waves. It was cold. He felt himself shivering. He put his hands in his jeans' pockets.

'Just as we were about to make our move, the shelling started again. She screamed. I realised I had screamed too. We stayed where we were. I looked out and saw bodies — dead ones in pools of blood, injured people moaning, crying, screaming. I saw people trying to run from the square, down into the metro, to escape the carnage. One Hungarian policeman, from the ÁVH — he was wearing the ÁVH uniform — he lobbed a can of tear gas into the Metro station. When people came up for air they shot them. The tanks kept pounding the building behind me. I thought I was going to go deaf. I thought I was going to die.'

Emil had never heard a story as wretched as this one. He could feel his whole body shaking. He imagined his father in the middle of this slaughter, just one of the many dead and dying.

'I could feel the heavy wood doors of the ministry rattle. I hoped they would collapse so we could escape. Then I decided the only way to survive was to pretend to be dead. So I told Magda to pretend to be dead. Magda and I went limp. We stayed that way for maybe half an hour, until the firing stopped and the Soviet tanks rolled away and the ambulances started to carry away the wounded and I saw soldiers throwing dead bodies onto the back of a lorry. Just chucking them in without any respect. I told Magda we had to get away. Magda couldn't stand, her trousers were covered in dried blood. The material stuck to her leg, which dragged at an odd angle. She gritted her teeth as she leaned on me, her arms rubbing against my back where the bullet had grazed. She was pale and shivering. She seemed past crying and that scared me. Somehow, I managed to get her to the metro station which smelled of tear gas. My eyes burned. When we got on the metro, we both cried.

'We got off a few stops later, just to get away from the police. We took a taxi to the hospital. The driver didn't charge us and didn't talk to us, either. The hospital was packed, full of people looking worse than we did.'

Gergő paused for a long time, staring out at the river. He seemed oblivious to the cold. He looked worn-out, old and exhausted by life. Eventually he slapped his thighs and leaned back on the bench.

'I never saw Magda again. I don't know what happened exactly; probably the ÁVH questioned her. Her parents would not let me see her again. She left the university because she couldn't walk anymore, I heard.'

Gergő blew out a long breath, like he had been holding it in for years. His eyes were filled with tears.

'We never found out who called the protest, but I know who it was. It was the Soviets. It was a set-up.'

Emil felt sick to his stomach. He knew some of the rest of the story. Probably one thousand people died that day. Including his father. Maybe more. He imagined his father was one of the bodies thrown into an army truck. It was a picture stuck in his head: the man in that photograph on his mother's dresser being tossed into a lorry like the bag of rubbish thrown out on Thursdays.

Emil looked over at Gergő on the bench. He was close in age to what his father would have been if he had lived. He didn't know why his father — a husband and soon to be a father — would have risked everything to go to that rally. Was he that naïve; that trusting, as his mother said? Did he really believe the Soviet soldiers would swap cigarettes with cute girls? Did it not occur to him that a Soviet soldier would be shot as a traitor if he did?

Emil turned off the video and sat back down on the bench. He wanted to hug Gergő. Take him out to dinner. He too wanted to cry. He wasn't sure what to do next. It all felt so raw, so immediate. At the same time, he felt numb. Cold numb.

Both Emil and Gergő sat side by side and stared at the river, as the sun began to reflect orange and red on the water. Even that though couldn't make the white caps on the grey waves seem warm. Emil couldn't stop shivering. There was so much to think about.

Eventually, Gergő let out another long breath and pulled out another cigarette.

'Thank you,' he said.

'For what?'

'I've never told anyone before. No one knows I was there, at *Kossuth tér*, back then.'

Emil nodded, trying to take that in.

'I'm honoured you shared it with me.'

He wanted to ask more questions, but needed to think about everything he had heard.

'Would you like to meet again? Maybe have a beer

sometime?' Emil asked.

Gergő's eyes, Emil could see, were red. He looked so old. The man nodded a yes, but said nothing, like he couldn't bring himself to speak.

When they eventually parted, Emil was confused; happy to have found Gergő, but angry at the scene he described where his father had died. This was key to understanding Hungary. So many people, like his mother, had wounds that hadn't healed, a nation too afraid to take off the bandages or maybe they were just too beaten down.

He stayed on the bench long after Gergő walked off, letting the video camera stay in place just a few minutes longer. Emil tried to make sense of his father in this different light. The Hungarians in Cleveland romanticised him as a national hero, someone who fell fighting for his country. He had never felt that way. In Cleveland his father had been a badge of honour to the exiles. Emil couldn't idealise him like they could, though. He missed not having a dad. Once, when he was still in High School, he watched as Mr. Molnar wrestled with Sandy over a basketball. Tickling each other, giggling together, hugging. Emil pretended he had not noticed. By the time he had reached the back door to the house, he was wiping away his tears.

Now, hearing Gergő's story, he felt... almost... he didn't know how to feel. He never was good with feelings. But Emil did know this: he was more than a decade older than his father had been when he had died. He didn't feel the passion his father must have had to attend that rally. Would he ever? Was there ever a reason to risk your life? Maybe swimming away, as he had done, was an act of cowardice. Fighting for your ideals was far more righteous, but Emil didn't have that kind of passion.

Sitting on the bench he felt acutely how privileged his life had been. He had never thought about that before. Things just fell into place for him. Being picked for the team hadn't been his choice. But there was his name on the team sheet. He had made no plans to escape, but it all came so easily once he had. The opulence of the Molnar's house had blown him away when he moved to the US, but it was so easy to slip into that comfort. It wasn't even hard to stop swimming and switch to art.

He'd never had to limit his words in case the secret police were listening; not that he remembered, anyway. He'd never had to wait decades to get a phone or a car. He'd never given a crate of salamis to a bureaucrat, as István had just done, in order to speed up the acquisition of an alcohol licence.

Emil loved his wife. He adored Tünde. He didn't think he would ever do anything to threaten their happiness. He would never allow his daughter to grow up without a father. Emil had spent his life wishing he had a father. Had his father waited, the Soviets would have gone anyway. History proved that. And his father would have lived to be a grandfather. Had it not been for his father's naïvete, he and his mother would not have had to share a bedroom in his grandmother's flat? That's what he had always thought. Now, after hearing Gergő's account, he saw things differently.

EMIL, THE RABBIT

Emil would never tell his mother that he fled the country because of his father. Now, sitting on a cold bench on an overcast January, Emil wondered if what he was feeling was shame. He, not his father, had been naïve all these years.

The day he swam away, Emil and his coach had a fight. They were in Yugoslavia for a competition. Emil was the fastest eastern-bloc swimmer under eighteen in the Butterfly. At the trials though, the coach had not entered him for it. He was only in the relay team because another swimmer was injured.

'What kind of an idiot won't let me do the butterfly?' Emil had yelled at his coach.

'What kind of idiot,' the coach had yelled back, 'would criticise the government at a rally with a defaced Hungarian flag?'

'What the fuck are you talking about?'

The coach had stormed off, leaving the assistant coach to break the news.

'You're the rabbit. You always have been,' he said.

'Didn't you ever get that? Your father was a dissident. They'd never let you go to an event held in the West. You're a security risk. You're lucky they even let you come to events here. Your family is an embarrassment to Hungary.'

The assistant coach left, leaving Emil, stunned in the white tiled changing room, hunched over on the bench, his elbows on his knees. One last swimmer, looking embarrassed that he had overheard every word, had remained standing naked in a turned-off shower. His teammate quickly dressed, and keeping his eyes firmly down on his duffle bag, passed Emil without speaking.

Alone, Emil got more and more angry: everything made sense and nothing did. When he was a kid, he swam to please his mother. He had somehow sensed that something was wrong, yet never knew, or asked, what it was. After a while he assumed his home life was like everyone else's. He had a feeling that he could make his mother and grandmother happier if he excelled in the water. It was his way of pleasing them; making them smile in a family that did not have a lot to smile about.

In the changing room, Emil tried to focus his mind, but couldn't. He heard a loud ringing in his ears, although he knew there was no such noise around him. It was as if his brain was trying desperately to block out the words he had already heard. It was like... like the truth were nails racing to a magnet, piercing his being to get there.

He couldn't see a future. Now he knew he'd never be able to swim at any major event from that point on. He already could sense his mother's disappointment; the knitted eyebrows. Could almost hear her suggestions about how to get back into the good graces of the coach; making it look like it was somehow his fault. Then, when the Olympics were over, they'd be finished with him. He'd wind up sitting behind a desk working a nameless, dull job and living in a colourless flat like his mother, like István, Péter and Erzsébet.

Slowly, the numbness he felt from the assistant coach's words wore off. In its place was a sharp, penetrating rage. It started in his gut and moved up his body, stiffening every muscle. He could feel his heart beating fast; his breath was shallow. He could barely stop his heart from pounding during dinner. Everyone else was pumped up; slapping each other on the shoulders, full of the nervous laughter which preceded an important race, careful to avoid eye contact with Emil, who they knew had been benched. Emil hardly noticed. He was quietly forming a plan.

That night, he stole all the money he could find from his teammates and nabbed a couple of vials of mink oil from the coaches. Then he walked down the sea. It was the most spectacular swim of his life and no one was there to cheer him on. He had swum away on an impulse, furious that he had been duped; conned; made into a fool. He had been surprised at how easy his escape had been.

Now, sitting on a bench overlooking the Danube on a winter night nearly two decades later, Emil again felt that pain of his coach's betrayal. As he looked out at the dark icy river Emil felt that he understood his father for the first time in his life.

Emil thought his father's treason had transferred from the bullet that passed through his father's face and seared into him, lodged into his soul, transforming his life. For so long he thought his life alone had been hit by that bullet. All the adults around him had acted like nothing had happened. Now, as an adult, he saw that his mother, too, was collateral damage. And like his father, he too, had wounded his mother. He thought he understood now why she never told him that she and his grandmother had moved into a smaller flat. That she had been left without a job in a country that had boasted full employment. Ilona Kovács knew a lot about betrayal and he was complicit. Only, Emil thought, there was a difference. His father died for a noble cause. He, Emil, defied the government not from ideals, but from sheer anger.

KINDERTEE

Melissa taught three days a week at the international school and got paid in dollars. It was all under the table of course as she didn't have a work permit. Melissa's salary paid for more than their fair share of household expenses so Ilona couldn't complain anymore. Well, she shouldn't be able to now but Ilona found a way to find fault in everything Melissa did. Melissa dreamt of finding their own flat, but Emil was opposed to the idea.

'Is it really necessary?' Emil had asked. 'We're only going to be here a few more months.'

'*Six* months,' Melissa had answered.

The conversation took place the same day that Ilona had brought home *Kindertee* for Tünde so that Melissa 'wouldn't have to' breastfeed anymore. Melissa had looked at the ingredients of the so-called children's tea and saw that it was filled with sugar.

'Why would I want to give my child processed sugar when breastmilk is perfectly packaged and nutritious? Besides, she's eating everything we put in front of her.'

'Well,' Ilona had sniffed. 'I'm only trying to give *my* granddaughter the best. This is from West Germany, you know.'

The next week Melissa had learned from one of her dance mums that the *Kindertee* had been pulled off all the shelves in West Germany. Apparently, babies' teeth were growing rotten after drinking the tea.

'She's trying her best,' Emil had said. 'She didn't know about the tea. It's the bastards who are dumping their products that you should be angry at. Businesses that will do anything to make a buck.'

'Okay, you're right, the company was taking advantage of Hungarians who think the West has all the answers, still, that misses the point. Why is your mother always trying to improve you? And me, by the way?'

Emil shrugged. 'The greatest burden a child must bear is the unlived life of its parent.'

'Well that's profound.'

'It's Carl Jung. I heard it in my psychology class years ago and it stuck with me.'

Thursday afternoon dance class was the last for the week, and Melissa was tired, happy not to have to make the long trip back up to the international school for a few days. It was the kind of afternoon when the sun was out and tricked you into thinking spring was on its way. Melissa decided she'd make a quick stop at *Moszkva tér* market to pick up some groceries for the weekend before going back home.

When she came out of the greengrocer's though, the trams seemed to have stopped running. Crowds of people were waiting hopefully, mounds of cigarette butts piling up at their feet; others were trudging away, resigned.

'Shit,' Melissa said.

'Shit, shit, shit,' repeated Tünde on Melissa's back.

'No honey, I didn't mean that. I just meant you're getting heavy. I got the dance bag *and* groceries *and* we gotta walk home.'

'Shit, shit, shit,' Tünde answered.

Melissa really wasn't into walking the rest of the way. It was easily five kilometres. Tünde would start to get cranky if she didn't get dinner soon; if she fell asleep now, they'd never get her to bed for the night.

'Let's look for a taxi, honey,' Melissa said.

She dreaded that; taxi drivers were known for driving foreigners more than a half hour out of their way and rigging the metres just to squeeze out a few more *forints*. She decided today she didn't care; she'd just monitor his route. Melissa glanced in the usual spots.

'Damn. No taxis.'

'Damn, damn, damn,' Tünde repeated.

The pair joined a crowd walking from *Moszkva tér* towards the river. A makeshift parade, silent. As she reached the top of a hill, Melissa looked up the instant the lights on the bridge were turned on in the distance. The suspension wires that curved like waves illuminated against a darkening sky were made more sinister by heavy clouds. It was dramatic. A Danube cruise ship turned on its lights, too, as it floated down the river. From her vantage point, Melissa thought she could just make out the faint chatter from the passengers, who she suspected were just starting on their cocktails. Wind lightly shook the trees next to the pavement, loosening the last of the leaves which floated down in front of them as they trudged on, crunching on the dead ones that already carpeted the ground. It smelled like it was going to snow.

Taxi Strike

Meanwhile, Ilona was wringing her hands as she looked nervously out the tram window. The tram driver rang the bell several more times, trying to capture the attention of the cars parked in front of the tracks, but the cars didn't even seem to be moving. They weren't the usual array of cars but were all cream-coloured Ladas with their strip of red checker pattern running across the doors. The oval TAXI signs usually lit up on the roof of the cars were switched off. There were probably six or seven all parked perpendicular to the tram lines.

Taxis had blocked the Liberty Bridge. Looking down toward the end of the bridge, Ilona could see that all sorts of cars, not just taxis, were parked bumper to bumper, The tram driver rang the bell again, a shrill *briiiiiing*. By now it was clear that even if one car tried to move, the others behind it were staying put.

Ilona could hear the other passengers murmuring in soft tones as they collected bags and pulled on coats. Eventually, the tram driver gave up and opened the doors, letting the tired commuters out onto the bridge to continue their journey on foot. Ilona looked downstream at Erzsébet Bridge, then upstream at Petőfi Bridge. It was hard to see, but from where she stood, it didn't look like any traffic was moving at either of them.

Nobody liked taxi drivers on a good day. But this was too much. The taxis were parked in perfect lines on each lane of the intersection beyond the bridge. Drivers, maybe thirty or forty of them, were hunkered down, some smoking, others with their hands stuffed in the pockets of their black jackets. None of them looked apologetic as the commuters passed by in silence. Ilona could see her breath as she walked. She wished she had brought her gloves.

As Ilona passed the drivers, she could hear engines and smell fumes on the highway at the end of the bridge, long lines of cars, one by one turning around. A few honked horns, more than a few of the drivers in the cars cursed the strikers. Ilona noticed the strikers kept their eyes on the pavement.

Ilona looked to see if any police were coming. Would they just allow the taxi drivers to block the road at peak time? She kept her head down and walked on, refusing to look at anyone, not speaking with a soul. She did not notice when the lights went on at the bridge. She was unaware of the cruise ship floating past her. She clutched her handbag which was hanging on her shoulder and marched on.

It was nearly seven when she finally arrived at her flat.

Emil was in the kitchen, cooking, bobbing to *The Talking Heads* which was blasting from Ilona's stereo. By now, Ilona was getting to know the different bands Emil played. She didn't like any of them. It was all noise that jarred her nerves.

'Where's Melissa? Where's the *kisbaba*?'

'Hi mum.' Emil said, a wooden spoon poised in the air as he turned to greet his mother.

'Is Melissa home?' Ilona's voice was tight.

'Not yet,' Emil said. 'They should be here any minute. Did she tell you she'd be late?'

'The trams aren't running,' Ilona said, turning down the music.

'Oh, that's probably why they're late, then,' he said, nodding his head. He turned back to the stove.

Clearly he didn't grasp what she was telling him, so Ilona repeated herself.

'Emil, the trams aren't running. There seems to be a blockade or a strike of some kind.'

'What strike?'

'The government raised petrol prices today,' Ilona said. 'It looks like the taxi drivers are on strike and have blockaded the roads in protest.'

'How much did they raise it by?' Emil asked.

'Sixty-five per cent,' Ilona answered, and watched as Emil blinked at her answer. 'The government can't get its cheap Russian oil anymore. They have to buy it at market rates, they have no choice.'

'Shit but that's a lot.'

'Yes. I fear this isn't going to end well.'

Emil turned off the stove and raced to the bedroom to grab his camera bag.

'I gotta go talk with the taxi drivers. Where are they?'

'On the bridges.'

'Oh, that's good. Melissa's coming from the opposite direction; she'll be away from any protests,' he said.

Ilona moved in front of the door.

'Emil, don't get involved. It's dangerous.'

'Mum, it's a demonstration. I've seen lots of them.'

'In the United States.'

Emil was pulling on his jacket when Ilona's phone rang. Emil hoped it was Melissa, but instead it was John calling for Ilona.

'Can you reach any of the bridges? Get some quotes from the protestors and phone them in?' he asked her. 'And Ilona, don't forget to get first and last names this time. See if you can describe the scene for me.'

He said he was on his way to the office, walking. He was sending János, the news agency photographer, out as well. All roads leading to Hungary's capital city were blocked, it seemed.

'Don't forget to bring coins for the phone. Call in a couple hours, especially if anything gets nasty,' John said.

Ilona winced when she heard that last sentence. Her hands trembled as she changed into comfortable shoes and walked with Emil back to the bridge. It was dark by the time they arrived. She had been unusually quiet walking there; breaking the silence only to instruct her son to stay clear of any harm.

'Never stand between police and protestors; find a way to stand back and up high. Use your scarf to cover your mouth and nose if tear gas is used.'

'Stay cool, mum. Nothing's going to happen.'

'How do you know?' Ilona snapped.

She was surprised to see women had arrived at the barrier lines, too. There were lots of people and not just the taxi drivers there now. One group was setting up tables; placing thermos flasks and cups on one of them. Two young women in jeans were lugging a vat of soup down to the river, each leaning into the heavy load, trying to avoid the hot, sloshing contents, yet laughing when they failed. Ilona was startled at the mood, decidedly different from only a few hours earlier. All the honking cars stranded behind the taxis had left or been abandoned on the roadside. A boombox blared pop music in one corner of the crowd; near the tables, she walked by men huddled around a small transistor radio that was tuned to the news. There was even a fire on the river embankment.

At first it felt like a street party, until she realised it was nervous laughter that she heard. Everyone, it seemed, had one eye on the Pest side of the bridge. Like her, they seemed to be waiting for the police.

Emil started snapping photos immediately. Ilona mulled around at first, trying to decide with whom to talk. She pulled a notebook from her handbag and approached a woman who looked slightly younger than herself, wearing a sensible coat and black shoes.

'In the past salaries went up with the prices. This time, that's not happening,' she told Ilona. 'I miss the old days when everyone had jobs and you knew when the prices were going to rise. How are we going to afford to heat our homes this winter? These prices are ridiculous.'

Ilona nodded her head in agreement.

Ilona thought about her own gas bill. Without Melissa's extra income, she'd also have problems paying it. *Good quote*, Ilona thought. *Done*. As John had requested, Ilona jotted down her name. It was time to go, but she couldn't find Emil, who seemed to have vanished in the crowd. An unshaven man with uncombed hair pulled out a megaphone which squealed, the sound piercing Ilona's ears.

'We need to decide our demands!' he yelled, as the megaphone squeaked again.

One of the drivers hollered back: 'No petrol price increases. Full stop!'

Please. Not sixteen demands. Just be happy with one, Ilona thought, as she frantically looked above the heads of the protestors, hoping that Emil was just tall enough to stand out.

Ilona's heart pounded as she ignored her own advice and plunged into the crowd. Cigarette smoke choked her lungs as she elbowed her way first left then right to nowhere in particular, just keeping her chin up, hoping for a glance of her son. *We need to get out of here*, she thought. Someone offered her coffee. She waved them off. She ploughed on, pushing her elbows into people so she could make her way forward.

Ilona was fighting back tears by the time she found Emil standing with the men who were lining up for soup; his camera down by his hip, laughing. She reached out to grab his shoulder but her grip was a little too tight.

'Son. We must go. Now,' she said, her voice quivering. 'Now. Please.'

Ilona pulled on his arm, and although she was nearly half his size, dragged him from the crowd. When they were a few streets away, she stared at him, gaze unwavering, forcing him to stay put while she stepped inside a telephone box to call the office. She was still watching him as she pushed coins into the slot at the top of the phone and dictated her quote. They walked silently toward home.

'There is a danger that they will become dissatisfied with

the system, not simply the government,' she said, her voice steady. 'Or, maybe the secret police has had enough of this democratic experiment and will send in tanks.'

Emil laughed.

'*Anyu*, there is no secret police anymore. You worry too much. It's just a peaceful protest,' he assured his mother, rubbing her back. 'The bad old days are over.'

'Don't be so sure.'

Friday, the taxis still blocked the bridges. The city centre was under a sort of lockdown. Ilona trudged to work, figuring she would learn what the government was up to when she got to the newsroom. She asked Emil and Melissa to stay at home, but knew their promises were hollow.

Saturday, Ilona woke up with stiff knees. She had walked far too much the day before and the sofa bed was much too soft for her joints. Her back creaked as she folded the bed back into its place. Emil and Tünde were just waking up as she took a position in front of the window that faced the Pest side of the river. She turned on the news.

'The strike is still on,' Ilona told Emil. Her voice was grave.

'Will you have to work?' Emil asked.

Ilona swallowed. 'Probably.'

'I'll walk down to the bridge with you.'

'No Emil, please. Stay with your wife and daughter.'

'*Anyu*, I'm here to document 'Hungary in Transition'. These are the kinds of things I need to capture.'

Ilona shot him a glance. Her jaw was set.

By Sunday, the third day of the taxi strike, Ilona had stopped eating. Her face was sallow and she developed a nervous tic. She had not slept at all. She didn't understand why Emil had spent the whole of Saturday at the bridge, ignoring his wife and daughter. She feared he would get caught up in the protest. She wished he had not come back to Budapest. She wished he had stayed in Ohio, where he would be safe. He seemed so oblivious to the dangers.

She stayed in the flat feigning illness, even though John called, asking if she could come in again. It was easier than telling John she couldn't leave the flat. She knew the government wasn't going to let this strike continue indefinitely and worried about what they might do. She sat next to the window and stared out above the treetops on the Pest side of the river. Waiting.

Emil and Melissa, though, were ecstatic. With the traffic at a standstill, the cloud of smog over the country's capital had floated away.

'I can't believe how clean the air is,' Melissa said. 'I never knew you could tell the difference.'

'Yeah, even the sun seems brighter,' Emil said.

'I mean did you realise we were only getting a filtered sun?' Melissa said, as she leaned over Ilona to glance out of the living room window.

Melissa had packed a picnic as Emil got his camera bag ready. They were hoping to take Tünde to the City Park to go ice skating. Emil told Melissa he used to go sledging on the ice, too.

'When we get to the bridge, I'm going to stop for a while and talk to the demonstrators,' Emil told Melissa.

Ilona sat upright on the sofa, her hands twirling a tissue. Her lips were tight.

'Please don't, Emil,' Ilona said in a small voice. 'Don't go now.'

'*Anyu*, really, it's OK.'

'We still don't know how the government is going to react. The strike can't go on forever.' Ilona rarely had a small voice, but within only a handful of days, she had seemed to shrink, so that her lungs only had the capacity for her to speak in whispers. Her face sagged. She had bags under her eyes.

Emil cocked his head and walked back into the living room. He already had his coat on.

'What are you worried about, *Anyu*?'

'That government tanks might roll in and soldiers might turn on the country's citizens again, as they did in 1956. You are aware that the Soviets still have bases here.'

'It's 1991, for God's sake. The *Russians* might still have a base here, but the Soviet Union is gone. Hungary is on a roll.'

Melissa lowered herself onto her haunches next to Ilona and rubbed her mother-in-law's back.

'I can't imagine the government reacting with a heavy hand. No way. Are you sure you don't want to come with us?' she asked politely.

Ilona remained on the easy chair next to the window and stared straight out. She clenched her teeth so hard her jaw hurt.

'You really are worried,' Emil said. He gave her shoulder a squeeze. 'I won't put my family in danger; I promise we will come back.'

Ilona pushed his hand away, and continued to stare out

toward the Pest side of the river; towards where the seat of the government would be, willing the officials to be kind.

Emil, Melissa and Tünde left with animated 'goodbyes' but Ilona still said nothing.

To distract herself she turned on the television. The prime minister would be making an announcement in the late afternoon, she heard. That did not sound reassuring to her, so she turned off the TV, found a duster and vigorously wiped the sideboard.

She cleared the clutter from the dining-room table — toys from the child, some lenses from Emil, a letter Melissa had received from her parents along with more of her medicine — and gave it a proper rub down. Toast crumbs flew into the air. When she reached the side table where her phone lay, Ilona thought about maybe calling someone. Get out of the house. Think of other things such as how to get her son out of harm's way. Someone who might convince him to stop messing about with protestors, and demanding things from governments. Whoever got a government to change? Hungary's last regime simply collapsed under its own incompetence.

Would the current prime minister József Antall betray his country, or, would he be captured and executed the way Imre Nagy had been? It was a test not only of his moral strength but it also meant he would be placing his faith in the Russian army. That they would remain in their camps. Russian troops were still stationed in Hungary, after all. She, for one, trusted no one.

She made a call to that man, Albert, who had returned to Hungary to do business with the American ambassador. She guessed correctly, that he was staying at the Intercontinental Hotel. To her surprise, he remembered her when she rang his room.

'Crazy business, this taxi strike,' he said.

Ilona frowned. She didn't want to think about that.

'I've heard the terrible news that the American ambassador had to leave his post,' she said. She was standing next to her phone, weight on one leg, tilting her head as she spoke, waving the duster for emphasis.

'Well, it wasn't completely a surprise,' Albert said. 'Still, this will allow him to work for us full time. We're very pleased at how it's all working out. He's in Czechoslovakia now.'

'Oh my, you are expanding so quickly,' Ilona said and could almost hear her heart beating. She would have to work on Emil. If they didn't act fast, they could miss their chance.

Before they rang off, Albert gave her the number of his secretary to call to make an appointment during the week.

'Of course you wouldn't know your schedule!' Ilona nodded her head as if he would see her. 'Yes, I'll ring first thing Monday morning!'

Ilona was pleased, but she knew it would take more than one meeting with this important businessman to convince Emil to give up his silly work. She stared at the phone, drumming her fingernails against her teeth, thinking, planning, scheming.

It's about networking, she reasoned, and Ilona knew the one person who could help.

She called her old friend.

'Judit,' Ilona moved her voice a pitch lower, and made it more sing-songy, something she did to sound sophisticated, duster swinging. 'How's your committee going?'

Judit and her husband were on the executive committee of the *Nemzeti Kisgazdapárt*, the Smallholders Party. They were junior members of the ruling centre-right coalition, but were counting on making a bigger splash in future. Their main platform was to force the government to make reparations for all the property that had been stolen from them by the Soviets, and they wanted their old titles back. Judit and her husband Zsolt were practically running the party by themselves.

'I'm ringing about Emil. He's researching how Hungarians are adapting to all the post-socialist changes. Naturally, I thought you and Zsolt could talk to him about reparations — and how that might work for —'

'— Your *kastély*?!' Judit squealed. 'Say no more. I'll arrange a dinner.'

Ilona felt better as she finally — Judit was a talker — rang off. For something to do, Ilona decided to see if Erzsi was home, but there was no answer when she knocked. *Clip, clip, clip* Ilona flitted back to her own flat.

Once back inside, Ilona felt its emptiness and she remembered that Emil, Melissa and the *kisbaba* were out; possibly with tanks about to roll into the city. In an instant, her foreboding returned. She switched on the television and slowly lowered herself down onto the chair by the phone, this time fearful it might ring.

Eyes fixed to the screen. A newsreader said the strike was in its third day. The government was in an emergency meeting with the strikers. A commentator complained about all the high prices. A commercial, then a documentary about animals of the Puszta, the great plains. The TV droned on as the winter sky darkened.

Ilona didn't notice the time going by; in her mind she was sitting in a different flat in this very building. The one she and Laci had just moved into thirty-five years ago, and she was fretful that he hadn't come back yet.

Each time she heard someone walk past her flat, Ilona imagined the footsteps were slowing down near her door; that she would hear a knock from police. Paralysed, she could hear her heart thumping. Ilona's hand caressed the embroidery draped across the armrest, before her fingers explored underneath and found the hole in the threadbare upholstery; the one just like that pit in her stomach.

After a while, Ilona managed to move to the sofa, nearer the television. The prime minister would be speaking soon, though she wasn't sure if she wanted to hear what he might have to say. She glanced out of the living room window half expecting to see gun smoke wafting from the Pest side of the river. She tugged on her sleeve.

Ilona jumped when Melissa opened the door.

'Hello?' Melissa said, lowering Tünde out of her sling and throwing her bag down onto to the floor.

Ilona blinked a few times until her eyes adjusted to the glare, as Melissa clicked on the overhead light.

'Ilona? You OK?'

Ilona couldn't speak; she only looked at them, a happy mother with a tired baby. They seemed so unaware.

'Emil wanted to stay with the protestors, to see if he could get some good shots,' Melissa said, unbuttoning her coat.

'Did he not consider that he was mortal?' Ilona said.

Melissa didn't hear her. She was pulling boots off Tünde. 'Your feet are soaking wet! We're going to have to get you into the bath!'

To Ilona, Melissa said, 'The park was packed. The whole country seemed to be, like, on a kind of national holiday weekend! There was this one family — they were so nice — they let Tünde ride with their daughter on a sledge. Tünde got to steer, didn't you? You liked that! The trees in the park are beautiful. The snow has fallen on them perfectly. And we learned a new sentence, didn't we? *Jó a hó*!'

'*Jó a hó*!' Tünde repeated, making Melissa laugh.

Ilona didn't smile; instead she stared silently at the television screen. Her body felt heavy as she waited for Antall's address to the nation due to start in a few minutes. Her eyes darted to the living-room window, wondering if she would hear tanks; if she would feel their vibrations. She didn't notice Tünde climbing up to the sofa to sit with her grandmother as Melissa busied about the flat. Tired from the excursion, the toddler put two fingers in her mouth and leaned on Ilona, but Ilona did not put her arm around Tünde. Instead, she sat upright, waiting for the awful words, pondering how she ever would be able to console Melissa if something happened to Emil.

The awful words did not come. Tanks did not roll in the streets. There were no executions. No gunfire.

Antall, who had spent years in jail in retribution for his part in the 1956 uprising, been blacklisted from work, gave in to the taxi drivers' demands. Petrol prices would not rise sixty-five per cent, but half that.

With that, it was over. The strikers agreed to go back to work and Emil would live to see his daughter grow up.

Ilona wanted to clap, yell and cry all at once. She pulled

the *kisbaba* on to her lap and gave her a big squeeze. Her hands shook from emotion. She felt jittery. She hadn't realised she had been holding her breath. The news was good! Emil is saved!

It was a good day after all! She had set up a dinner with Judit and on Monday she would invite Albert the investor to the party; she was certain her friend wouldn't mind.

This wasn't like one of those bad days she had experienced in her life. Sitting on the sofa with her granddaughter in her lap, Ilona smiled.

See what you can do when you take initiative, Ilona thought.

THE STUDIO

Ilona's plan to convince Emil of the importance of getting a real job was not going smoothly.

Judit and Zsolt's dinner party was in a week and she had yet to convince him to attend. That new investor Albert and his wife would be there. That had been an easy match: Judit and Zsolt knew so many people with properties that had been stolen by the Soviet-backed government; Albert has so much money.

The tricky bit was Emil.

'I'm a photographer, for Christ's sake.'

'And how much money do you earn being a photographer? Or are you going to keep selling pictures of your family? I don't want to discourage you, honey, but, really, couldn't you make this your hobby?'

'For the last time, those cards are just for you and Melissa's parents. Will you stop it now? I don't want to hear you bring this up again. Enough.'

That conversation had taken place in the kitchen as Ilona and Emil were washing up the dishes from dinner. Emil had asked Melissa if they had enough money to buy some lens he felt he needed. It had been a long discussion over reheated goulash. Ilona tried to stay out of it.

Melissa and Emil were careful with their money. For Christmas, Melissa had sewn pillow covers for the living room sofa as a Christmas present. Emil gave Ilona a photo of the family he had taken.

Ilona had purchased real gifts. She had bought the *kisbaba* a pretty red Christmas dress, Melissa some perfume and Emil a dress shirt. Proper gifts. She did mention to Emil that István had given Erzsi a gold bracelet. Ilona could barely look at it, she was so jealous.

Emil's face had reddened when Ilona mentioned his stationery business. He had stared into the suds-filled sink and refused to look at her. Ilona knew Emil had a quick temper, but sometimes she couldn't help herself. She knew she could be annoying sometimes; that her nagging didn't always work, but Emil needed to understand that to make money, real money, you have to go into business. Emil had slammed the door on his way out. This was all so much more difficult than she had imagined.

The next day, on her way home from work, Ilona stopped by Emil's studio to try again. He seemed to be more relaxed there.

'I've got too much to do for the exhibition,' he refused to even look at his mother.

'It's in the evening.'

'I'll still be working.'

He reeked of that acidic smell of developing fluid with turpentine mixed in. His thick dark hair was greasy and hung down in clumps over his pale face, but still, her son's eyes sparkled. In spite of the lack of sleep, Ilona noticed that Emil looked energised when he was at his studio.

'You haven't eaten well the past few weeks. You need to get out; relax.'

Emil's head was bent down as he slouched his lanky body over a strip of negatives. He was holding a loupe to his eye. He didn't answer her.

'Besides,' she continued, 'you can meet more people.'

'*Anyu*,' Emil said without looking up. He used the same tone to tell Tünde not to throw her building blocks into the toilet.

'Well, fine,' Ilona said, blowing air out of her nose. 'I'll call Judit tomorrow.'

Emil moved the strip along, staring into his loupe at the next photo.

'Of course, I thought you were here to document change in Hungary,' Ilona tried again. 'Did you know that Judit and Zsolt are *leaders* of a political movement? But if you aren't interested in their political party, I'll let them know.'

Emil gathered up his negatives in a huff.

'OK, one dinner.'

Ilona looked pleased.

'One night. Now I have to get home to take over from Melissa as it's her dancing night at the *Táncház*.'

Emil and Ilona left the studio together. Ilona hooked her arm through his. She had more bounce in her step now that Emil had acquiesced.

Their walk through the university campus seemed magical that wintry night. Yellow lights from inside offices warmed the light snow that coated the shrubs and trees.

'I am so glad you have come back, Emil,' Ilona squeezed his upper arm. She briefly rested her head against his shoulder as they waited for the tram. She ignored the other commuters waiting at the stop. This was her moment with her son.

'You know, sometimes when I walk around the city, I remember bits of my childhood that I had forgotten. Like when I was at *Moszkva tér*, I remembered that peach sponge cake thing you baked every autumn when Józsi bácsi brought a huge basket of fruit.'

'You remember that?' Ilona looked pleased. 'I can make one for you.'

'Melissa found that old scrap book you kept of every bit of my life. All the old medals, news clips, and a photo album, too,' he said. 'It all looks so battered and it is falling apart. It made me feel old.'

Ilona tensed for a moment. Of course Emil didn't know that the police had ripped up the scrapbook looking for a note or clues as to why he would escape. She said nothing. Emil continued.

'Then, when I was bathing Tünde the other day, I got this flashback to the time I had croup and you held me in a bear hug while the bathroom filled with steam. I remember I was so scared because I couldn't breathe, and you wrapped your arms around me and sang a song. What was I? Probably five at the time.'

Ilona was too moved to speak, so she squeezed his arm instead.

'It's nice being back with you,' his voice was warm.

On the tram, Ilona allowed Emil to talk about his exhibition. There was less than three months to go and there was so much to do, but it was starting to come together, he told her.

'I just finished a video that I'm really pleased with. I want to make another.'

'Video?' Ilona looked surprised.

'Montages, really,' he said. 'I'm trying to give my viewers the opportunity to experience expressions of oral history within a modern-day context; what is betrayal and how are those feelings manifested? How do we cope with feelings of treachery? It's a mixed media exhibition, so I'm working in ways I've never tried before. I was really frustrated when we first got here, both because of the topic and what I was producing. I met this guy — Gergő — and he's put me in touch with other people. I feel like I'm finally seeing a part of Hungary that always existed but was, like, underground. No one expresses their feelings here.'

Emil turned to his mother.

'I'd like to talk with you, too, if you'd like.'

'Me? Why?'

'To hear about dad. Gergő told me about the uprising and he's introducing me to other people, too. I'm learning a lot. I'd like to hear about how you experienced it, too.'

Ilona sighed, almost resigned.

'There's nothing to say, Emil. Your father was so innocent. He thought the government would change because he wanted it to. That's all. He trusted too much. I guess that's why I loved him, but that's also why he died.'

'It happened at *Kossuth tér*, right?'

'Yes.'

'That's one of the reasons I want my exhibition to be

there, in the metro station. Underground. There are all sorts of metaphors —'

'What? You're going to do what?'

'My Fulbright. I want to spend part of my grant on an exhibition, you know that. I want to show my work at the *Kossuth tér* metro station. I'm going to ask the transit authorities if they will let me have an exhibition there for a week. You know, at a time when everything is being bought up, I want to keep art accessible to the public, make it non-institutional, non-corporate.'

'An art exhibition in the metro?'

They had reached their stop. Emil helped Ilona climb down the wooden steps of the tram and the two began to walk up the hill toward their block of flats. She had forgotten about Judit's dinner. She was now more interested in keeping the family name from such embarrassment.

'This is certainly, well, *unusual*, Emil. You want your paintings to hang on the concrete walls next to graffiti and advertisements? Sometimes I simply can't understand you.'

'First, I don't have a lot of paintings, *Anyu*. Mostly photographs, video, mixed media, you know. Second, the head of the Fulbright here and I are trying to convince the transit authority to forgo advertising revenue for a week at that stop. As a former communist country, these politicians sure have embraced capitalism with gusto.'

'Emil, I'm not sure you've noticed, but the country is almost bankrupt. Even the government needs to figure out how to make money. I'm sure I can find you a nice gallery where you can show your work.'

'That's sweet, but I have a concept —'

'— Emil, if you want to make money, you need to court the right people. That's what galleries do.'

'Thanks, *Anyu*. I have this under control.'

'Do you really?'

The two stood in silence as they waited for the lift to take them up to their flat. It had been nearly a year and the entire building was still relying on one lift. Ilona knew it would be a long silence.

'I'm going to stop for a moment at Erzsi's,' she said, quietly.

As Emil was unlocking the door to her flat, Ilona remembered something.

'Emil,' she said in a lilting voice. 'You and Melissa are still coming to the dinner party?'

MARCH

Emil didn't know it but Ilona often stopped by Erzsi's flat before going home. She enjoyed the respite. Work exhausted her — after all those hours of speaking English, she found her brain turned to mush. She frequently wanted nothing more than to fix a small plate of toast, pepper and cucumber for supper and relax — alone — in silence with a cup of tea.

Instead she knew she'd arrive home to loud music while Tünde hopped around all the toys that had been strewn across the flat that day. Ilona had never seen so many toys in her life.

Melissa was likely to be writing or drawing or reading something. Only occasionally did Melissa have supper waiting for them. When she did, it was some vegetarian, low-fat, low-sugar, low-cholesterol meal that tasted like cardboard. Ilona liked paprika.

Melissa even changed the recipe for *lecsó*, leaving out the kolbász in order to have no meat at all and use sunflower oil instead of lard. She called it her 'go-to Hungarian stew' but Ilona knew that no Hungarian would recognise the taste without the spicy sausage and bacon fat. Ilona was mortified to learn Melissa had given her recipe to the mothers in her dance class, passing it off as authentic. This, in spite of Ilona frequently pointing out to Melissa that children needed to eat meat.

She envied the tranquillity of Erzsi's place. So Ilona was surprised to hear laughing and loud voices coming from Erzsi's door that evening. Before she even knocked, she knew Melissa was there. Ilona took it as a betrayal on Erzsi's part.

She took a deep breath and walked in. The flat was filled with boxes and bags — on the kitchen counter, on the table, the floor surrounding Melissa, the sofa beside Erzsi, on the coffee table, on top of the TV. Children's clothes spilled out of them and the women were putting them in piles — babygrows, trousers, tops, sweaters, dresses. As Ilona entered the room, Melissa tossed a pair of blue leather shoes into a box with the name of an international moving company emblazoned across it. The box looked new, unlike the saggy ones with heavily creased flaps that Ilona was used to seeing.

There were more toys than Ilona had ever seen in the living room and, Ilona could see, into István's room, where his bed sagged under the load of more boxes and bags. Tünde, with two fingers from her right hand in her mouth, used her left hand to bang on a xylophone.

Erzsi greeted her friend with a smile.

'Ilona! Come and help us!' Erzsi pushed a bag off the couch, and patted the cushion.

Ilona remained in the doorway. Tünde had stopped banging on the xylophone and was inching toward a plastic pyramid of colourful rings on a stick, dragging a white bunny with her.

'What's going on here?'

'Isn't this wonderful, Ilona?' Erzsi gushed. 'Melissa asked her mothers if they could donate clothes for the orphanage and this is what we got in just two weeks!'

'Mothers?'

'From the dance classes,' Melissa said. 'Erzsi told me she volunteered at an orphanage, so naturally I thought about those poor children we have been reading about in Romania, but apparently it's not like that here.'

Ilona had no idea what Melissa was going on about.

'Anyway,' Melissa continued. 'I thought these kids could benefit from having some toys and clothes. I guess they didn't get a lot for Christmas and aren't likely to get anything for Easter, so I made a few fliers and put them around the international school. One of the mothers volunteered her garage as the collection point, then drove it all over here in her Land Rover. I never expected to get so much.'

Melissa pronounced the name of the car slowly so that Ilona and Erzsi could hear she didn't approve of such conspicuous consumerism. Ilona longed for Emil to buy a car like that.

'And most of the clothes look new,' Erzsi waved her hand, indicating how amazed she was at the largesse. 'Don't they save clothes for their next children? Or their friends' kids?'

'What?!' Melissa feigned shock. 'And have your second child be caught wearing *used* clothes? Good heavens!'

'Or used toys!' Erzsi added, attempting a falsetto.

The two women looked at each other and howled with laughter at their fake rich-woman accents like it was a running joke. Ilona remained paralysed at the door. Tünde was oblivious to the laughing adults. She was now lying down, using a bag for a pillow and stroking the bunny again. Her fingers firmly placed in her mouth.

'Has the *kisbaba* been given her dinner yet?' Ilona tiptoed across the floor to her granddaughter. Melissa felt the reproach immediately, but Erzsi was immune to the sting.

'Come sit a few minutes, Ilona!' Erzsi repeated.

'What are you going to do with all this?' Ilona asked, still standing.

'Take it to the orphanage!' Erzsi said. 'In Isi's car. Did you hear he bought a new one? He gave the Lada to Emil and Melissa to use while they are here.'

Although her face remained unchanged, Ilona could feel her ears starting to burn. This was getting to be too much for her. István seemed to be getting richer by the day and here was Emil, insisting on showing his *art* in a dirty underground station and receiving a Lada as a gift.

'István's business is doing so well he can give away cars like these women toss away clothing?'

'No, silly,' Erzsi seemed oblivious to Ilona's sarcasm. 'It's not like that. Isi can still use the Lada for his business.'

Erzsi placed her hands in her lap. She was still holding a tiny green sweater in her hands. Erzsi looked earnestly at her friend.

'Ilona, you need to start loosening up a little. Have some fun, enjoy Emil and Melissa while they are still here.'

Then Erzsi looked at Melissa and said in English. 'She all vork and no play.'

'I know,' Melissa said.

'I remember ven Ilona could play de vicked cards,' then

Erzsi smiled with a mischievous look in her eyes. 'Stilllll. You had to vatch out,' Erzsi shook a finger playfully. 'Vandering eyes.'

Melissa looked at her mother-in-law in mock surprise. 'Ilona Kovács, you don't cheat at cards do you?'

'Only ven she losing,' Erzsi said quickly before Ilona could answer.

Ilona didn't find any of this humorous. Her bottom lip pressed up to her upper lip as she stepped over the toys, took Tünde's arm and attempted to lead the child back to Ilona's own flat. Tünde screeched and held on to the bunny. As grandmother and toddler left Erzsi's flat, Ilona turned and asked, 'Is it okay with you that your daughter cuddles a used toy? One meant for an orphan? After all, that's the best you'll ever be able to do for her.'

Before Ilona could slam the flat door shut, she could hear Melissa and Erzsi talking.

'Does she ever lighten up?' Melissa asked.

Ilona stood motionless, listening. Erzsi took a moment to answer.

'She my oldest friend. She never left me ven Laci died. Or even years before dat, ven we lose second child.'

'I wish she would show that side to us sometimes.'

Ilona pretended not to hear as she closed the door to Erzsi's flat. She was still annoyed when she opened the door to her own place and found Emil bobbing his head to Eric Clapton as he sautéed onions.

'So,' Ilona said, turning off the music. 'It doesn't bother you that your wife hasn't got around to making your dinner?'

Emil turned around. 'Wha —?'

Ilona still had not taken off her coat.

'Emil, have you no pride? Melissa earns the money and you make dinner. You live off a government cheque. The three of you are sharing a cramped bedroom in your mother's flat. What are you doing with your life?'

Emil's shoulders tightened as did his grip on the wooden spoon in his hand. His neck reddened. His lips stiffened across his mouth as his jaw snapped shut. As his glare intensified, Ilona knew she had gone too far.

'What I mean is, István works so hard. And he now owns a new car, I hear! So successful! And you can be too…'

'Stop talking.' He said it so quietly, she almost didn't hear.

'What?'

'You know how to wreck the moment, mum. I thought we had a nice tram ride together.'

He turned around to stir the onions. Ilona thought he was going to break the wooden spoon in half.

THE ORPHANAGE

A long driveway led up to the orphanage. Tall majestic plane trees — still bare in the cold March air — lined the way. Although the snow had melted, spring seemed far away. A wide mulberry stretched out on the front lawn; the morning frost had turned its weeping branches into a white veil that covered the archway, acting as the front entrance of what once was obviously a lovely old villa. Not as large or ornate as the one Ilona had been so proud of, but sturdy and impressive nonetheless. The windows were leaded, not bevelled glass as the Pálffy had been, nor were there any baroque embellishments around the façade.

Melissa propped open the trunk and lifted out the first box. Erzsi had marked each container carefully: trousers, boy, six months to one year; shirts, girl, eight to ten years. Babygrows, infants. Crammed into bags in the back seat were toys that Melissa and Erzsi had wrapped as early Easter presents.

'Children wanna to open things, don't you t'ink?' Erzsi said. Melissa was holding a box of gifts under one arm as she slammed the door shut.

A woman wearing a smart grey A-line skirt and satiny top hurried down the chipped steps to greet Erzsébet. The pair kissed one another on the cheeks and began speaking in rapid Hungarian. Melissa walked over and politely held out her hand.

'Thank you so much for collecting everything. This means so much,' the woman said in broken German. 'The orphanage is taking in more children than we can really accommodate.'

'Why is that,' Melissa asked, surprised.

'Most of them have parents who can't afford to feed them. If the government doesn't raise wages soon, I fear we'll get more.' She turned back to Erzsi, who Melissa could tell was an old friend.

The hall was clean and tidy, however it was in disrepair, just as the Pálffy had been. Chunks of plaster were missing from the walls. The purple carpet leading up the staircase was threadbare. Naked bulbs hung from the ceiling; Melissa could see the wires leading up to them stapled along the doorways. Tiny hats were placed on a long rack neatly above probably thirty children's coats that were hung in a long row on wooden hooks.

Low benches lined the wall underneath them. Boots were tucked neatly underneath the benches on rubber trays. Hats and mittens, clipped together with wooden clothes pegs, were carefully placed on shelves above. Tidy. Melissa thought of the mess in the dressing room at her dance studio back home, when the kids dumped hats, mittens and coats in piles. *This*, she thought, *is what it means to value your things*.

She let Tünde down, but her daughter hung tightly to Melissa's thigh.

The director led the visitors to a side room off the main hallway. Inside, Melissa was slightly amused to see the same plush blue sofas that Ilona had in her flat. The director — Melissa hadn't caught her name and was too embarrassed to ask again — and Erzsi seemed to have a lot to catch up on, so Melissa, unable to understand their conversation, walked around the room with Tünde. She admired the ornate mouldings in the corners of the ceilings, then, standing in the corner, squinted to try to imagine the grandeur of this room. The director seemed to notice.

'It was a beautiful room once. Wasn't it, Erzsébet?' she said in German. Erzsi nodded.

'What was it like?' Melissa asked.

'Don't ask me, ask Erzsi. She lived here.' The director said.

'I didn't know you used to work at the orphanage,' Melissa said, looking at her friend. Erzsi stared down at her lap. The headmistress looked at Melissa, then at Erzsi, surprised.

'No dear, this was Erzsébet's childhood home. Confiscated by the Nazis, then the Soviets. Headquarters or something. Erzsi, you tell her. Horrible story. Looted everything. Erzsi has sort of adopted us in spite of it all. We are so grateful she has.'

Melissa looked over at this plump, dishevelled, sixty-four-year old woman.

'Do you have rights to this place like Ilona has to the Pálffy?'

Erzsi looked into Melissa's eyes and smiled, shaking her head.

'Vat vould I do wid it? Vere vould poor children go? I could no pay to restore it. Lord, how do you even keep up de heating and electricity on dis t'ing?'

There was an awkward silence, as Melissa tried to put the pieces of Erzsi's life together.

'But —'

Erzsi patted the bag of clothing by her side and asked the director with a broad smile on her face. 'Any children around?'

On the way home, Melissa again tried to ask Erzsi about her childhood home.

'So that was your home? Before the war? What happened?'

'Dere's nothing to talk about. Focus on de good things in life, Melissa, because dis is vere ve are and ve need to be happy.'

Melissa turned on the cassette to keep Tünde occupied for the car ride, but the little girl was exhausted from playing with the other children and quickly fell asleep. In the quiet of the car, Melissa waited for more of an explanation.

Erzsi sighed.

'My father vas landowner, but dey mocked and called us '*kulaks*', saying ve vere selfish for keeping de food to ourselves. It vas nonsense. Ve vere farmers; ve sold our food for to live. My father he vork so hard his life to move up in de world — he and his papa built de home. He sent me to a boarding school. Soviets took all.'

Erzsi was quiet. Melissa waited, hoping Erzi would continue.

'Funny, but ven I t'ink back to that time, I t'ink of being hot,' she said, looking out at the flat bare fields. 'My father made me wear my broder's vinter vools as long as Soviets vere in town, even in the summer. I vas stinky and sweaty.'

'Why did you have to wear your brother's clothes?' she asked.

Erzsi didn't answer. Instead, she continued her story.

'After Soviets took home, ve lived in the carriage house. Ve bunked with de foreman and his family. Denn, Soviets decide ve no could stay. Dey ordered us leave. Dat's how ve got to Budapest.'

Erzsi's voice was so quiet, Melissa strained to listen.

'I vas assigned to vork at de Zwack factory, making Unicum. You know dat? Very good herbal drink. I vas eighteen.'

'I've tried a little once,' replied Melissa, who didn't care for the drink.

Erzsi's voice got cheerful again, as if she was forcing herself out of her melancholy.

'I vorked next to Béla Zwack, one of de owner's sons,' Erzsi said, closing her eyes. 'Dey didn't know dat Béla and I had known each other since ve kids. My father sold grain to his father. Béla introduced me to Péter, my husband, who family also vere supplier to de factory. Dat was before Béla escaped to Italy.'

Erzsi giggled at a memory from long ago.

'Boy, Béla t'ought he had to get outta dere fast. Béla's father had give Soviets a fake recipe.' As Erzsi laughed at the memory, her face turned scarlet. 'De whole family had to leave before Soviets realise it.'

Tears welled in Erzsi's eyes. Melissa wasn't sure if she was crying or giggling at the memory. Erzsi dabbed them with a tissue. 'I don't t'ink de Soviets cared.'

Erzsi's voice turned cheery and loud again. 'Béla's brother

is now de Hungarian ambassador in de US, did you know dat?'

Melissa, mesmerised, did not notice how adeptly Erzsi had changed the topic.

'What a story,' Melissa said. 'So you met your husband through a factory worker friend who actually was the son of the former owner of the factory? Amazing. I need to write these things down.'

Darkness descended in the early afternoon and the road seemed black as they sped past the last village before the long stretch of dual carriageway that led to the capital. Melissa almost didn't see a young woman with a white furry jacket smoking a cigarette and nearly hit her. A few metres down the road, another woman, one leg resting against a wooden fence, stared at the headlights of their car. Then, not far from her, three teenagers barely sixteen, Melissa thought, jerked their heads up as she drove past. The tallest abruptly spun around and stuck out her bum, ready to moon the car, as the other two laughed.

'Are they waiting for shift work?' Melissa asked, her mind still thinking of the Zwack factory.

Erzsi was quiet for a moment.

'I t'ink all da factories here laid dem off.'

A light rain began to fall; the fields glistened in the headlights. Car tyres made tracks down the road. For the last stretch before they reached the city lights, the Hungarian countryside seemed at peace.

ISTVÁN

Damn Emil, István thought as he gripped the steering wheel of the black BMW, whipping the car into the left lane to get around the Nissan Cherry moving at half his speed.

How dare that arsehole pretend he was above it all? As if making money was some kind of weakness. All he had to do was photograph some of the girls at the Pussycat Nightclubs.

'I'm not into being a commercial photographer,' Emil had said. 'I'm an artist.'

All István wanted him to do was photograph some of the girls at his nightclubs. Emil did, eventually, but not without acting like he was above it all.

He actually said that as if he didn't shit in the toilet like everyone else and earning money was beneath him. Like the US government was always going to give him his bread and wine, just like the socialists had when he was a swimmer; just like the UN had when he was some fuckin' hero for escaping. Well, István's parking space for his BMW cost more than the rent for the flat they weren't paying for. And István had just put a down payment on a villa in Buda. So fuck Emil the artist.

István had looked at Emil squarely, into his smug eyes and shrugged, smiled even. Didn't let on that he was irritated.

'And I'm a businessman.'

Isi had learned from his parents that if you work hard you make it in the world. Go the extra mile, his mother always told him. Never be satisfied, be better, his father would say, be a go-getter. A go-getter.

When he was twelve, István had ridden his bike around the neighbourhood looking for ways to make some money. While Emil swam, Isi would bike up the hill in Buda to the villas and find people who needed a lawn mowed. He had two regulars; an old lady whose hand shook when she handed him a one hundred forint note. He learned to pretend to not want the money, act modest and smile sweetly, as she pressed the bill into his hand. The second place was a small house with a long yard where four East German medical students lived. The first time he mowed their lawn, they tried to pay him in Ostmarks, but even at twelve Isi knew those things were worthless. Only *forints*, he told them. Then, on his way home, he'd stop and buy an ice cream on *Szépvölgyi út*.

When he was fifteen he had chosen to do a catering apprenticeship. He liked people, liked food, so why not? He couldn't picture himself sitting behind a desk.

'Be a go-getter,' his father reminded him on Isi's first day at work, 'never be one of those guys who needs to be told to do something.'

'Find ways to be helpful,' his mother had said. After all, it was how his parents could afford a Lada. His dad used to buy stuff — watches, jewellery, shoes, and such — from the

Soviets and sell them to his colleagues at his office. His mum sold them too, at the factory. The black market was a great way to supplement your income. When Goulash Communism opened up small plots of land for private sale, his parents bought one not far from Lake Balaton. He and his dad spent two years building that summer home. As far as Isi could tell, no one asked where the extra money came from.

'Always do a little more,' his dad told him.

So on his first day at work, Isi had collected up all the dirty plates from the tables; before he had helped to wash them.

'Slow down buddy,' one of the old waiters said, 'don't wear yourself out.'

István wanted his boss to see how eager he was, and he did wear himself out. It was exhausting. It took years to work his way up. Like his parents, he found ways to make a bit of money on the side. The easiest way was to present tourists with special menus that listed higher prices than what they charged Hungarians, or prices listed only in *Deutsch Marks*. He also ran a modest currency exchange for regular customers.

When the government changed over, István was ready. Now was payback time. He liked the free market. He liked having nice things.

Emil had always had it easy. Those swimming camps he attended were in luxury resorts; the food Emil got to eat was just a cut above anything István's mum could buy. How many competitions did he, István, have to attend because his parents felt bad because Emil had no father? Then Emil threw it all away when he escaped to Italy.

Emil had no idea how frightening it was to hear furniture being thrown about when the police searched Ilona's flat after

Emil had run away. Isi had crept up a floor to Ilona's old flat and listened to the police's sharp staccato questioning.

Emil had no idea that Erzsi, István and his dad had helped clean everything up. After that, Ilona lost her job and couldn't pay for food or her rent. Emil had no clue that Ilona had used up all her savings to keep her flat for as long as she could. Then she and her mother had to move to a smaller place, and Ilona slept on a sofa. Then Erzsi invited them for dinner and that became a regular thing for Ilona and her mother.

So damn Emil, he just didn't know.

Emil had kept his mother waiting for months before writing to her to say he was safe. In that time, István saw Ilona grow old. He saw grey hairs form at her temples. He watched as bags appeared under her eyes; skin dripped off her high cheekbones. His parents worried Ilona would be sent to prison for Emil's escape. Ilona worried that Emil hadn't made it or that something would happen to him in Ohio, once she knew he was moving there. She worried that her mother would be left alone if she was imprisoned, or worse, that her mother too, would be imprisoned. With that government you never knew how they would choose to hurt you.

Every week that went by, István thought, Ilona's back curved more. Her hands twitched, unable to be still. He, István, knew that it was up to him to do the right thing and make everyone proud of him. He'd bring food home from the restaurant when he could. Often it was only extra bread, but sometimes he could get the chef to give him something better. When they changed flowers on the tables Isi would make a big bouquet for Ilona. She'd place them on Laci's grave.

Only later — after she had got a job from foreigners —

did she start to dye her hair again. Straighten her spine. It was odd, like one day she just snapped out of a bad dream and it was as if nothing had happened. His parents, too, acted as if everything was normal.

For Isi, nothing was normal after Emil escaped. He had seen what those bastard secret police could do. He worried they might try to arrest his parents for selling things on the side. And that they might arrest him for exchanging currency. So fuck Emil who spent his days taking pictures like he was something special, as if anyone couldn't take a picture with a camera.

He, István, had skills. He had drive, grit, and he was going to make it. He had been a good restaurant manager. He understood what was required. He knew, for example, when to charge a government official for a meal and when not to. He knew when to give them a good exchange rate when they asked for money back. Now he was a great owner. He told his staff there was no task he would ask them to do that he hadn't already done himself. That was his mantra at work, fairness and teamwork.

At busy times, when everyone did their jobs efficiently, it was a work of art. A well-choreographed dance. The *maitre d'* seated customers where they needed to be; the waiter greeted them promptly to get their drinks, and later, their meal ordered. Then came the perfect steps: the commis waiter set the table; the chef made the food, the waiter brought it to the table. They were a synchronised team because he got them to understand how important it was to help each other. To play your part. To always stay vigilant for something that needed to be done. He was their leader and it was fun.

That's why he had to be the person to own and run that restaurant when it got privatised. That's why last year he had quietly, with a smile on his face, asked that guy Albert-the-German who came for lunch, if he'd stay a minute, after his lunch partner left. Albert had come often enough that he recognised István. Albert called himself an investor, but István knew that for years he also helped communist ministers with private banking matters. Isi had overheard snatches of conversations. As a restaurant manager, you watched and listened; took mental notes and learned.

Albert did stay after lunch that day. István brought over a second cup of coffee for him and a Unicum. Albert didn't say much. Instead, he leaned back in the cushioned booth, legs crossed, fingertips pressed against each other and listened.

'I been running dis restaurant for de last eight years. Ven it comes up for privatisation, nobody can keep it going better dan me,' he said.

'Ja,' Albert had nodded.

'But I gonna need money to do dat,' István said carefully.

Foreigners were buying up Hungary, staking claims like they had the right because some Nazi or some Russian had grabbed their home or company fifty years ago. So what? Get over it. Life is unfair. His whole life had been unfair. He didn't get special treatment when he was young; his mother wasn't asking for her estate back. Too many of these ex-Hungarians weren't even alive when it all happened, yet here they were, Zwacks taking back the distillery; the Coats family grabbing the thread factory; Tungsram — makers of the world's first tungsten filament light bulb — bought up by some American firm. Nothing was Hungarian anymore, while the advisors to the prime minister say they have to do it or the country will go bankrupt.

And the ex-communist ministers who destroyed the country in the first place and the new ones who replaced them have lunch with men like Albert and suddenly a new government plan is announced; and new villas sprout up in Buda along with new business ventures. He wanted in.

'You are thinking too small, my friend,' Albert had told István finally. 'If you are looking for investors, you need to be bold. Not one restaurant, but a chain.'

Then Albert was quiet for a moment, like he was sizing up István, trying to figure out exactly how hungry he was.

'What about a flagship eatery and a chain of nightclubs?' Albert suggested.

'A chain of nightclubs?' István couldn't believe his ears. Hungarians barely eat at restaurants, why would they visit nightclubs?

'Place the nightclubs strategically,' Albert said. 'At the Austrian border, the Romanian border, the border with Czechoslovakia; at Lake Balaton, throughout Budapest, in the areas where foreign visitors go.'

István stayed quiet, trying to understand.

'It's all about *Baksheesh und Beziehungen* — cash and connections, my friend,' Albert said. 'I can arrange a few meetings to get the cash. I assume you have gathered a few connections of your own, regular customers, *ja?*'

István maintained his poker face, the one he had long mastered from working at the restaurant. Inside though, he could feel his heart pumping.

Before that next investor meeting, István did some

research. He ordered drinks at the bars at the Interconti and the Kempinski and watched. Then he saw them. How could he have been so blind before? Certain ladies, tight black dresses and stilettos, yes, but the bosoms couldn't show too much. The neckline had to be tantalisingly high at those hotels. The zippers, however, were easy to locate. They were class acts.

At his nightclubs his girls were classy too. He checked every day to make sure they dressed just right. If they looked cheap, he kicked them out.

It was Albert who suggested taking photos of the girls in soft light, with feathers and things, so customers could think about whether they'd want a blonde or brunette. And what they would want to do to them. No big deal.

'Emil, just take a few snaps and develop them,' he told his friend, getting irritated, when he saw that Emil was surprised when they entered the club. It was 10:00 am, and although open for business, there were few customers. 'I'll pay you.'

Emil had shrugged it off, but István thought he saw pity, or maybe disgust, in his eyes, which István found hard to stomach. He, not Emil, had bought a BMW. He, not Emil, was going to buy a villa. He's the guy who works hard. He knew who he was. *Emil forgets sometimes*, István thought.

So István didn't tell Emil he was going to be an artist too, only one that will actually make money from his art. He was going to make films. He had a meeting next week with an Italian producer; about their plans to start DeeluXXX Films. The guy had been coming to the Pussycat Nightclub, trying to steal Isi's girls. Isi was learning quickly. Budapest was turning into the Thailand of Europe and István was going to get in on the action. Albert didn't know about that meeting, either.

István and his bartender, Bálint, had already figured out the first film script, one they were calling 'The Streetcar of Desire'. István had already contacted the city transportation department about renting out a tram for a day for the filming. He asked for the number eighteen tram. The story was about an eighteen-year-old bombshell who 'charged' eighteen men to get on the tram. They got a good laugh about that one. They knew just the girl to star in it, too. She was a Romanian who had just started working for him. A dark beauty with tits that filled his hands. He got a hard-on thinking about her.

Like his Pussycat Nightclubs, his films were going to be classy. Best to leave a lot to the imagination. Isi thought he could get a building for a good price to use as a theatre. It was next to his Budapest Pussycat Nightclub and had been a furniture store, so it was empty now. Easy to install a few chairs and a screen. His films would get the men in the mood before they came over to the Pussycat.

István parked his BMW. He looked at himself in the rear-view mirror as he combed his hair back. He'd stop by the restaurant before ending his night at the bar. He had a good life and his hard work was paying off. Life was all about making money.

APRIL

On the evening of Judit and Zsolt's dinner party, Ilona reminded Emil to take a bath. She encouraged Melissa to wear that black dress that Ilona thought was the closest thing her daughter-in-law had to an acceptable outfit. She even suggested they take a taxi to the old villa in the leafy part of Buda.

The home stood illuminated on a steep hill that rose abruptly from the tree-lined street; Ilona, Emil and Melissa climbed steps that wound their way up through the lawn of the front garden.

'God, are we meeting our maker?' Melissa joked. 'Are those wrought iron or pearly gates up there?'

'Hard to tell,' Emil answered back.

Ilona said nothing, she saved her breath trying to keep up with the youngsters. She was pleased she had worn her lighter coat for the evening. Spring was late this year and a winter coat would have been more appropriate but her lighter coat was newer and more fashionable. By the time they had reached the door though, they were all flushed. Emil waited a moment for Ilona to catch her breath before he rang the bell.

'Édes,' Judit said when she opened the door. 'So good to see you again.'

The two friends kissed each other's cheeks while Emil and Melissa took off their coats.

The villa was filled with antiques and threadbare rugs on creaking wooden floors.

'What a beautiful home,' Melissa gushed.

Ilona introduced her daughter-in-law but before she could get to Emil, Judit jumped in, clasping both his hands.

'I'm sure you don't remember me.' The bracelets on Judit's thin wrist jangled as she shook Emil's arms. 'I think the last time I saw you, you were maybe ten or twelve years old. It was at your mother's name-day party.'

Ilona knitted her eyebrows, trying to think back.

'It was that picnic at *Margit-sziget*! I remember now. Emil, you and István wanted to swim, but it was only May and too cold —'

'— So you acted bored and miserable,' Judit laughed. 'My son Tibor was there too. Do you remember?'

Emil narrowed his eyes for a moment, then slowly nodded his head.

'Wait. Tibor. He's younger than me, right? Skinny guy?'

'He's not skinny anymore, but yes. That's him. You went to different schools, of course. I think that might have been the only time you met.'

Remembering her manners, Judit looked at Melissa and switched to English.

'I met your husband one time when he was young. Ilona and I had just got together. It was rather hush-hush, our meeting. My husband Zsolt and I were trying to find the last of the aristocracy here. We weren't sure who had escaped, who had been shot and who was still around.'

'Oh wow,' Melissa said.

'Oh yes. In the 1960s, that was rather revolutionary,' Judit giggled. 'We had to keep it all quiet. We found the last of the Pálffys and we were very excited about that! Ilona and her mother.'

Ilona beamed and swatted away the compliment modestly, as she knew she should. Ilona usually prepared in advance appropriate affectations for whatever occasion she would be attending: hand movements, facial expressions and the like.

'Judit? Are you going to keep our guests standing in the foyer?' Zsolt was a short, unimposing man with a bloated belly and a wide smile.

'*Kezét csókolom*,' He kissed the air just above Ilona's right hand, bowing slightly as he did so. He did the same with Melissa before firmly shaking Emil's hand.

Two other couples were already there, warming themselves by a fire that had been lit. Ilona noticed the room was draughty and wished she had kept her coat on. Spring was always unpredictable. What with the cost of oil these days, Judit and Zsolt probably had already turned off the heating. Everyone made introductions — some government minister and his wife whom Ilona didn't know; Albert the investor and his wife — and began having animated conversations.

Melissa and Emil politely decided they would rather stand than sit.

'Can I get you a drink?' Zsolt asked the pair in English, and stayed next to them once he brought Emil a beer and Melissa a glass of wine.

Ilona could barely hear what they were talking about, though she thought Melissa had one of her '*this is all so European*' looks on her face. Ilona considered herself adept at studying people and situations, and this was going well.

'So you were looking to see who had left after the uprising?' Emil said. 'Does that mean you were part of the uprising, too?'

'We all were hoping to overthrow the government,' Zsolt said. 'I was too young to join the protests. I was only in secondary school, my parents forbade me from leaving the house. My father joined one, though.'

Ilona thought Emil looked disappointed at the answer. Apparently Zsolt did too, because he added. 'Of course it was terrible what they did to your father. He's a hero.'

Emil nodded.

'I'm starting to understand that the people who were left behind were heroes, too,' Emil said. 'There seem to have been, I dunno, everyday acts of defiance.'

Zsolt grimaced, 'Like what?'

'Like, so many people are proud to say that they had ten years of Russian classes and don't speak a word of it.'

Zsolt laughed. 'I think it was because the teachers were all drunk and worthless.'

Ilona relaxed. Judit lit candles on the large linen-clad table before she ushered them all into the dining room. Ilona was disappointed she was seated next to the politician. She had been hoping to chat with Albert, or at least Zsolt. On her other side was an empty seat.

Just as Judit lifted her napkin, a young man in his early thirties rushed in.

'*Anyu*,' he said, kissing Judit's cheek. 'I made it! I told you I'd try.'

'Then we do have an even number!'

Judit nodded at the empty seat between Ilona and Melissa as Tibor quickly walked around the table shaking hands and kissing above the ladies' wrists.

Ilona noticed Judit had turned on Bartók's 'Hungarian Folk Songs from Csik' as background music for the dinner. Excellent choice; so soothing.

Ilona smiled pleasantly at her dinner partner, the government minister, a brutish sort whose name she didn't catch. He rambled on about the motorway being built to the Austrian border, but Ilona was trying to block him out. She was more interested in what Emil was discussing with Judit across the table.

'So you and Zsolt have started a new political party?'

'It's not new, actually. It was quite a force just after the war, until the communists banned opposition. We see ourselves as continuing the Hungarian way of life that had been interrupted by the Soviets. We want the government to give back our estates, that were stolen from us by the Soviets. Like your mother's estate.'

'So what happens to the retirement homes and orphanages if that happens,' Emil asked.

'Well that's what governments are for, isn't it?'

The soup course went well, although Ilona noticed Melissa didn't eat it. Ilona had not told Judit that her daughter-in-law was a vegetarian. Next, Judit brought out the meat course: a large platter with a skull in the middle. Around it, perfectly sliced cuts of rare, juicy meat.

'Beautiful.' 'Lovely.' 'Gorgeous.' Everyone around the table complimented Judit, who was flushed from all the activity in the hot kitchen.

Melissa, Ilona noticed, looked pale.

'What is that?' Ilona could hear Melissa asking her dinner partner.

'*Malac*,' Tibor answered in Hungarian, struggling to find the English word.

Melissa looked confused.

'*Malac*,' he said again, only louder. 'Ruff, ruff, ruff.'

Melissa looked down at her plate sorrowfully.

Albert, on Melissa's other side, laughed.

'It's pork,' he told her. 'Hungarian pigs say ruff, ruff.'

Melissa smiled weakly. She cut a piece and pushed it forlornly across her plate.

Ilona was relieved Melissa wouldn't be spoiling this lovely meal. Ilona took a bite of meat. So tender.

Zsolt leaned across the table to speak with Melissa conspiratorially. 'You know, Judit and I are officially divorced. That way we can also have a flat in the city.'

'I don't understand.'

'Well, the old government, under the socialists, only allowed one housing unit per family. So we officially divorced in order to buy the flat. We rent out the flat to foreigners for *three times* what it's worth. It's important to have investments these days, you know,' he said. 'It was Judit's idea. She's very good with money.'

Judit demurred.

Zsolt took a bite of potatoes then, with his fork still in the air, he gestured for emphasis.

'You know getting property confiscated by the Soviets returned isn't the only thing we smallholders are fighting for.' He said this in a loud stage voice, so that Emil and the minister could hear, too. 'We Hungarians are conservative, Catholic people. Our platform is to return Hungary back to its former state, as it were, with conservative ideals. Install Otto von Hapsburg as head of state, if he wants the post, which I suppose he will.'

'Former state?' Emil looked confused. 'As in pre-World War One?'

'Yes. When there was order in this country.'

'You mean when the aristocracy ran roughshod over the peasants.'

Ilona could see Emil was getting testy. This made her nervous, but Zsolt didn't seem fazed.

'The aristocracy knew how to keep order in the country. Hungary was well respected in the world.' Zsolt sat a bit straighter in his chair.

The politician next to Ilona said, 'Hear, hear,' in agreement.

'So how would that work now, in the late twentieth century? I mean, how many aristocracies are running countries these days?' Emil's voice sounded sarcastic.

'What do you mean?' Zsolt asked.

'I mean, are you really interested in running a nation or simply out for personal gain?'

Emil wasn't smiling. Instead he was staring disdainfully at Judit, to his right, and Albert's wife, to his left, like he was hemmed in, trapped. His eyes darted between Judit, Zsolt, Albert and his mother. The others at the table stopped talking.

Albert's wife looked perplexed.

'I don't understand,' she said. 'Please sit down.'

Ilona had been so stunned at her son's rudeness she hadn't even noticed that he had jumped up from his chair, but there he stood, rigid.

'So Judit, why exactly did you and Zsolt invite us to this dinner?' His voice was dangerously quiet.

Judit's hands fluttered a bit with her napkin.

'Your mother said you were here to learn about how Hungarians were adapting to change after years of socialism.'

'And you and Zsolt lead a group that's working on reclaiming your old family titles and properties.' Emil's lips were tight; not a good sign, Ilona knew.

'Yes,' Zsolt spoke this time. 'And why not? They were stolen from us.'

Ilona shifted her weight on her seat. She didn't like where this conversation was headed. Emil remained standing. All eyes were on him. The record needed to be turned over, it was emitting an irritating scratchy noise, but Judit remained seated. The dining room was eerily still.

Emil's jaw, Ilona noticed, was jutting out. He turned slowly to Albert. His voice was barely audible.

'And you have come to Hungary to buy property, your wife told me.'

'Well, we're looking for business opportunities, if that's what you mean. I already have some private projects and we have a group that has started a new fund that will encompass all of Eastern Europe.' Albert's voice was velvety. 'Your mother told me about your plans with the Pálffy, and I think we have a lot to talk about.'

Emil nodded. Then he turned the full force of his glare at his mother. His hands trembled, like he was forcing himself not to upend the table.

'My mother told you about *my* plans?' Emil's voice quivered slightly.

'Well, what I meant —' Ilona said.

Emil stared hard at his mother.

'— You took me away from my work for this?'

Then he turned to Albert: 'You need to be talking with my mother and my neighbour about their plans, not mine. I'm the wrong man.'

To Zsolt he said, 'I wish you all the best with the aristocracy.'

To Judit, he added, politely. 'I'm so sorry to have wasted your time, but Melissa and I need to leave now.'

'*Anyu*,' Emil nodded goodbye stiffly. Ilona could see fire in his eyes.

Melissa kept her eyes down as she followed Emil out of the room. No one at the table spoke. Zsolt hurriedly followed after him and brought them their coats; Ilona could hear him talking in the foyer.

'Look, I don't understand the objection. Emil, we are sure that with our... *heritage* and investor *backing* we can complete some very interesting projects and get the country back on track. Your mother mentioned something about your American sponsors.'

Ilona could not hear Emil's response. She imagined him giving Zsolt one of those thin, wan smiles with a slightly raised eyebrow that Emil was practised at. Then she could hear Emil and Melissa leave the villa. No one at the dinner table had spoken.

Zsolt walked back to the dining room shaking his head.

'Kids,' he joked. Everyone at the table twittered in agreement. No one looked in Ilona's direction.

Ilona sat icily straight-backed in her chair. She took a deep breath to steady herself, then concentrated on eating a piece of meat on her fork, counting as she chewed. When she got to fifty, she could feel her pulse slowing down. Then she swallowed, but still felt a lump in her throat, so she took a sip of water and calmly turned to her dinner partner — she really should have been listening to his name during the introductions — and asked, 'When will this motorway to Vienna be completed, do you expect?'

The bureaucrat had long finished his meal and had just lit a cigar when he turned to answer her. He blew smoke into her dinner, which she could not finish.

BUDAPEST, 1974

The burly man greeting Ilona when she opened the door to her flat landed a quick hard punch to her jaw. She could feel blood on her lip as she reeled backwards, just barely able to stop herself from falling.

'That's to make sure you tell us the truth,' he said.

She steadied herself against the door frame, tears welling in her eyes. She waited. She saw the two men were wearing special police uniforms. ÁVH. No name tags.

'Where's your son?' the second man asked. He was tall and wore glasses.

'My son? He's at a swimming competition in Yugoslavia. Is there something wrong?'

The tall man smiled at Ilona. When he did, his moustache twitched.

'Have you heard from him since he left? Has he called you?'

'He just left two days ago. No, I haven't heard from him. He can't call. I don't have a phone.'

'No phone?' The man looked surprised. 'May we

come in?'

It wasn't a question. The two men stepped through the doorway and looked around the tidy flat. Ilona quickly closed the door. She didn't want the neighbours to see the secret police visiting her. Her lip was swelling up and she could feel blood dripping down her chin. She pulled a handkerchief from her sleeve and dabbed at it.

The burly man pulled a drawer all the way out of the sideboard and let it fall to the floor, scattering a letter opener, an address book and some stamps. He walked past the living room and into the bedroom which Ilona shared with her son. She could hear a dresser drawer open — the one that separated the two beds so they could have privacy — and crash to the ground. Ilona winced.

'Ilona?' A voice called from the next room. It was Ilona's mother. 'Is everything okay, dear?'

'Yes, mother.'

Ilona's mother opened her bedroom door, saw the tall man with glasses.

'Oh, we have company. You didn't say, Ilona.' To the man she said. 'Hello.'

The tall man smiled back. '*Kezét csókolom*,' he said politely and kicked his heels. I kiss your hand.

Ilona's mother darted her eyes from her daughter's swollen lip to the drawer on the ground and back to the man standing in front of her. Another crash came from the bedroom. Ilona winced, but her mother ignored it.

'Would you care for some tea?'

'Yes, please,' the tall man said. 'We were here inquiring after your... grandson?'

'Emil? He's not here,' Ilona's mother said as she walked to the kitchen. Although her back was straight, she carried herself in a slightly off-kilter way that hinted at a long-ago injury that these men could never worsen. 'He's at a swimming competition, the "Under 18s" in Koper. He left on Thursday.'

Ilona could hear Emil's mattress being thrown on the floor. She fought back tears.

'Are you sure you are looking for my son?' she heard herself asking. She noticed her speech sounded funny with her fat lip. She swallowed some blood.

The tall man didn't answer.

The burly guy came back into the living room. He was hunched over; his arms swung sideways. Ilona thought he looked like a gorilla. He swept away the trophies that were displayed on the sideboard, then he tipped out the contents of each drawer. In the bottom one he found the scrapbook Ilona had been keeping of each of her son's competitions; ribbons, time sheets, team photos — all were carefully mounted; keeping track of her son's ever-increasing success. First in the breaststroke, then the fifty-metre butterfly.

'We're hoping Emil will represent Hungary at the Montreal Olympics,' Ilona said to the burly man as he flicked through the pages of the scrapbook, 'in the fifty-metre butterfly and the relay.'

Looking Ilona straight in the eye, the burly man tore the scrapbook in half, then opened his hands and let the pages drop.

'Well he won't be,' he said.

Then he walked very close to Ilona.

'Where's your son?'

Ilona was shaking, her teeth were chattering and she felt like her knees would not be able to keep her standing upright. She didn't know what to tell the man, so she stayed silent. He struck her again. And then a third time. Ilona could feel a tooth loosen as she fell to the floor.

The tall man looked at Ilona on the ground. She could see through one eye that he was holding the cup of tea. She didn't know where her mother was.

'Apparently your son has gone missing in Yugoslavia. Why would a young man give up the chance of an Olympic gold medal?' He took a slow slurp of tea. 'Are you a good mother, Mrs. Kovács?'

'Gone missing? Is he OK?' Ilona didn't understand.

The tall man kicked her in the ribs. As he did, hot tea spilt on her shoulder.

'Where did he go? How much money did you give him? Who helped him in Yugoslavia? Who do you know in Yugoslavia? One of your husband's old acquaintances, perhaps?'

'We don't know anyone in Yugoslavia. I don't know what you are talking about. Where's my son?'

Ilona curled up on the ground and shielded her head with her arms as the man kicked her a few more times — she wasn't sure how many.

'Please,' she pleaded.

She blacked out when his boot kicked her in the head. When she woke, she could hear the door slam shut. Her mother raced to her and cradled Ilona's head in her arms. Ilona could feel tears falling on her cheeks. Her mother rocked her daughter, as she had when she was younger. It was painful to move but the touch was comforting. Ilona wasn't sure how long the two women sat on the floor crying; worried and confused about Emil — what had happened to him? They were distraught at Ilona's badly beaten body and despaired at the state of their flat.

Ilona noticed the sideboard's gaping holes where the drawers should be; the doors in the middle open at odd angles. Had that brute managed to break the hinges? With her mother's help, Ilona managed to crawl onto the mattress the burly man had thrown on the floor and she fell back to sleep. At some point, her mother must have placed a blanket over her.

When she awoke, she saw that her mother had returned the drawers and their contents to the sideboard and tidied up the room.

'Thank you,' she said. It hurt to breathe, to speak.

Her mother, with a broken porcelain figurine in her hand, just shrugged. 'Women always clean up after the mess the men leave.'

Later in the day, Erzsi and Péter fixed the hinges on the sideboard, but no one knew how to fix the pain in Ilona's ribs, or could even advise her about whether she should go to the hospital. They could not answer the questions about what had happened to Emil.

Her son was due to return late Sunday night. When he didn't, Ilona called in sick at the factory on Monday, and though it hurt to walk, she managed to find her way to the swimming pool during normal practice time. None of Emil's teammates would look her in the eyes. The coach wasn't there, either.

Ilona limped to the assistant coach, worried that she might

slip on the wet tiles. All he would say was that the coach had been fired.

'Is Emil OK?' She asked, almost yelled, as she stood by the side of the pool. She didn't care about the coach. She wanted to know where her son was.

No one answered. No one would even look at her, standing there at the side of the swimming pool in her street clothes looking more exposed than they did in their swimming trunks.

'I can't leave until someone tells me about Emil,' she said, nearly whimpering, barely able to hold back tears.

The assistant coach, looking intently at the guys warming up, spoke quietly, in a whisper.

'Look, all we know is that Emil stole money from all the swimmers in the dormitory in the middle of the night,' he said. 'We think he probably swam to Italy.'

He then turned and walked away.

Later in the day Ilona made an appointment for a dentist to replace her missing tooth. Seeing her bruised and swollen body, the dentist didn't ask any questions. The next week when Ilona stood in line for her pay, the head clerk told her there wasn't any money in her name and she no longer had a job at the factory.

Ilona never spoke of the beating again with her mother. One moves on; it's best not to discuss unpleasant things, although she and her mother did follow Emil's life abroad.

April, 1991

By the time Ilona got home from Judit's dinner party, the flat was eerily clean and still. She peeked around the corner to the bedroom, expecting the trio to be cuddling and snoring when she opened the door. Instead the bed was empty. She noticed one of the suitcases was gone, too. She looked in the bathroom and saw that Melissa had taken her whole supply of pills.

At the weekend, she heard nothing from her son. She decided to take advantage of the quiet and clean the flat. She put away a collection of cassettes and CDs that had piled up on the sideboard, making sure that each disc was in its proper case. She threw Tünde's toys into a big red plastic container, which she pushed to the back of the living room, next to the TV console. As she dusted the telephone, she idly picked it up to make sure there was a dialling tone. She even changed the sheets on the bed. Even though it was free, Ilona did not sleep in it. She decided it was best to have it waiting for when Emil came home.

By Monday, the flat was in proper shape, it felt great to wake up to a tidy home. Ilona just didn't feel clean unless her flat was too. When she returned home from work, she was expecting to hear music booming from her flat as she reached her floor, but all was silent. For nearly a year, she had longed to come home after work to a quiet flat. Now it felt empty. Noiseless. Inside, her flat was just as orderly as it had been when she left. Except it didn't feel right.

The toy box by the TV was gone, so too was Melissa's CD player, the CDs and cassettes. When she looked in the bedroom, Ilona saw the clothes were missing as well. As were all the shoes that Ilona used to trip on walking into the flat. The living room seemed to have expanded in the silence. At least a few drawings were still on the refrigerator.

On the perfectly dusted dining room table was a message, written in Melissa's handwriting, on the back of a piece of scrap paper:

> Dear Ilona,
> Thanks so much for your hospitality!
> Love,
> Emil, Melissa and Tünde

Hospitality? That's what she called those months of sleeping on the sofa? The dinners she made? The babysitting? She must put an end to this nonsense. She wasn't angry anymore and didn't understand why they were holding a grudge.

Not bothering to take off her coat and shoes, Ilona picked up the phone. Then it hit her that she didn't know who she could call. As far as she knew, Emil didn't have a lot of friends here other than Isi and a few artists from the university. He never looked up his swimming teammates. She didn't have any phone numbers of Melissa's friends. To be honest, she had never really bothered to ask Melissa about them.

Ilona stood alone in her flat, clutching the receiver of her phone mid-air.

All sorts of practical things raced through her mind: Emil and his family were registered at her flat. Would he re-register at a different address? His exhibition was only a few months away. Could she attend?

Would she be able to hold her granddaughter again?

Would they leave in July, as planned, without ever seeing her again?

Having a phone means being available day or night in case — perhaps — someone might want to reach her. Now, Ilona thought as she replaced the receiver back on its cradle, no one would want to ring her. Emil had run away from her again. Ilona had learned in 1974 that love was as fleeting as those fish that scatter when you put your foot into the water. She had thought that she could prove that, with time and patience, they can return. Now she wondered if she had scared them away again.

When that thought hit her, she cried. It was emotion that had been a long time coming.

It started with jerking movements from her stomach, as if her body, long immune to emotions, was trying to remember how to express sadness. Then she emitted a moan, a long, low, sorrowful sound which so surprised Ilona that she didn't realise it was coming from her. Its source was deep, from her gut, which retched, heaved and released years of agony, ache and anguish.

The flood of grief, once released, would not stop. She

cried for Laci, because she missed him; because he had to die faceless; because she had to bury him in a wooden box because she had no money to do anything else. She wept because she had not been able to hold or nurse her premature son when he was born, she had been too bereft over Laci's death. She sobbed over Emil's escape, leaving her without warning or any explanation even now, seventeen years later, about why.

And now, he left her again. She had only been trying to help him. She cried for her *kisbaba*.

When she thought she had nothing left inside her, her stomach spasmed and Ilona, undignified, threw up on the carpet when she remembered and acknowledged what the Soviet captain had done to her decades ago. After forty-five years, Ilona cried for herself.

Ilona, then seventeen, was up in her bedroom when two Soviet soldiers and a local policeman had arrived at the Pálffy. She heard the captain's voice and ran to the top of the stairs to listen in. She was angry with her father and secretly glad he was getting yelled at.

She had quarrelled with her father earlier in the day. It had been unusually warm that early June morning, and Ilona had come down for breakfast wearing a pale-yellow cotton dress. It was one of her favourites. She loved the ornamental needlework of daisies sewn on the hem.

Her father, barely looking up, immediately ordered her to change her clothes.

'Why?' she had asked, annoyed that he didn't even compliment her on the pains she had taken to look nice.

'There are too many soldiers around,' he said simply.

Ilona's brother laughed at the implication. Actually, Ilona had thought that was kind of the point. She was tired of wearing thick sweaters and her brother's old trousers, as she had all winter.

'It might turn cold in the afternoon, dear,' her mother said, trying to smooth the edges of her husband's sharpness and her brother's rudeness. 'You can change after breakfast.'

After she had eaten, Ilona had, as ordered, gone to her room, but she had lingered, reluctant to pull on the scratchy wool sweater, which anyway, she had convinced herself would be too hot on such a sunny day.

When the Soviet captain spoke, it was so loud it was impossible not to hear his voice.

'The people need food,' the captain said. 'You must give the farm produce to help the people.'

Ilona saw her mother hurry past her bedroom door and Ilona decided that she, too, would listen in. The two women stood just to the side at the top of the staircase, so they could get a good view of the exchange.

The captain peered into the grand salon just off the foyer and added, 'We will also need this villa to compensate the Soviet people for their hardship.'

Ilona knew the Tura policeman who was standing next to the Soviet captain. He was maybe a year younger than her brother, still too young to be drafted, and he worked during the harvest here each autumn for extra money. Now, standing between the two Soviet soldiers, he was trying to look important.

Ilona could tell from her father's stiff back that he was angry. Ilona's father was a monarchist through and through, even though the Habsburg Empire had long been disbanded. Ilona knew that he thought very little of the Soviets and their Bolshevik rhetoric.

'We can discuss selling food at a fair price, but you can't just waltz in here and take it.'

The captain took out a cigarette and lit it.

'You must give your farm produce for the good of the people.'

He blew smoke directly into Ilona's father's face. Though his back was to her, Ilona could see the skin on his neck turn crimson. She noticed that his hands were shaking with rage.

'Over my dead body,' her father had bellowed.

The captain nodded to the Soviet soldier, who aimed at her father's forehead and fired. Ilona and her mother jumped. The policeman's jaw dropped.

Ilona watched as her father fell back against the bottom of the stairs, blood forming a puddle around his head like a grotesque halo.

Her first thought had been that he was ruining the rug. Her mother had purchased it before the war broke out and it still looked new. The red smear did not look like blood; it was too thick. She expected her father to apologise; her mother would be furious at the mess. Ilona glanced at her mother, expecting annoyance but encountered sorrow instead. Tears trickled down her mother's cheeks, her shoulders shook, her jaws were clenched. Her mother's gaze was locked on her father's eyes, which were still open. He appeared to still be breathing.

'What just happened?' Ilona asked, confused. The policeman and soldiers looked up the staircase and saw the women.

'Come down here now,' the captain said.

As Ilona descended the first couple of stairs, she was acutely aware that she still was wearing her yellow dress. Her mother grabbed Ilona's forearm and forced her daughter behind her as they neared the bottom step. Her grip was tight, almost stopping the circulation of her blood.

Her mother glared at the men, with her chin held high. Rather than stepping around her dying husband, Ilona's mother stopped beside him. Ilona stood just behind her on the bottom step.

'I will ask you now to please leave my house,' Ilona's mother said in a strong voice. 'You may have the food.'

The captain took a last drag on his cigarette and flicked it down so it landed near Ilona's father. He then stamped rather too hard on it to extinguish the cherry tip. Ilona winced. She thought he was going to smash her father's head, who she now could see was no longer breathing. The captain spoke in a low voice to his subordinate in Russian, then, in Hungarian, he ordered the policeman to take away the body. He glared at Ilona and her mother as the soldier and policeman dragged Ilona's father by his feet out of the front door. Her father's hair, like a paintbrush, smeared a brownish red across the marble floor.

Ilona shivered. Perhaps a cloud had slid in front of the sun, draining the heat from the June morning, because when she remembered the day her father died, she thought of it not as an unusually warm day, but as cold and dark. She winced as she heard the *bump, bump, bump* of her father's body being dragged down the entrance stairs. She thought her knees would buckle, and she grasped the railing for balance. The front door was still ajar; the sun poured in through the door, blinding her, so she could no longer see what was happening to her father. Perhaps it had been a sunny day. These were the details her troubled mind mislaid.

The captain remained silent for too long. He seemed to be considering what to do with them. Ilona wondered where the maid had gone; why the gardener had not come to the door. Her brother, she guessed later, had heard the shot and run off. At least that had been her hope. She did not recall hearing any more shots and she never saw or heard from him again.

Ilona could not stop shivering; her jaw hurt as she clamped her mouth shut to keep her teeth from chattering.

The captain reeked of cigarettes and damp wool as he slowly walked toward the women. The uniform he wore was too warm for June and probably had not been cleaned for weeks. His hair was oily, although neatly combed. His shoes were too worn for an officer of his rank.

'How many people live here?' he asked, directing his question not at Ilona's mother, but at the seventeen-year-old standing on the bottom step.

'What do you mean?' Ilona asked.

Her question was genuine. Did he want her to include the foreman and his family, the maid and the gardener or just the Pálffy family? The captain thought she was being impertinent and slapped her face. He apparently didn't care that one of his feet had stepped in her father's blood.

He sneered at her when she cried out in anguish. He was missing a molar.

He ordered the two women back to their rooms and told them to pack. Ilona, grateful to leave, began climbing the stairs only to realise he was following her. She could feel his breath on her neck; the putrid smell of his sweat. She thought she heard his belt buckle jangle behind her.

'No,' Ilona's mother said from the bottom of the stairs, refusing to move.

Ilona turned to stare beyond the captain at her defiant mother. What was she doing? Why refuse this awful man? Didn't she see what he had done to her father?

Her mother looked at the captain and said in a firm but trembling voice.

'Take me instead.'

The captain laughed, but it wasn't a happy tone, it was one that instinctively made Ilona's upper lip curl. 'I'll do that, too.'

She didn't remember a lot of what had happened the following days; she had only vague images. Sharp pains. Her head being held down, her cheek feeling like it was being crushed. Putrid smells. Laughter from the captain and his aide who had returned. The lock of the door. Then the door unlocking. More sharp pains, which felt more intense than the low, constant throb of the burns on her back as the captain stubbed out each of his cigarettes. She stopped trying to figure out how many days she had been locked in her room or how many times the captain or the soldiers had entered. She reeked of sweat and semen, and was beyond feeling. She lay with her arms around her stomach, knees to chest, like a foetus, hoping to die. She had not eaten. Eventually the door unlocked again, and instead of the captain, Ilona heard the foreman's voice.

'Oh God.'

The door shut again. Then, perhaps a half hour later, her mother, whose hair was the most unkempt Ilona had ever seen, came to her with a sponge bath, water and a piece of bread.

'Up,' she said, as if nothing more had happened than a bad cold.

It was dark when the foreman brought the two women to a camp for displaced people in a wagon that was meant for hay. The camp nurse gave Ilona and her mother — and nearly all the women in the camp, Ilona learned later — antibiotics to treat gonorrhoea and herpes. Once, Ilona saw a thin woman with wild eyes toss a new-born into a toilet. Ilona noticed the woman had cigarette scars creeping up the nape of her neck, too. The nurse swiftly dug out the baby, scraping the excrement from its body and wrapping it in a towel. She did it adeptly, like she had done it before. When she saw Ilona's shocked eyes, the nurse shrugged.

'It's what men do. It's our job to clean up and move on.' Then she regarded pale, thin, Ilona, who had chewed up her lower lip. 'If I were you, I'd start moving on.'

Ilona spent her days lying on her bunk bed feeling confused, angry, desolate and alone. She barely spoke. Certainly she never discussed anything beyond the topic of dinner with her mother, whose only comforting words offered, were that time heals all wounds.

Ilona learned to stop thinking about her feelings. They were useless anyway. Not helpful to any situation, as far as she could tell. She needed to get out of that camp, and lying in her bunk feeling sad was not helping. Once she stopped thinking about her feelings, they stopped existing. Ilona learned to watch, listen and learn. To figure out power structures. To calculate odds, play out the moves.

Ilona took the nurse's advice and made herself useful.

She moved to the front of the desk at re-education classes. Smiled sweetly at the teachers, the leaders, the people who knew what-was-what. Ilona, who had never done anything useful in her life other than help her mother arrange flowers or plan a menu, turned her event planning skills into becoming efficient at running her camp group. She organised time tables and soothed squabbles. She learned to type. She smiled pleasantly at everyone who counted. When the time came to assign jobs — getting Hungary back on its feet after a brutal and heartless war — Ilona's mother was sent to sew in a textile factory in Budapest. Ilona, young, pretty and helpful to the new government, entered the office typing pool at the same factory. They lived in people's Soviet-style housing, that had been erected quickly. Ilona learned how to cook.

The two women never acknowledged what had happened to them. A year after she had left her *kastély*, Ilona thought she had become impenetrable. Her inner world had left her entirely. Ilona never discussed her feelings with anyone, not even Laci when he asked about the burns on her back.

'One doesn't talk about these things,' she had told him.

'I hate those bastards. I want to kill every Soviet,' he had said, tears running down his cheeks as he hugged her tightly. Although he obviously felt distressed, Ilona herself felt nothing. Emptied of basic emotions, stoic endurance had become her cloak of survival.

Laci had helped to soften her edges. He made her smile, feel and accept warmth. As the years passed her numbness dissolved. That took a while. Then, he too had been taken from her. At first Ilona had been bereft, inconsolable.

Then, as before, she learned to hold up her chin and

do what was required to raise her son. When Emil left, too, Ilona simply became impervious not just to her own, but to everyone's feelings. She knew what she needed to do: pick herself up and start again. Three times she had been fooled by her emotions. She had vowed to never let that happen again.

Except now, Ilona was surprised that all those wounds had reopened. Still quivering on the living room rug, she wasn't aware that her moans had turned to sobs.

The next morning, Emil still was not there. Ilona, embarrassed that she had spent the night lying on the floor in her coat and boots, was disgusted at the dried vomit. Then she realised no one would care anyway about the mess. She wondered if she should even bother getting up. She no longer cared about anything; not her flat, not herself. She was late for work, and Ilona didn't worry about that either.

Eventually, she found the energy to clean up the floor and put herself back together. She boiled the water for tea, but as she attempted to sip it, she found her hand shaking.

This, she now knew, was how she would grow old: alone, drinking weak tea, in a lonely flat. And that thought brought back that empty space, that void in her stomach she had felt for so many years. She began to weep again, and felt as if she would never be able to stop. She tried to force herself up from the chair. *Buck up*, she told herself. *Put on your face and get to work*. She couldn't. She sat at the kitchen table with a half-drunk cup of tea and stared into space.

After she had wiped her tears Ilona only felt blank, lifeless, sterile, spent. After a few deep breaths, she managed a voice steady enough to call in sick. She sat back on the couch, held one of Melissa's pillows to her stomach. Her thoughts had left her, she simply let the tears roll down her cheeks. Then, exhausted, Ilona slept some more. At some point she woke, but night had already arrived.

She walked into the bedroom — the one she had begun thinking of as Emil's and Melissa's — and sat on the bed. She tried to feel rage against him: why had he left her? She didn't have the strength to pretend. Maybe wealth and contentment didn't have the same meaning for him. Her chin quivered again. Would she ever have the chance to say sorry? Could she ever fix it? She threw her head on the pillow and was surprised she could smell her son. She breathed in deeply and fell back asleep.

The next day, Ilona dried her puffy eyes and numbly left for work. She walked stiffly, going through the motion. She did not smile. She did not greet the man at the newspaper stand as he handed her the stack of newspapers and magazines. He looked at her with concern as she plodded heavily into the building. She lumbered glumly up the stairs to the office and didn't bother to make herself any tea. She stared at the blank piece of paper she had put into the typewriter and considered that both she, Ilona, and her Olivetti were outdated.

She blinked at her arthritic knuckles and wondered if her life had been pointless, devoid of love. Had she simply spent her adult life undertaking meaningless tasks while she waited to die? Is that what she would be doing in future, too? That thought made her eyes well up with tears. If she started to cry, would she ever stop?

John had been encouraging her to learn to use the computer, but Ilona had thought she wouldn't be staying much longer at the news agency; that her son would take care of her in their *kastély*, so she had demurred. Now, she looked over at the machine on his desk with dread. It was grey and impersonal. Its keys were light and insubstantial. She was too old to learn about control and escape keys. Her stomach ached. She couldn't stay there.

Ilona left the paper in the typewriter, pulled her coat back on and picked up her handbag. She dabbed her eyes again, and headed for the door. On her way out, she met John rushing up the stairs. Before she could tell him she was taking another day off, he took hold of her by the elbow.

'Thank God you're here,' he said. 'Totally forgot. We need to get to that interview at the telecommunications ministry.'

Ilona inhaled deeply while John grabbed a notebook and pen from his drawer. It would be a long day.

The new telecommunications minister was a member of the Smallholders Party, John told her. He was now a junior member of the ruling coalition. To her abhorrence, Ilona recognised him from Judit's dinner. They had been seated next to one another and she had found him boorish; of course it was her son who had acted poorly, not the minister.

He remembered Ilona when she walked in with John for the interview.

'*Kezét csókolom*,' he said to her, with a flourish. And he did actually kiss her hand, rather than the air just above her wrist as a real gentleman would have. Ilona forced a smile.

The minister's English was good enough that John did not need Ilona to translate, so she sat in her chair and ignored the men. She knew she was supposed to keep notes, in case John had missed something, but she had no interest in GSM nor did she have any idea what it was. Did it matter? Her eyes blurred as the two discussed bids and construction time-tables.

She was tired in spite of her long sleep, and stiff from sleeping on the floor. She felt drained, old, and washed up. She wondered if she would ever feel any energy to do anything again.

After an hour of the two men droning on in the overheated office, Ilona felt as if she could drift off and never wake up again. As her head began to nod, John and the minister stood up. She hoped she would be able to go home rather than back to the office.

'I believe I might have met that relative of yours,' the minister said to Ilona in Hungarian as she and John were walking toward the door.

'A relative of mine?' Ilona said doubtfully.

'Your son. I recognised him immediately. He made quite an impression at the dinner party. He said he was an *artist*. He wants to exhibit at the *Kossuth tér* metro station,' the minister said. 'I told him it wasn't possible, of course. I hope he understands.'

Ilona felt her heart skip a beat. Then she understood: the telecommunications minister also had the transportation portfolio. That's why he was going on about the motorway to Vienna at the party. Emil needed approval from the transport ministry to hold his exhibition at the metro station.

As they walked back to the office, Ilona asked John, 'do you know the term *schadenfreude*?'

'Of course. But it's an ugly concept. Why would anyone want to be happy about someone else's sorrow?'

It was true: Ilona wasn't happy that Emil's request to hold his exhibition in the underground had been denied.

On her way home from work, Ilona bumped into Erzsébet as the two of them had reached the walkway to their block of flats.

'Ilona! I haven't seen you in days! Where have you been hiding?'

Ilona was so relieved to see her long-time friend, she was caught off guard by tears welling in her eyes. If Erzsi noticed, she didn't let on.

'Let me show you the most adorable little vest I found for Tünde,' she said. 'Come on in for a minute.'

Ilona followed Erzsi into her flat. On the table was a fireman's red felt vest with bright red, blue, yellow and green embroidery on each front panel. It was the kind of thing tourists bought.

'Beautiful,' Ilona lied.

'As you know Melissa is collecting things she can use when she gets back to Cleveland...'

Ilona did not know this; she nodded her head anyway.

'...so I thought I would find old traditional outfits for her and Tünde.'

Erzsi looked pleased with herself. Ilona simply stared at her.

'Are you going to their housewarming party? Should we go together?' Erzsi asked.

Housewarming party? Ilona had heard nothing from her son since they had left.

'I wish I could!' Ilona said in a cheerful voice. 'Unfortunately I need to help John with something then.'

'I can't wait to see their new place,' Erzsi said. 'It sounds like Melissa did a lot with so little. I'm sure your back is happy to be sleeping on a solid mattress again!'

'Oh yes,' Ilona lied again. 'It's nice to have my peace and quiet. You know how loud children can be.'

'I miss all that clamour, I wish Isi would settle down and give me grandchildren,' Erzsi said. 'He's too busy making money, I suppose.'

'And Emil's living on government grants,' Ilona reminded her.

'Ilona, it's not the money that makes someone happy,' Erzsi said. 'It's possible to be wealthy without having a lot of material goods. The thirty-five years I spent with Péter were the happiest in my life. We never had a lot of money, but I felt like I was the richest woman in town.'

Back in her empty flat, Ilona stared at the clean, clutter-free dining room table. So. Emil and Melissa were having a party. They were still friends with Erzsi, yet they haven't called her.

Well.

Ilona tried to feel indignant, but she couldn't. She ran a finger along one of the pillows Melissa had sewn for her as a Christmas present. The cover was a pale eggshell blue muslin that offset the heavy dark blue of the sofa nicely. Yellow silhouettes of a man, a woman and a child — Emil, Melissa and Tünde — were embroidered in the corner. Ilona ran her fingers over the second pillow. It had embroidered on it a grandmother with a toddler. When she opened her present, she had been disappointed that it was not bought in a shop and special. Now, for the first time, she was impressed by the pillows, their simplicity and artfulness.

She looked anew at the finger painting Tünde had given her, which her mother had glued to a piece of cardboard. Would her granddaughter ever make another one for her? Ilona could feel her chin starting to quiver. She took a deep breath to calm herself.

Finally, Ilona moved her eyes to the family portrait, which Emil had hung in the hallway near the bedroom. It was beautiful, black and white, slightly off-centred, complete with a mount and frame. She missed them.

Ilona wanted to see her son, but didn't know where he was. She couldn't bring herself to admit to Erzsi that she hadn't been invited to the party. That she hadn't spoken to her son or his family in nearly a week and that she did not know where they lived. That she had driven Emil away. It wasn't supposed to have worked out this way. He was supposed to come back to her, but she had pushed him away. Now she needed to find a way to get him to return.

ISTVÁN

The lunch rush was over and the two tuxedoed waiters were changing the tablecloths on the tables, getting ready for dinner. A commis waiter was sweeping up. The hum of the dishwashers in the back and the *clank* of the pots from the cooks preparing dinner was as soothing for István as Liszt's *Liebestraum*. The routine was familiar; no one spoke. Everyone knew their dance moves. Each worker, tired from the rush, was now grateful for the respite. Zoltán, who had come in early, threw on his jacket and waved goodbye to Tibor and Ádám. His cigarette was lit before the restaurant door had closed completely.

Isi made a cup of coffee and poured two small packets of sugar into it before heading to a back table where Albert was waiting, puffing on a cigar.

'It was a good day,' Albert nodded his head approvingly.

'Yeah, volume has picked up a lot with de good weather. We getting a lot more tourists.' Isi's English was improving.

Albert drew on his cigar. He leaned back, crossed his legs and nodded for Isi to continue. István noticed Albert had nicked himself shaving that day.

'We working with de tourism bureau to get more recommendations in de pamphlets. Dere's an American tour guide who we are trying to give us a write-up. We working all de angles.'

'And the Pussycat Nightclubs?'

Isi smiled. 'What can I say? You called it. De border clubs are packed every night. Lorry drivers and a lot of Austrians come across for good time. Tings are lookin good.'

Albert tapped the ashes from his cigar into a ceramic bowl. He sipped some water, then looked down at a spot on the table.

'I'm happy to hear all this because we had an investor meeting and we need to free up some capital. We decided, well... I need to call in the loan.'

'What does dat mean, call de loan?'

'István, I need the money back. Your loan. You have to pay it back.' Albert drew on the cigar. 'Luckily, as you tell me, business is going well, so I'm sure you can get me that money.'

István stared blankly at Albert.

'Didn't you just say business was going well? Didn't you just say that? Well, I need you to pay back the loan.'

'But we have agreement.'

'Yes, but there is a buy-back clause in the contract. I can call in the loan at any time.'

István rarely lost his temper. He had a look, honed from years of practice, that told people not to push things. He never had to say anything. Anyone looking at Isi's face could read it; the intensity of his eyes, the reddening of the neck, the clenching of the jaw, the uneven breath. Albert didn't see it because he didn't look up. He didn't want to see it.

'Anyway, I'm really happy that you've been able to get these places running so smoothly.' He paused.

István spoke in a low bass. He was barely audible; his nostrils flaring.

'You know most of de nightclubs just broke even dis month, Albert. Your man was here last week.' Then István finally was able to lock eyes with the German. 'Dat's why he came, right?'

Albert didn't blink.

'I need you to repay the loan, István.'

He paused, then shrugged his shoulders. He uncrossed his legs and leaned forward.

'If you can't come up with the money, you have options. You can sell us this restaurant; it's profitable and in a prime location. As you've said yourself, it's an institution. Or — we will take over the chain of nightclubs. If you'd like, I'll bring in our man to explain your options better. But either way, we will be repaid.'

Albert checked his wrist. 'I need to run. I have a meeting with Matthew. We've got a bid in on a small *kastély* we'd like to turn into a boutique hotel. That's why I need the capital.'

Albert stubbed out the tip of his cigar, stood up and pulled on his Hugo Boss jacket. He clapped Isi on the shoulder.

'No hard feelings, man. It's just business. We'll stay in touch.'

István stayed seated at the table, hunched over. He could taste bile. After a few minutes he yelled at Tibor to bring him a bottle of pálinka.

'Everything okay?' Tibor put a bottle of *Csalló Körte-pálinka*, Isi's favourite, on the table.

'*Nagy kutya*,' István said. Loose translation: big dogs fuck anything they want.

Isi poured a glass of the pear schnapps, which he knocked back in a gulp.

Albert wasn't going to get this restaurant. It's where Isi had started working at fifteen as a commis waiter. It's where he learned how to wait tables, how to work the back office, how to run a successful business. It's where he'd been for the last twenty years, humouring the tourists, ingratiating himself with the customers; smiling, always smiling.

As his parents had taught him, he had been a go-getter for Albert, working his arse off — running around the damn country, chatting up government officials, securing permits, getting the refits completed on time. He had found the girls. He had bribed the right people to get the alcohol licences. He had worked the sixteen-hour days, seven days a week to get the whole chain of nightclubs running on time. Albert had done none of this.

István tipped back a second pálinka and slammed the glass on the table, which Tibor pretended not to notice. Isi never drank during the day.

Once, when Isi was thirteen, his class spent two weeks at Csilleberc, a Pioneer Youth summer camp. He thought it was magical. The camp was in a forest and kids from all over the country slept in tents. They were all equal, they were told. Each had duties to fulfil; and afterwards they played games and sang songs. Isi plunged into his work and played with the eagerness he had been taught by his parents. On the last night of camp, he was rewarded with an increase in rank and a leadership pin. Isi fastened his aluminium belt on his shorts and proudly wearing his white shirt, red scarf and his pin, saluted his dad and uncle — fingers to the temple, palm facing out — when they picked him up at the train station.

As soon as the Lada pulled out of the car park and away from prying ears, his uncle burst out laughing.

'Hey, what's next, Nikita, a leadership role at the Youth Communist League?'

His father, who was driving, laughed, then pulled down the corners of his mouth and looked at Isi through the rear-view mirror.

'Don't rat on us. We're only joking.'

The taunting stung. What was the problem? He'd done as he had been taught. He had worked hard, helped out. Done a bit more than the others. He wanted to be a leader; to be respected. He had earned his pin. Now his own father and uncle guffawed at his efforts. He pretended he had only been joking. He threw the pin in the rubbish when he got home, not bothering to show it to his mother. Still, his uncle and dad recounted the salute as they drank that afternoon. For years afterwards, his uncle saluted him when he visited. He was relentless. Khrushchev himself had to die before his uncle stopped calling him Nikita.

That humiliation was nothing to how he felt now. Isi twirled the empty shot glass with his fingers. The foreign investors weren't going to take over his businesses. His businesses were Hungarian businesses, not West German. What the hell is the difference between the Western investors buying up the country now and the Soviets demanding a voluntary takeover of his mother's farm forty years ago? This was the same betrayal. It was the same subterfuge, only now the men smiled and wore tailored suits.

What the fuck do these Westerners know about hard work? Their pitying glances, their better-than-you attitudes; their furtive glance at István's scuffed black shoes or his jacket before giving their partner that raised eyebrow *look*, like they were going to mock him, as his father and uncle had done, as soon as he was out of hearing. They had merely humoured him, taking him for a willing fool.

István stared at this empty shot glass, contemplating his next move.

Those foreigners forget Hungarians are smart. We developed the A-bomb. At many Manhattan Project meetings, Isi knew, Leo Szillard, Ede Teller, Jenő Pál Wigner and János Lajos von Neumann dropped the pretence of speaking English and lapsed into Hungarian. Why not? They all attended the same High School in Budapest. Hungarians are smart, alright. Isi thought he needed to get smart, too.

He needed to think it through though. He needed to find the *kis ajto*, the little back door that exists everywhere; the one where you can slip in, even if people do not think you belong. Every deal has one.

Isi poured another shot of *pálinka*; the smell of the sweet alcohol reminded him of summer on Lake Balaton, when his neighbour would put bottles over some of the pears on the trees when the fruit was only the size of his finger. All summer Isi would stop by and check the pears ripening in the bottles. By the time Isi was ready to leave in the autumn, the fruit in the bottles would be greener and larger than the ones hanging free. Each winter, his dad would bring home a bottle of pálinka, a present from the neighbour, with the pear floating in the clear liquid. Isi never figured out how his neighbour turned that into schnapps.

Now thirty-four, István realised there was a lot he didn't know, and he needed to start getting curious. He was still getting the hang of this free market economy. He couldn't have afforded to buy his restaurant or start his Pussycat Nightclubs or begin building a villa without using someone else's money. Hell, he wouldn't have been able to get the BMW if it hadn't been for OTP Bank, at least their money. Without the funds behind him, István wouldn't have been able to sit down with the right government officials or even have the chance of opening more nightclubs throughout the country.

Under the last government, connections mattered too. Yet under this new regime, you needed connections and cash; that's how Albert had explained it to him. Now Isi could see that's not the whole story. Without him, István, the work wouldn't have been done. He ran the restaurant and found the right locations bidding for them when they came up for auction. He met the right guy who would get him the alcohol licences; and that wasn't easy. He had to make a few deals for that, including buying three times the amount of Pick Salami than his restaurant would need in a year. Why? Because he found out the man who gave the alcohol licences was also working with his brother-in-law to get the salami factory profitable again. Just in case that didn't work out, he kept his government job. Isi even used a few cases to speed up the refits of the nightclub buildings.

Albert and his investors needed people like him.

The country, it seemed to him, had gone full circle. The Soviet-backed government couldn't have existed without people doing the real work. Nowadays, the International Monetary Fund and World Bank existed to help these Western businessmen, not the dopes like him. In the end, communism and capitalism are the same; ultimately, both keep Hungarians down.

He thought about what Arpád Göncz had just said in a speech, that as president he would serve those who have no voice in this world. When Göncz had said it, István hadn't comprehended what Göncz was trying to say. Now he understood too well.

István slammed back his third *pálinka*. He was breathing fire now. He felt the alcohol flow through his veins.

They weren't going to keep him down, though. No. Albert wasn't going to get his restaurant. And he wasn't getting the Pussycat Nightclubs, either.

In 1848, Hungarians peasants fought for independence against the nobility and lost. A hundred years later, the Soviets took over the country and again the Hungarians lost. The Westerners weren't going to take away that sweet taste of freedom. Magyars weren't going to be duped again.

This time the fight won't be fought with guns. We are smarter than that, he thought with the taste of venom in his throat. This time the war will be deliberate and calculated. As smooth as Albert's best suit.

As he sat in the back of his restaurant; comforted by the whirr of the dishwasher, István devised a plan. István would invite that new MP, Viktor, the one who had given that speech demanding that Soviets leave the country. Isi had seen him at the restaurant. They were about the same age; he'd understand. This Viktor guy seemed to know how this worked. Next time he was in, Isi would ask him to stay for a drink after lunch. These government officials needed to stop giving away the country to Westerners. Now it was time to let Hungarians in through the little back door. Keep Hungary for the *Magyars*! Put that into law, even.

The schnapps warmed Isi's belly. He liked the way it made him think. Here's what the country needed to do: kick out the foreign investors along with the Soviet troops — or, at least, don't ever allow either of them the upper hand. Money may have more clout in this new free market economy, but Isi was now understanding what the West meant by capitalism.

István sat back and lit a cigarette, letting the smoke blow in two straight lines from his nose.

Sometimes bribes don't only involve money. Power is a good motivator, too. That was his plan and that was how he'd keep his restaurant and the Pussycat Nightclubs. Viktor was a young guy, newly elected to parliament, just back from a year at a university in England. He's surely seen how the West works. Let's see if he can create a *kis ajto*, that little back door for Hungarians. From now on, Isi decided his business partners were going to be Hungarians, not foreigners. He was going to get the government to understand that Hungary needed to stay in Hungarian hands.

ILONA

István wasn't the only one making plans. Alone in her flat, once again, Ilona realised she had to move forward. It's what one does. It's what she had always done. Ilona knew that she had to make amends to Emil. She could get back into his graces through helping him with that exhibition of his. The art show was important to her son and he wanted to hold it in a metro underground station. It's not at all what she wanted for Emil, although this time, Ilona realised, she had to go along with him.

Emil needed permission to hold his exhibition in the metro underground. If Ilona got him that permission, then perhaps he would come back to her. This was going to be tricky, though. It would take more than a well-placed bottle of *pálinka* this time. This would take some planning. Planning was what Ilona did best. It reinvigorated her mood. Ilona made her first call.

'Judit,' Ilona said sweetly when she heard the voice on the other end of the line.

'Are you up for lunch this week? I need to make amends.'

This was going to be very difficult, she thought with

glee. To help Emil, Ilona required more information on the transportation minister and Judit would have it. Ilona wished she had paid more attention to him at the dinner. The only thing she had noticed was that he liked cigars. At the very least, she calculated that she'd need to buy a box of Cuban cigars. That would cost a lot. Her mind raced. Maybe even the cigars wouldn't be enough.

Ilona wished she could ask Emil what he intended to do at the exhibition — she would need more information for that too. She had always prided herself on her memory, but now she drew a blank. She hadn't really listened that night on the tram. Something about mixed media, whatever that was. Photographs, videos, paintings? She wasn't sure. She only remembered him saying he wanted it to be underground. *This was going to be very difficult*, Ilona thought, feeling energised.

On her lunch break the next day, Ilona walked over to the ministry and met his secretary for tea, which Ilona naturally paid for. Afterwards, the secretary showed Ilona Emil's official application. Ilona knew Emil had filled out the form himself because it was the same scrawl she had read in his letters for seventeen years. Her heart skipped a beat when she saw it.

His request was to close that station for the night of the opening only. For the exhibition he wanted to decorate the walls of the underground metro station — the photographs would be mounted on top of the graffiti and in place of the advertising posters. He also wanted to arrange video players and installations. He'd need to erect more lighting around the platform, too, the application said. He hoped to keep the exhibition up for a week for commuters to see. He would pay for the workers to help him with the installation.

Good God, Ilona thought. This wasn't really asking the government for a lot. He just hadn't gone about asking correctly. Although she was pleased he had gone straight to the national government rather than bothering with city officials. Sometimes they could get especially greedy.

A week later, Ilona breezed into the minister's office.

'I just stopped by because I found these at a store on *Vaci utca*,' Ilona told the minister, handing him a box of the best cigars she could secure.

They had been purchased in Austria. John and his wife made monthly trips to Vienna, she knew. It was, they had once told her, so they could stock up on things they couldn't get in Budapest. At the time, Ilona had been insulted. Hungary wasn't some backwater, you could get everything here. However Ilona discovered she couldn't buy Cuban cigars anymore. Trade between communist countries had collapsed. She had only recently heard that Pick Salami, the best in the country, was in financial difficulty because their old clients couldn't pay anymore.

'Would you mind bringing back some cigars? Nice ones. The best you can find,' Ilona smiled prettily at her boss.

'Ilona, what do you need cigars for? Not work, I hope,' John asked. He was aware that sometimes she needed to place gifts in the right hands to keep the office functioning smoothly, still, he chose to pretend he knew nothing of it.

'Good heavens, no.'

He looked at her curiously, but he didn't dare probe any further.

'While you're there, I've heard there is a new fragrance of perfume I'd like to try.'

Ilona wrapped the box of cigars and the bottle of perfume with special care. She added little notes: one to the transportation minister, the second to his secretary. She found a pretty bag for them as she made her way to the politician's office.

'I think I missed your birthday, so please accept this from me now, belatedly,' Ilona said with her head slightly inclined towards the secretary.

The minister happily accepted his present without any hesitation. He invited Ilona into his inner office and waited to see how he could help her.

'Oh my, it's been such a busy few weeks,' Ilona said. She leaned back to make herself look at ease. 'I've been helping John with that GSM story he's writing.'

The minister raised his eyebrows to show she had his attention. It was a lie. John's story was long finished and waiting for subbing in London. Ilona suspected John would fire her if she knew what she had said. But the minister, eager to get good publicity for the bids, was all ears.

'You might remember that my son is looking for permission to hold his art exhibition about Hungary in the metro, underground,' Ilona said. 'It will be sure to get a lot of attention among Western investors.'

Although it was the second lie she had told that day, Ilona knew it was the best way to get these officials' attention.

MAY

Viktor was trying to look at ease sitting in a back booth of one of the top restaurants in Budapest, talking with the owner. Isi had seen that look before. The young rebel who had given the fiery speech was still learning how things really worked. Viktor was leaning back, his right leg crossed, but the left leg was bouncing nervously. István waited an extra couple of minutes before walking over to join him.

'Thank you for coming,' István said.

'Thank you for the invitation. Your restaurant is the best in Budapest.'

István nodded his head in modest recognition of the compliment.

'I wanted to talk with you about the direction of the country.'

Now it was Viktor's turn to nod. Isi could see he was pleased with the way things were going and was warming to the praise. Certainly life had been good to Viktor. He had been elected only a few months after he had returned from studying political philosophy in England.

'Let me be frank. The country is going to shit,' István said. He wasn't used to beating around the bush the way politicians are. As a restaurant manager, he barked orders.

Victor's eyes bulged slightly. He wasn't expecting that.

'How so?'

'Prices are going up so fast, I can barely afford to buy food for the restaurant. Hungarians can't afford my prices. And no one is here to help us. The Soviets are broke. The East Germans have West Germany to help them. We have no one. I have friends who spent last winter in unheated flats; skipping meals. To the foreigners though, we're cheap, and this government is selling us to the highest bidder. Then the foreigners — Jews mostly — they fire half the workers in the companies they buy.'

'Well,' said Viktor, ignoring the slur. He knew that many Hungarians had unfavourable views towards Jews and Gypsies. His own parents were openly hostile to the Gypsies, who every Hungarian knew, would steal your last piece of bread. And a Hungarian Jew who had fled during the war had paid for Viktor's year in England and Viktor had been a quick learner. In England, you don't say bad things about either group; at least not out loud. Still, the one thing that did unite all of Europe was their hatred of the Soviets, so Viktor started there. He knew he'd find common ground there.

'The communists stuffed all the state enterprises with too many people. Hardly anyone had enough work to do to fill a full day, you know that. How many waiters did this restaurant have when you bought it? How many do you have now? To make it in the market economy, you need efficiencies.'

Viktor used that word like he had just learned it, Isi

thought. The restaurant owner gave the younger man a thin, patient smile.

'To make it in parliament, you need happy voters. Your party barely squeezed in.'

Viktor squirmed.

'Well, it will take a while for people to understand how liberal institutions work. Our party is working to make a New Europe, one where we are united in democratic values.'

István coughed. 'The people understand that the policies of this new government made them lose their jobs, but they see all those government officials driving Western cars. They see the new villas going up in the Buda hills while they're stocking up on sugar and flour before the prices go up again. No one trusts politicians anymore.'

'Transitions take time,' Victor said, but his eyes betrayed him.

'Look, Antall is sick. This is your chance to win more votes at the next election,'

Viktor's eyes widened. No one talked about Antall's illness. At least not out loud.

'What are you hearing?'

'That he is going to die,' István leaned across the table and spoke in a near whisper. 'They say he has cancer.'

There was feverish planning for his succession even though such an illness was never discussed out loud. If Viktor knew, he didn't let on. He just nodded his head in acknowledgement of each statement he heard. István liked that. Discretion in business and politics was important.

What Isi didn't know, couldn't know, was that the young man had, only days before, been invited into the inner sanctum of the prime minister's office. Viktor had never met Antall in person, just the two of them, like that. Antall was old enough to be his father. He was the leader of the conservatives. He had been part of the uprising in 1956, imprisoned for nearly a decade. Viktor was born after the uprising. He was merely a member of the opposition Young Democrats.

'You speak well,' Antall had complimented him. 'I think you can go far. However, Viktor, Hungarian people are not like those in the West. You talked about free speech. Fascists talk freely but it doesn't help us. Tread lightly.'

Viktor had looked at Antall askance as the frail man, clearly tiring, continued: 'Hungarians are by character conservative people. The church is important; family is important. Now even crime is rising, pornography and prostitution are rampant. People don't take care of their neighbours the way they used to. We were once part of a great empire. We are noble people. Focus on those issues, and you will go far.'

As Viktor shook the prime minister's hand to leave, Antall, a tall, once imposing man, looked at the short, young, eager politician. The elder statesman held on to Viktor's hand, then placed his left hand on top of it.

'You are still young. You need to make decisions about your future. Do you want to be a university professor?' Antall said those words like they were a slur. 'Or, do you want to lead? You are intelligent. You have the potential to be quite powerful.'

Viktor had left the meeting in a daze.

His year in England had changed him; he was hopeful about his country's potential, but now that he was back, he felt dejected.

England had surprised him in both a good and a bad way. He was shocked at how poorly the students lived. At his first party, hosted by an emaciated woman named Fiona, an Indian print was draped over an ancient sofa to hide its shabby condition. Second hand furniture that didn't even match finished off the sitting room. If you have the money, and these students clearly did, why not flaunt it?

Fiona, whose severe features and sharp nose were emphasised by the blunt chin-length cut of her mousy hair, had been engaged for more than an hour with Edmund over political philosophy as they sipped wine. They would ask what, to Viktor at least, were rhetorical questions, then proceeded to answer them considering all sides whilst tossing in Rousseau, Hobbes, Locke, Kant, Mills, Hegel and Plato as casually as one scatters grass seeds in a front garden: curious to see what ideas take root. His studies in Budapest were mostly rote: memorising each philosopher and their tenets. The conclusions always came from the socialist perspective.

Viktor had wished that all Hungarians could have the same mind-blowing chance to experience what he had. Exposure to a way of life entirely unlike theirs. To a variety of perspectives. To see the possibility of a different outcome. He came back with such enthusiasm, primed to change the country, the system.

But, complacency shrouded the country in a tight, constricting vice. In only a few short months, people had lost interest in politics, in the possibility of change, and no longer cared that democracy opened up society, created a chance for everyone. They didn't notice that there were now no empty shelves in stores but only that the prices kept on going up.

Now, here he was in a restaurant, trying once again to explain to this businessman, who had benefitted from capitalism, who had purchased one of the crown jewels of the hospitality industry in the nation's capital, that democracy — democratic capitalism — was a force for the good of the country.

'There are economic adjustments that need to be made,' Viktor conceded. 'But we must keep our eyes open to be ready for future developments. In the long run, the rising tide will raise all boats.'

'The rising tide is only raising the boats on the Buda side of the river.'

Viktor frowned.

István paused, trying to phrase his thoughts in a way Viktor would understand.

'You studied politics, right? I'm a businessman. I have to keep my customers happy, right? Otherwise, they don't come back. It is important that the state ensures no one is deprived. Otherwise they won't vote you back in. So, you gotta keep people happy.'

'How?'

'All the Westerners are gobbling us up. They are taking over our industries faster than the Soviets did,' István declared with feeling. 'Democracy is what's wrong.'

'These are two separate things. Democracy and capitalism.'

'I don't care what you call it, it's wrong.'

'So what can I do about it? How do you want to change it? We're not going back to communism.'

'Change the rules so that Hungary stays in Hungarian

hands.' The businessman's jaw was tight.

Viktor was quiet. Isi wondered if he had gone too far, too fast. He tried again, speaking in a way a politician would understand.

'You guys didn't do so well in the last elections, with your talk about high-minded concepts like free speech and plurality,' István reminded him. 'If you lose too many more seats, you will be out of parliament. So if you want to stay in power, you must make people happy.'

'You need money to make people happy,' Viktor said. 'The Soviets went bankrupt trying to do that.'

'People were complaining back then, too. They miss not having to worry about whether they will have a job, or that they can keep their flats or even heat them. They worry about crime. No one should be spending so much time worrying about food prices.'

'But you need money,' Viktor persisted. 'Industry brings money.'

'Industry can be Hungarian. We can make money, too,' István insisted.

'You can't have it both ways,' Viktor said. 'You can't be good capitalists and socialists at the same time. The communist way just doesn't work. I'd never support that again.'

'Correct,' István said, making it up as he spoke. 'Those foreigners made the rules so that they come out on top. That's what they mean by capitalism. We Hungarians need to make rules that suit us. Hungarians vote. If you want power, you have to make us happy, not the Westerners. Then, we'll make you happy.'

Then, remembering all the lessons he had learned this last

year, István added, slowly, 'And along the way, you might be able to make some money, too. Viktor, you can have power and money. You need to be smart about it, that's all.'

The way István spoke was eerily like Antall. Still, Viktor continued to keep his poker face and just nodded.

'I'll think about it.'

István noticed that Viktor's left leg had stopped jiggling and that the young man was leaning in slightly. That's how István knew he had Viktor on his side.

A WEEK LATER

Ilona got a letter. The address was written in heavy familiar handwriting, and as it had for nearly two decades when she got mail with that handwriting, Ilona's heart beat faster. She held the envelope tightly as she waited for the lift to bring her to her flat so she could read it in private. She worried that Emil was writing to end his ties with her entirely. Or to say he was leaving early. She was hoping for a reconciliation.

Inside the envelope was a postcard. On one side was a collage of photographs — archival and contemporary — of Hungary with the words *In search of our fathers* scribbled across it in red. She didn't really examine the photos. What was important was the invitation on the other side to attend the opening of an exhibition in the underground at *Kossuth tér*.

Ilona was pleased. Her scheme had worked. Emil got his exhibition and she got an invitation to it. She would be able to see him and the baby again. She examined the postcard again. She was delighted with the topic. Emil was going back to his roots after all! She was hoping he had included some of those photographs she saw him take of the Pálffy Kastély when they had visited.

She wondered if Erzsi got an invitation too. She hurried off to ask.

In the hallway of the block of flats, Ilona saw Emil and Melissa standing at the lift. Tünde was toddling after them, waving bye-bye to '*Erzsi néni*', Auntie Erzsi. In the weeks since she had seen her granddaughter, Ilona was surprised at how much the *kisbaba* had grown.

'Hello,' she said, formally. Her heart was pounding.

'Lili!' Tünde said excitedly, as she raced to meet her grandmother.

Ilona stooped down and hugged her granddaughter.

Although he was down by the lift, Ilona could faintly recognise the tell-tale smell of Emil: developing fluids mixed with turpentine. Ilona briefly wondered if it was permanent, she didn't mind, though. He looked beautiful.

Melissa and Emil stayed transfixed at the lift doors. Erzsi remained in the doorway of her flat.

'I got your invitation, thank you,' Ilona said to her son.

She could see that all three adults relaxed.

'Have you seen it?' Ilona asked Erzsi.

'Yes!' Erzsi said, 'It's so beautiful. And they were so lucky.'

If Erzsi felt guilty about babysitting Tünde while Emil organised the exhibition, she didn't let on. Ilona felt more than a pang of resentment.

'It was touch and go,' Erzsi continued. 'At first the Transport Department turned down the request to hold the exhibition in the underground, so we were searching for an alternative space. We still don't know why they changed their mind.'

The *we* in those sentences felt like a slap in Ilona's face.

'Well,' Ilona said, looking at her son and not her neighbour. 'As I'm sure you're aware, a well-placed gift works wonders.'

The three adults stared at Ilona, astonished.

'How did you know?' Emil stammered. 'Why did you…'

Ilona beamed at her son. She couldn't remember the last time anyone looked so genuinely grateful at her. She had done a favour without being asked and it felt good. Her heart was beating loudly, but in a different way: happy and heavy and thumping.

Emil walked back from the lift and hugged his mother. That felt even better. When the lift door pinged open, Emil told Melissa to go ahead.

'I think I need to talk to my mum,' he said.

Melissa and Tünde waved good night as Emil followed his mum into her flat. Erzsi dabbed at her eyes, then closed the door to her flat.

Emil stood awkwardly in the frame next to the front door.

'*Anyu*, thank you so much.'

'Son, I'd do anything for you,' Ilona said. She asked shyly: 'Would you like some tea?'

Emil followed her into the flat. He leaned against the kitchen doorway while Ilona poured water into the kettle. Neither spoke as they waited for the water to boil.

'I'm sorry,' Ilona blurted it out a little too loudly.

Emil looked down. 'I'm sorry, too.'

'What are you sorry for?'

'For leaving you seventeen years ago; not staying in

touch as much as I should have.' He fiddled with his ear. Ilona remembered he did that when he was little, too. 'Was it really bad? I mean, after I left.'

Ilona shrugged it off. 'Well, you know…'

Then she stopped herself. Her hand shook as she handed him his tea. These last weeks seemed as if she was frequently on the verge of tears. She took a deep breath as they walked into the living room.

'Yes. It was really hard,' she said.

Surprised, Emil waited for her to continue. Ilona didn't trust herself to speak.

'*Anyu*, can you tell me about it? And about dad, too?' Emil's voice was quiet, patient.

Ilona took a deep breath and told Emil stories about his father. About how Laci liked to play football, how he loved to take apart things — radios, the phonograph, the speakers — and how he made her laugh; how much Emil looked like him and how it hurt sometimes when she saw the way Emil flipped the hair from his eyes because it was just how Laci had done it. She could feel her voice quiver when she told him why Laci went to the demonstration.

'I've always wondered if he had done it for me; if Laci thought he was defending my honour because a Soviet captain had once…' Ilona didn't know what to say '…hurt me very badly.'

Emil stared into Ilona's eyes, like he was giving her strength.

'I remember when I was little, and I asked you about those scars on your back. You never told me how you got them,' Emil said softly. 'Does it have to do with the scars?'

'Yes,' Ilona nodded, she wasn't sure if she could speak anymore. She felt over-exposed, like a photograph that had been left out in the sun. 'Yes, it had to do with the scars. I think your father wanted to get back at them because of my scars. In the end, of course, they got him.'

Ilona told Emil about seeing the wreckage of Laci's face and how she had nightmares about it.

'I'm sorry I wasn't a better mother,' Ilona said in a voice so tight her throat hurt. 'I was so upset about Laci's death that I couldn't keep you protected inside my body.'

Emil looked confused.

'You were born a month premature, so they had to keep you in a plastic box under bright lights with little cotton balls taped to your eyes,' she said. 'You looked so… exposed. So helpless. You had oxygen tubes taped under your nose and the other tubes that ran into your veins to feed you because I didn't have the…'

Ilona blew her nose, took a deep breath.

'I wish I could have held you more. Told you I loved you more. I'm sorry I nagged you.'

Emil stared at his mother. She dabbed at her eyes.

'I'm sorry I pushed you into swimming. To be honest, I could see you weren't happy. I thought it would change things for us after Laci's death. Put us back on track.'

Then Ilona went very quiet. In a soft, almost mousy voice she didn't think she had ever used, Ilona, with tears flowing down her cheeks, apologised for being his mother.

'Now I've pushed you away again. Will you ever forgive me?'

Emil fixed his eyes on the worn material of the settee.

'It wasn't like that,' he said. 'You didn't push me away. I didn't even plan it. It just happened. I swam away because of the coach, not because of you. I'm sorry I never told you that. I'm sorry you had to suffer for it. I didn't know you lost your job or had to move in with grandma.'

Ilona sipped her cold tea to calm her nerves. She held the cup between her hands to steady them. Emil continued.

'*Anyu*, you were a good mother. You took me swimming at *Margit-sziget*, we went sledging on Balaton in the winter, you took me to concerts even. Every weekend, we were out doing something. I hope we do as much with Tünde. You taught me you don't have to have a lot of money to be a good parent; the key is that you have to be there for them. You were always there for me.'

'Well,' Ilona said, her voice stronger. 'That's what mothers do.'

Emil smiled at his mother.

'You're a tough cookie, Ilona Kovács, or are you using Pálffy these days?'

Ilona held her chin high and smiled shyly at her son. It had been a long time since someone joked with her like that.

'I'm Ilona Kovács. The proud mother of Emil.'

'*Anyu*,' Emil said. 'It's really important to reconcile with the past. You can't keep these things inside. They fester. They affect your health. I'm glad you told me just now, but that should be just a start. You need to keep talking about it.'

'What's the point of bringing up the past? You can't change it. We have to move forward.'

'You can't change it, you're right. Still, in order to move forward you have to understand why it happened. You don't want it to happen again.'

'No,' Ilona said, agreeing with her son. 'I don't want Hungary ever to go back to being subjugated again. We've had enough of strongmen.'

'So, I've got this friend, Gergő, who has taught me a lot about Hungary's past. I'd like you to meet him. He is trying to get people to do something with their memories. Democracy is easy to lose if you don't keep working to keep it.'

'I would be pleased to meet any friends of yours,' Ilona said.

Emil walked over to the settee and hugged his mother.

JUNE

There had been so much to organise for the exhibition, and Ilona was only too happy to take over the planning. She was pleased that Emil recognised how adept his mother had been at handling bureaucracy. Doing it himself had taken him away from his work, he told her. Ilona smiled.

Emil and Ilona got volunteers to stay with the exhibition when he or Melissa couldn't be there during the week of the installation. Melissa felt bad that she couldn't help more because she couldn't speak good enough Hungarian, however she was able to convince the new American ambassador's wife to attend the opening. Melissa had met her through one of the dance mums.

At work, Ilona asked János, the photographer, if the news agency would be interested in attending the *Vernissage*. She used the French word to underscore the artistic importance of this exhibition. János gave her a curious look and said Emil had already invited him. John was coming too, because of his help. Help? Ilona had no idea what kind of 'help' her colleague had given her son. Simply too much was going on in the office without Ilona knowing about it, she felt. Ilona liked being in control.

To be sure all media corners were covered, Ilona made calls to Hungarian papers to let them know of this special event. She was sure her son wouldn't mind. They had already been contacted by the university, still, Ilona was certain a personal call would ensure their attendance.

Melissa helped Ilona with the food and drinks for the exhibition opening. Ilona found an East German man at *Moszkva tér* selling sparkling rosé from the trunk of his Wartburg station wagon, and Melissa used the Lada to pick it up.

'It's Little Red Riding Hood brand!' She laughed. 'One bottle costs less than two bucks, so you know it's gotta be great!'

Ilona looked perplexed when Emil laughed too.

'*Rotkäppchen Sekt* is one of the finest champagnes I've ever tasted,' she reprimanded them.

Ilona wanted to make shrimp hors d'oeuvres but Melissa insisted on vegetable *crudités* and nuts. Erzsi somehow got a shipment of Pick Salami, which she was selling that week from her flat. She gave some of them for the event.

Then, it was show time. As arranged, Ilona picked up Tünde from their new place so Emil and Melissa would have time to set everything up. It was the first time in months that Ilona had the *kisbaba* to herself. She took her to the playground outside their flat and pushed her on the swing. Tünde had grown so much this past year and was no longer shy. She was even starting to speak Hungarian with the other children, and joined them going down the slide.

A cool breeze wafted off the Danube as Ilona, Tünde and Erzsi walked across the red brick square, passing the parliament building toward the *Kossuth tér* metro station. A small gathering of people were smoking their last cigarettes before riding down the steep escalators to the exhibition. A few already held flutes of the *Rotkäppchen* sparkling wine. They all seemed to be the arty sort — a smattering of Fulbrighters, university colleagues and Melissa's friends from the dance group — a group Ilona knew nothing about, but were recognisable by their black clothing and cigarettes.

Ilona ignored them as they walked past, pausing briefly to wave at John who stood near the underground station entrance. John stood next to István, and Ilona saw Isi give her boss a business card as they walked up. István's hair was slicked back and his aftershave made Ilona's eyes water even from where she was standing. He had a tall, busty blonde at his side, whom Ilona noted, he did not introduce to his mother.

A placard announcing the exhibition 'In Search of Our Fathers' was mounted at the entrance. Mist from the river mixed with that universal stench of an underground station. Melissa, who stood at the top of the escalator greeting guests, looked anxious.

'The ambassador's wife is late, she's supposed to open the exhibition.'

'*Háát,*' Erzsi said, shrugging. 'You know how busy these people are. She'll come eventually. Don't worry.'

Ilona, Tünde and Erzsi stepped onto the steep escalator leading down into the station. As they neared the bottom, Ilona could hear cries, sirens and an occasional scream. Tünde's grip on her grandmother's shoulder tightened. Ilona too, was confused. This was an art exhibition? Smoke seemed to waft ominously out of the station.

As they stepped off the stairs, Ilona had to adjust her eyes to the dim lighting. The cool concrete of the underground added to the dark atmosphere. She could just make out old 1950s vintage televisions perched on pedestals scattered throughout the space. Secured, Ilona guessed, from the flea market Melissa liked to visit. On the grey concrete walls where posters usually proclaimed the attractions of Big Macs and the new KFC, were instead giant portraits and collages. Perhaps twenty-five people walked through the narrow metro platform that now was transformed into an art space. Their silence was punctuated by incoherent chatter from the various video stations. The smoke from some invisible machine, the darkness and cool temperature: the effect was an eerie cacophony. Even the acrid stench of the underground — urine mixed with bleach and whatever chemicals Emil was using for the smoke — caused a visceral reaction as Ilona and Erzsi stepped off the escalator.

Screams could be heard as Ilona neared the first television that marked the start of the exhibition. Playing on a loop was BBC World Service archive footage of the 1956 revolution, showing tanks rolling in and an excited reporter barely coherent as he tried to describe the chaos. Suddenly, the video flipped — as if someone changed the channel — to a Magyar TV show on the biological wonders of the Hungarian Great Plains, the *Puszta*. Birds twittered by, an odd-looking sheep with dreadlock curls grazed. The video cut back to the tanks, which were gunning down terrified protestors; Ilona wondered what this had to do with Emil's photography. As the camera panned a sickeningly still mound of bodies, a clear voice could be heard above the confusion. It seemed to come from someone in the heap of rubble next to a building on *Marko utca.*

'All we wanted was more humane treatment; more humane society… that socialism should live up to its name.'

The voice faded and they were back with the chaos and noise. Ilona found it difficult to watch. This was not her idea of an art exhibition. There were no beautiful paintings or lovely photography. She knew by now that Emil wanted to remember the 1956 uprising, but to focus the whole exhibition on it was something else entirely. Silently, stoically, she plodded on.

She saw a still of a young man stooping over a girl in stockings and an overcoat. She was maybe thirteen or fourteen years old, and she was covered in blood. In the background of the photo, Emil had added the unmistakable brown uniform of the secret police, the ÁVH.

The next TV monitor featured Pathé footage. A camera panned a city street that was devoid of life — burnt out army trucks blocked an intersection; a Soviet tank with its top blown off lying a-kilter on the side of the rubble-strewn road. Windows from the buildings were blown out; balconies were missing, exposing the interior of a once tidy living room. A blackened telephone box was a mere skeleton of itself. Felled trees with charred branches blocked side streets. The footage was shot in black and white but Ilona saw it all in colour. The camera stopped and the video cut to a woman sitting awkwardly on the ground, cradling the head of a man, whose legs were missing. Then, somehow interposed on the body, first out of focus then increasingly sharp, was a photo Ilona had stared at for nearly forty years. Her husband. The framed picture was from her dresser. It was Laci relaxing on a picnic blanket in the City Park, hands holding his head, head slightly cocked, smiling into the camera, with oddly mismatched shoes. The photo of her smiling husband filled the screen. Then — the screen went black.

'Oh my,' she heard Erzsi say weakly.

Ilona froze, unable to move any further. Shaking.

'What was that?' she said. 'What if people saw this? This can't be shown here. This must stop.'

Ilona had learned forty years ago to trust no one. In this new democracy that everyone was crowing about, betrayal could happen again. Why was Emil displaying this? Dredging these things up? Even he admitted that democracy was still fragile in the country. Ilona's head felt hazy. She needed to find Emil immediately. Her eyes darted around to find him. This video must not be played again.

Instinctively she placed her arm in front of the screen, blocking anyone from seeing it. Trying desperately to prevent it from starting again.

It did start up again. The screams were unbearable, then the video footage. Then Laci.

'What is this?' Ilona said, too loudly. 'Where are the pretty photos? This is wrong. Everything is wrong.'

With Erzsi's urging, Ilona, who still was clutching Tünde, willed her feet to keep walking.

In the next area, life-sized cut-outs of ÁVH and Russian soldiers — distinguishable by their uniforms — surrounded Ilona as lights flickered in incandescent yellow, fluorescent white and a cool light blue. A Magyar Radio broadcaster reciting at a frantic pace but nearly monotonous voice the events unfolding outside his studio:

'ÁVH fired on unarmed demonstrators. Then, as Red Cross ambulances drive up to help the wounded, more ÁVH police wearing white coats jump out. Are they pretending to be medical workers? Before they can inflict more damage, the ÁVH are overcome by an angry crowd.' In a cool, monotone voice, the Magyar announcer described how the crowd attacked the secret police. Then, as with the last installation, a clear voice of an elderly man could be heard in broken English.

'We knew dere were large barracks on the same boulevard as the radio station, so we all ran down dere and broke down de door. Police were waiting for us, aiming deir rifles at us. The commander ordered dem: Shoot! But we said "No! You won't shoot your own people to help de Russkis!" So de soldiers pushed de commander aside and let us take all the weapons in de barracks.'

The sound of machine guns burst over Ilona's head as the lights flickered, then went out. The posters of the police went black, as spotlights focused too brightly on a placard to Ilona's right: the list of sixteen demands — written in Hungarian and English — the protesters had made to the government: Soviet troops must leave the country, freedom of the press, the right to form political parties; free voting, independent judiciary…

Ilona wasn't sure she could bear any more. She felt certain Emil would be arrested. Why had she helped him get the permit for the exhibition? Whatever would the transport minister think of this? She hugged Tünde tightly , who in turn, had her arms securely around her grandmother's neck.

At the next television, a video of a man about her age sat

quietly on a bench near the Danube in modern day Hungary. It was Gergő, the man Emil had told her about. His voice in the background repeated,

'*It was a set-up. It was a set-up. It was a set-up. It was a set-up.*'

Then in a quick-fire montage: dizzying shots of historical footage of Soviet tanks firing on unarmed students during the *Kossuth tér* massacre mixed with the wounded, the dead, a burnt-out telephone box, along with contemporary black-and-white photos of the same ornate, proud buildings around the city that make Budapest so beautiful. Only, these photos of buildings on *Bethanyi tér*, *Moszkva tér*, *Rákoczi utca* and *Andrássy út* emphasised the pockmarks, gashes, a few small fissures, a dent or a dimple, others deep penetrating gaps sealed in the black grime of time. Wounds that nevertheless had failed to heal.

As Ilona soaked it in, immersed, a Metro train sped through the station, startling and jarring the visitors. A woman not far from her screamed in shock. Ilona could hear nervous laughter from a few people who also had been spooked by the unexpected noise.

She could feel her stomach start to rumble again. Her nerves tingled.

Ilona looked up where the train had passed through. Across the tracks were oversized photos of people lining the concrete walls. Lights mounted from the ceiling focused on the people's photos. Everyday activities with Hungarians: at a desk, in a market, splashing about in the thermal baths.

In the centre of the group was a giant pixelated photo of Imre Nagy, the leader of the 1956 uprising. Ilona couldn't get close enough to see them — the train tracks prevented it — however the picture appeared to comprise the more than two thousand five hundred men and women who were murdered during the week-long revolt.

Next, a collage of Soviet tanks, troops and ÁVH soldiers was defaced by red and black paint, scribbled with words like 'murderers,' 'traitors,' 'filth,' 'assassin,' 'scum' and 'executioners'. Surrounding it, like a crowd whose powerful voices could not be silenced, were colour photos Emil had taken during the three-day taxi strike. The strikers were smiling, a couple danced, women ladled soup, faces stared confidently into the camera lens giving the unseen photographer a thumbs up. Slowly an archival photo of a group of women gathered on a dreary city street came into focus. From the shops that could be seen in the background, Ilona knew they were near *Vaci utca*, even though a few store windows were boarded up, awaiting repairs. Women, some wearing heavy coats and silk scarves around their heads, hair deftly tucked in, others too tired to bother to protect themselves against the brutal December winds, a scattering of slender leather gloves held flowers. There were hundreds of them, perhaps more than a thousand.

It could have been a happy May Day parade except for the deep grief, sorrow, anger, defiance, determination in their faces; mouths curled down, noses flared; tears streamed down the face of one woman, whose whole being seemed contorted in anguish. Ilona had never seen this particular photo, although she knew where they were, because she had been there. Erzsi had accompanied her. The photo faded into other photos, which merged 1956 with the present day. Women carrying signs at the taxi drivers' strike. A woman sitting alone in a tram. Women with children at the City Park. Women at their desks at work; in the garden; waiting in line at the green grocer on *Moszkva tér*; sitting at a kitchen table. The stills seemed to move, always forward. Just as she, Ilona, had with Erzsi's support, marched on with time.

In the background Ilona could hear the song sung by those women on that brutally cold December day in 1956. Was it in her mind or playing up above from the speaker? '*We shall never be slaves.*' She heard it; just as she had sung it, with the words initially caught in her throat, only louder and more clearly as they walked to a memorial for Laci and the other husbands and sons, sisters and daughters, who these women had just buried. *Stay away*, they had told the men that day. *Leave us to mourn*. They had defied the ÁVH lining the parade route. They had ignored the Soviet tanks at each corner.

Even the song itself scoffed at the men. It was a forbidden song. Still, who can censor a grieving woman singing a song? How do you stop thousands of women merely walking down a street? Among the collage on the TV screen was a photo of a young soldier with a sheepish stare, his head lowered while another portrayed men who doffed their hats as the women walked softly past.

When the sad, tragic melody ended, the montage on the television faded into one single picture; first fuzzy and unfocused. Then clearer and more defined as the photo came nearer to the lens.

And a young Ilona, the photo that was still on her dresser, was now there on the monitor, for everyone to see. Ilona, laughing while at a picnic in the City Park on a warm spring day, six months before she lost her smile, then Ilona at a picnic at the Pálffy only a few months ago with a grandchild on her lap and one with Ilona and Erzsi sitting at a kitchen table with a pot of tea between them sharing a long hearty laugh.

Ilona felt her knees buckle. She didn't want to be strong anymore. There was a new heaviness to her chest. A vibration in her neck that made her think for a moment that her head would explode. An old pain returned; she missed Laci with the fierceness of yesterday. His eyes, his smile, his smell, his touch. The way she could comb her fingers through his jet black hair. How proud she felt when they walked together, that this man had chosen her. She missed their long talks, their plans, his jokes. and his lightness, the way he could coax her out of a bad mood.

'Why?' Ilona asked aloud, 'Why are you doing this?'

Ilona wasn't sure she could stand any more pain; for so long she had thought her senses were dead.

Erzsi, herself shaking, put her arm around her friend and led her to a bench. The two worn women hugged each other, clutching onto memories that had been too painful to ever mention. Ilona could feel Melissa handing her a tissue, and she wasn't sure why Tünde put her hands over her ears. Was that she, Ilona, who let out that wail? This certainly was not how anyone was supposed to behave in public.

Emil had walked up and was standing next to Ilona.

'*Anyu*,' he said softly, rubbing her back. 'It's okay. Shh.'

Ilona took a deep breath. Then another. She didn't trust herself to speak. Melissa bent down on her haunches; facing her mother-in-law, holding a hand.

'Tell me what you're feeling right now,' she said, softly.

Ilona snapped her head up and stared into the brown eyes of her daughter-in-law. Ilona realised they were sincere. They probably always had been.

'What are you feeling right now?' Melissa asked again. 'Please share it with us, Ilona.'

Ilona was silent for a long time. Ilona didn't trust herself to talk. She had to breathe first. So few people had spoken so gently to her. The last person had been Laci, and she had told him to look forward, never back.

How did she feel? Upset that Emil would dredge this up? Confused that anyone wanted to talk about this bit of history; that anyone cared?

She let out a long breath. Sniffed. Then let out another long breath. She dabbed her nose and looked at her son. She didn't know what to say.

'I feel... sad. Lonely. You will fly off and I'll be by myself again.'

Erzsi squeezed her hand. 'No, you will always have me.'

And Emil smiled at her. 'And you will always have me. I will call you on your phone. And you can visit the US now.'

'Well,' Ilona pulled herself together, blew her nose and dried her eyes. 'Of course. That goes without saying?'

John had come up behind her. Seeing Ilona in tears made her boss uncomfortable, she could see that. 'C'mon, up you go,' he said. 'You Hungarians are resilient. You're the only people I know who can be on the losing side of every war and still have a country.' He laughed a bit too loudly, then dabbed at his eyes.

Another man was standing a few steps away from Emil, looking slightly out of place. His eyes too, were red. He cleared his throat and Emil turned around. The two men hugged.

'*Anyu*,' Emil said. 'This is Gergő. He's been introducing me to many of the people you see in this exhibition. I think I told you about him.'

Ilona smiled shyly at him. He kissed the air above her hand. '*Kezét csókolom.*'

Emil asked if Ilona was ready to see the rest of the exhibition. She held her son's hand to steady herself. As she stood up, she gave it an extra squeeze. She smoothed her skirt and patted her hair.

In contrast to the rest of the exhibition, the last installation was shot in vibrant, bright, dazzling colour. It started with playful pictures from Ilona's and Erzsébet's photo album of István and Emil. The two of them sitting in a cot together. The two friends swimming in Lake Balaton; István playing football; then it flashed to Kodachrome photographs of the children of Budapest that Emil had seen in the last year. Then finally a little girl sitting bare-chested in a sandbox with sticky red juice running down a pudgy chin, a contented grandmother sitting on a park bench nearby. Tünde. Ilona's little fairy.

The American ambassador's wife had finally arrived to give a speech as the official opening, although the exhibition was already open to the public. In a crisp dark blue cocktail dress with perfectly coiffured hair, she added sophistication to the crowd. She told the small crowd gathered around that she had escaped from Hungary, when she was fourteen.

'I am honoured to have been asked to open this important exhibition,' she said, her hands unsteady. 'My father had paid for papers for my mother and me, so in December 1956 we embarked on a train ride under the pretence of visiting relatives in Vienna for Christmas. My father, of course, was collateral, ensuring our return. However, unbeknownst to the authorities, he spent that time walking to freedom; sleeping by day, travelling at night, eventually crossing the border in a lorry, hidden under pallets of vegetables headed for Austria. We were the decoys.

'I share my story today because I was dumbfounded to see footage of my father at the protest outside the radio station. It was only a brief shot, so I had to watch the loop several times to confirm it, however, yes, it was indeed my father.'

Ilona suddenly was interested.

'My father is still alive today; living in New York. He felt vindicated when the Iron Curtain fell and feels even more pride that his daughter is here on behalf of the United States, to help in whatever way America can to assist in this country's transition to democracy.'

Gergő clapped loudly, prompting others in the crowd to do the same.

'The first step is always coming to terms with the past. This exhibition today is an important first step. It honours the sacrifices of those who lost their lives and those who had to keep living to hold on to hope.'

Erzsi squeezed Ilona's hand. Ilona squeezed back.

'I'm sorry my husband isn't here today; however, I will strongly recommend not only that he view this exhibition, but also that the embassy retain the works and keep them on display. Our family will provide the funds to do so.'

Ilona looked open-mouthed at Emil, who she could tell, was trying hard not to smile too broadly.

'Thank you to the artist, Emil Kovács, for putting on this powerful exhibition. He will go far.'

Everyone clapped a final time, especially Ilona. She loved those last words.

MONDAY

Ilona was back in the office bright and early. The stacks of newspapers were heaviest at the start of the week because they often included the Sunday papers. Ilona didn't mind. She was well-practised in climbing the stairs in her sensible heels with heavy packages.

Ilona put a new white sheet of paper into her electric typewriter to begin writing the Daily Digest for John. The main stories that day were the reviews in *Népszabadság* and *Magyar Nemzet* of Emil's exhibition. Both were favourable. Both included photos of the collage Emil had used on the invitation — clearly the most powerful for the reviewers. Another picture was of her son, looking straight into the camera, unflinchingly, his arms crossed. Cool, calm, self-assured. Those always were qualities to be admired, she thought.

She cut out the clippings and placed them in a folder to take home. More items to add to her new scrapbook. She thought about the cards Emil had sent her through the years. The ones she had stored in the sideboard along with receipts of bills paid and old birthday cards. Had all of them been his photographs? She'd need to check. Of course, they'd be glued into the new scrapbook too.

That evening Gergő rang on Ilona's phone, inviting her to tea.

'Ooooh,' Melissa said. 'Ilona's got a d-d-date!'

Ilona blushed as she grinned. Her back was hurting again because Emil and his family had moved back to the flat. She didn't mind though.

She met Gergő at *Ruszwurm* for tea and cake the following Sunday afternoon and Ilona found the man charming, as Emil had told her he would be. They spoke for hours. Ilona was actually late for supper that night. The next week, she invited him over for Sunday dinner with Emil, Melissa and Tünde.

Erzsébet never mentioned István's source of wealth, although Ilona knew that she had eventually discovered most of István's riches came from the nightclubs that were popping up everywhere and not the restaurant. No one knows how he did it, but Isi had managed to come up with the money to pay back Albert. Erzsi suspected it had a lot to do with that new politician friend of his, Viktor. In the years after the first prime minister died, István became close friends with the young politician. Together they crafted legislation that limited foreign investment.

'We need to protect our national treasures,' Viktor had declared when his party, the Young Democrats, introduced the bill to parliament. 'Hungary must be protected and left to the Hungarians!'

As a gift to Viktor, István and his Hungarian partners built a football stadium — almost a cathedral, really — in

Viktor's hometown village Felcsút. István continued to have
Sunday dinners with his mother, bringing a new girlfriend
with him each week. Erzsi stopped trying to learn their names.
Eventually he married Viktor's sister and became the fifth
most wealthy man in the country.

Although István offered to move Erzsi into a modern villa
in the Buda hills, Erzsi stayed in her flat across the hall from
Ilona. Neither Ilona nor Erzsi ever learned about Isi's dabbling
in filmmaking, which anyway ended when the Internet became
popular. Isi turned his DeeLuXXX studios into Hungarian
Hollywood, and rented out the space to streaming services.
As the years passed, István gave up the Pussycat Nightclubs
and moved onto more lucrative property speculation, mostly
with Viktor. Together they amassed a large property portfolio.
Some of the *kastély*, including the Pálffy, were converted to
boutique hotels and spas. Then the pair expanded into the
media, with Isi buying up most of the country's newspapers
and TV stations.

In July, Ilona took the morning off to accompany her son
and his family to the airport. She splashed out and ordered
a taxi, for which, in the end, Melissa insisted on paying. As
Melissa and Emil pulled suitcases from the trunk, Ilona peered
into the wide brown eyes of her granddaughter and had to take
a deep breath. She was going to miss this little girl. When
she looked into Tünde's eyes, she saw Laci and Emil. Now
she wondered when she would see those beautiful little eyes
again?

There was nothing more to say. She tugged at her sleeve
after she kissed her granddaughter's cheek. She decided not to
walk the family to the gate. She needed to take the next bus

into town so as not to miss too many hours of work.

'Do you have your medicine with you in case your luggage gets lost?' Ilona asked Melissa.

'I do. Thanks for worrying about me, Ilona,' Melissa said to her as they kissed on their cheeks, European-style. 'I can't wait for you to visit us in Cleveland!'

Ilona wondered if she would ever fly to Ohio.

'Or, you could come back next summer. We could go to Lake Balaton together.'

She knew the family had some money. The American embassy had bought Emil's entire exhibition. It was scheduled to be displayed at the *Amerika Haus* in Vienna and would make the rounds of other cultural venues, including some in the former Soviet Union.

When Ilona hugged her son goodbye, she closed her eyes; she wanted to remember how comforting he felt when he wrapped his arms around her.

'I'll call you every Sunday,' he said. 'We'll give that phone of yours a workout.'

Ilona cupped his cheeks into her hands.

'I'm so proud of you son.'

'I love you too, *Anyu*.'

After work, Ilona smiled as the tram carried her back across the Danube. She didn't mind the stifling humidity or the fishy smells of the river water. At home, Ilona tied on her apron and changed into her house slippers. Her flat was quiet, however she didn't mind. She had work to do. Without realising it, Ilona found herself humming a tune she had heard from Melissa's CD as she grabbed a duster from the broom closet. It was a song from one of the new records Melissa had purchased of Hungarian folk songs.

Clip, clip, clip the backs of her house shoes slapped the soles of her feet as Ilona whizzed through the living room with her duster. The windowsill, the coffee table, the sideboard — and the telephone, which Ilona now knew would ring every Sunday. Next, she made up the bed for her to sleep on that night. Her back was going to be happy about that.

While she was in her bedroom, Ilona peered out the window, straining her eyes so that she could see the car park six floors below. Just then she spotted a familiar man locking the door of his Polski Fiat, and she knew it would be only a few moments until Gergő arrived.

They had finally repaired the second lift.

—END—